MW01126578

The Storm After

Gina Hooten Popp

ALL RIGHTS RESERVED

No part of this book may be reproduced or transmitted in any form or by any means, electronic or mechanical, including photocopying, recording, or by any information storage and retrieval system, without permission in writing from the author, except in the case of brief quotations embodied in reviews.

Publisher's Note:

This is a work of fiction. All names, characters, places, and events are the work of the author's imagination. Any resemblance to real persons, places or events is coincidental.

Copyright © 2013 Gina Hooten Popp

ISBN-10: 148193581X
ISBN-13: 978-1481935814

ACKNOWLEDGMENTS

My gratitude goes to my family members and friends for their support during the writing of this story. I will forever be indebted to them for the countless hours they spent reading and re-reading.

A special thanks to my father James A. Hooten for the use of the front cover image of my ancestors Bud, Dove and Etaw Roland. Cooper, Texas.

The background image is a historical photo showing actual devastation from the 1900 Hurricane located on Galveston Island at the foot of 39th Street. **Courtesy of the Rosenberg Library, Galveston, Texas.**

PROLOGUE

GALVESTON ISLAND

Saturday Afternoon

September 8, 1900

Looking out over the ocean, Sister Elizabeth noticed two things: magnificent, violet-tinged clouds streaking across a gray-blue sky, and a strange swirling of waves in a most unusual green color. Walking back along the beach, she began to mentally prepare a list of things needed to ready the orphanage for the coming storm.

When Sister Elizabeth went to town for supplies, she would seek the advice of John, the church's volunteer handyman. Close to her in age and thought, John was her friend and a Godly man, even though there were some who thought otherwise. But she knew his heart and was grateful for his help. As Sister Elizabeth made her way back to the dormitories, she felt the first drops of rain. She couldn't help thinking they tasted like tears as they slid down her face. A gull in erratic flight screeched overhead.

Sister Elizabeth only intended to make a quick trip into town, but the rain had intensified, making it difficult to navigate the streets. People scurried about making last minute preparations for the storm. No one had ever seen flooding come in this fast, or this far inland, and people were starting to take the weather seriously. Many appeared to be leaving their

1

jobs early to go home and help their families get ready for the approaching storm. Some were saying the hurricane had changed paths and, now, it was headed directly for them. If the townsfolk's speculation of the storm came true, the orphanage would be completely unprotected in its position near the beach. Sister Elizabeth looked down at the too-fast rising water impeding her progress and shifted her packages higher.

"Sister Elizabeth. Sister Elizabeth."

She turned to the voice she knew so well. John stood, drenched by the rain, giving him the appearance of a different person. But she knew when he took the heaviest packages and loaded them for her he was the same sweet John.

Jumping into the buggy, John took the reins. "I've got to get you back, sister," he said. "Got to help you and the sisters batten down. Ships coming in report this storm's a real bad one. Sailors told me it's the worst they've ever seen."

•••

Later that night hurricane-force winds pounded the orphanage like demons with sticks. This is as close to hell as Sister Elizabeth ever wanted to be. Fear rose like bile in her throat and she wished John had not insisted on going back to town. His presence would have been comforting. However, she knew no mere mortal could protect them against the angry winds and needle-like sheets of rain being forced down upon them. The outcome would be in God's hands.

Rising high, the water covered the whole first floor. She was thankful John had the foresight to convince the sisters to gather all the children on the top floor of the girls' dormitory. He had deemed it the stronger of the buildings. Now at the height of the storm, even its sturdy construction groaned from the strain of the sustained high winds. She thought back to what the store clerk had said about the hurricane changing paths. Judging by the unrelenting roar, the hurricane was passing right over the heart of Galveston, and the island didn't have a seawall. Her heart lurched as she watched one wall start to bend perilously inward. Nails popped. Wood splintered.

Knowing she could not hold all the children in her arms, she had used clothesline to connect each child's hand to one another. She had told them they were playing a game. Now linked together, the little ones huddled around, hiding their eyes in her robe. With each new crash of thunder and burst of lightning they cried uncontrollably.

"Shhh, now … shhh," she said. The roar of the storm deafened her so she could barely hear her own words.

As the pressure outside dropped lower, she felt the urge to sleep— even as her anxiety increased. Her nerves raw, she stayed strong for the little ones. Silently, she prayed the clothesline would keep them from becoming separated if the storm intensified. If they had to move…closing her eyes, she tried not to think about "what ifs."

In the chaos, she saw one girl's mouth moving. As she leaned close to listen, she felt the toddler's silky blonde ringlet brush her cheek. "Momma. Momma. Make it stop," the toddler cried into Sister Elizabeth's ear. The heartbreak was instant. Her breathing became labored and she feared each breath would be her last. And she wasn't sure if she was holding the orphans or if the orphans were holding her.

A kerosene lantern hanging in the rafters cast ghostly shadows over them as it swayed ominously back and forth. Looking across the room, she locked worried eyes with one of the other nuns.

The wall of ocean water crashing through the roof on their side of the building took them both by surprise, as did the darkness it brought with it. Burning saltwater filled her lungs as the force of the wave pulled her and the children down. Death was imminent.

1 GALVESTON ISLAND

Sunday Morning

September 9, 1900

I was Sister Elizabeth, but no longer. Along with thousands of others who perished in the storm, I transitioned from my body last night. The people we left behind were dazed by what had happened to us … to them. Later they would learn they had lived through one of the worst hurricanes in history. Right now that didn't matter, because the real storms of life begin just after the howling winds and driving rain die down.

Today would be no exception, as the sun rose in a clear sky and a balmy breeze off the Gulf of Mexico greeted the still-shaking survivors.

It was Sunday morning. A perfect Sunday for going to church…if only the church weren't in shambles, along with so many lives. Intuitively, I knew my mission. I would help my earthbound brethren with the shackles of their human existence until they, too, could be set free.

Right now, I must stay with John as he begins searching for the orphans and me. His heart will be broken when he discovers what has become of us.

JOHN

Ah, Mother o' God, how did I survive? Morning sun beat down on my Irish soul and heavy sea-laden humidity hit me full in the face. I was floating on a door. It rocked back and forth as it settled on a mile-high pile of debris. Last night in the storm, the door caught in a whirlpool. Round and round I went as the hurricane and the ocean raged.

A fly began buzzing near my right eye and it took everything I had just to move my head away. My insides quaked in fear as I viewed the devastation.

I stood. My inner thighs hurt. The tops of my arms hurt. I was bleeding. There was no one to help. All the living were hurt. A seagull screeched overhead. People moaned and called out for help, for fresh water.

What the hell? I heard the tolling of the bells calling people to mass. God, I'm thirsty. Thirstier than I've ever been before. And, as my fellow dockworker and Greek friend Constantine would remind me, that's saying a lot because I'm Scots-Irish. Where was the ever-joking Constantine? Where were Dean and Jim?

My drinking buddies were mostly sailors and dockworkers. An odd assortment of fun-loving characters brought together from every corner of the world. We gave each other hell, but we loved each other, too. I had been playing cards and drinking with a group of them last night. It was how we were going to ride out the storm. What I wouldn't give for yesterday.

I tripped over something … dead man … oh, no … dead bodies everywhere. How many? I needed to get to mass. Needed to find living people. There was an arm waving from under a pile of tree limbs.

"Oh, God! Help me pull this stuff off." A face. Eyes blinking. Blue eyes. I'd seen the eyes before.

"I'm going to get ye out. Ye hear me? I'm going to get ye out," I was crying for myself, for being damn helpless, and for her because her beautiful hair was tangled in the limbs of a tree. To set her free, I'd need to cut her hair.

I turned wildly. Where would I find something to cut with in this chaos? I ran to an overturned chest of drawers and started rifling through it. Clothes, hairbrushes, old photos still in frames. Then I saw it. A hunting knife.

She remained very still as I cut. I tried to leave as much as I could, which made for a rather odd haircut. Long in some areas and not so much as an inch in others. She was a pretty woman in spite of the bruises. I had seen her before, but I didn't know her.

"Come now. Let's get ye to your feet."

She stood and leaned on me heavily. Then she began to walk on her own. In the direction of the ringing church bells. The same way I was headed. An ungodly stench made me nauseous. Covering both nose and mouth with a wounded hand, I tasted blood and sea salt. But I couldn't escape that strong smell.

Oh, God. My insides wouldn't quit quivering. I am not cowardly. But the events of last night left me undone in a way I had never experienced before.

I watched her up ahead as she picked her way through the debris and dead bodies. She stopped for a moment and lingered over the face of a child.

"Do ye know him?"

She didn't answer. She just stared straight at me. Or rather through me. Then she stood and turned and started to walk again.

This lady with the blue eyes. Something was wrong. She was like a ghost. A living ghost. Her eyes were hollow. Soon I would discover half the faces on the island would have this look and it would never leave them altogether. It might leave for a while. But when they were by themselves or deep in thought it would return.

We stopped to rest and, in my mind's eye, I saw the thunder and lightnin' cutting the darkness of last night's sky. I remembered where I had seen this Blue Eyes. She had been clinging to a rooftop at the height of the storm … a man and a child beside her. As my door raft raced by them, I could see her eyes, large and frightened. The wind howled like screaming banshees. So loud I barely heard the human screams. Was the child on the roof the same child she had lingered over earlier? I didn't think so.

Others had joined our silent sojourn to the church. Tangled, muddy and battered we walked together in a small band that grew larger as we got closer. The dead along the way far outnumbered the living.

Up ahead, the lady touched her hair, feeling its jagged pieces. Please, God, let it grow back fast. When we reached the church, people were eating out of cans. Beans and such as that…ah, there was also cider. I made sure me new friend, whom I referred to in me mind as Blue Eyes, had something to eat and drink. Then I sat and ate and drank.

That's the thing about me. I can always eat and drink. I'm not one to let me emotions go to me stomach and that's why I think I manage to get by so well. Blue Eyes barely ate a nibble.

I glanced to my right and saw a lad of about fourteen, muddy, bloody, tangled and unkempt. Yet still he managed to give me a small smile. He held out his grimy hand and I gave him some of my food. I have this philosophy on life. Everybody eats. Even if there is only a little money or food, it's split between everyone so no one goes hungry.

Then I stood and started in the direction of the orphanage to check on the sisters and the orphans. I sure liked the sisters. Sister Elizabeth in particular. She never seemed to judge me and seems like if anyone should be allowed to judge, it would be a nun like her—a real spiritual person. But she never did and for that I was grateful. It was easy to be with her and the kids and I wanted to help and be there with them. Especially whenever I was troubled.

I had not gotten very far down the way when I realized both Blue Eyes and the boy were close behind me.

"Hey, ye following me, lad?" I didn't ask Blue Eyes as I felt it improper.

The boy didn't answer. I called back to him, "If ye are, it'd be okay."

We went on down the road, the three of us picking our way through what was left of our lovely Galveston, one of the wealthiest, most prosperous cities in America. I was as proud of living in America as I was of being born in Ireland.

"Are ye an American, kid?" I asked to make conversation and, honestly, I was trying to bring some control to the overwhelming terror beginning to press down on me. Polite conversation was a way to normalize the situation for me. For the three of us.

"Yes, sir. Born right here on the island."

"Ye remind me of meself."

"And you remind me of myself," he parroted back.

Blue Eyes stopped to examine a small figure. She checked to see if it were indeed dead. When she assured herself nothing more could be done, she continued in our direction using a limping trot to catch up. Clearly, she did not want to be left behind, but she did not want to talk either. She touched her hair again. My heart hurt.

I slowed my pace to accommodate her. I hated myself for cutting her hair. But she was alive and the hair would grow back. I kept thinking that thought in me head so hard that finally I said it out loud.

"Ye're alive, Blue Eyes. Yer beautiful hair will grow back."

Aside from looking startled at being directly addressed as Blue Eyes, there was no other response from her. Still she seemed to cling to the boy and me as we headed for the orphanage. They didn't know where I was going, yet they followed.

Sister Elizabeth would need my help. To my luck, when we realized the storm might be worse than we thought yesterday afternoon, I caught a ride with her from town and helped her get things ready at the orphanage. She had been at the store buying supplies and the nuns in the downtown church begged her to stay as the storm started whipping up a strong wind. But she wasn't afraid. She wanted to be with the children. So I went back with her to the orphanage.

Turns out she really did need my help. The children were frightened and quite a few were just toddlers. I told her to take them to the top floor of the girls' dormitory, as it was stronger and better made. I even helped her make a small swinging sling to hold a newborn. We took a piece of cloth and nailed it to the topmost rafters. We left a few small air holes and hung it in a way that the baby wouldn't fall out.

Sister Elizabeth came up with the idea of hanging the baby in the rafters so her hands would be free to help the other children. The ingenious design of the little swinging sling with air holes was mine, though. She would probably need help getting the wee one down now. I had used a ladder to hang it securely.

After I had helped with all this at the orphanage the morning of the storm, I headed back to the house I was living in and renting out to four other friends. The water began to rise and I thought more than once I should go back and stay with Sister Elizabeth and the orphans, but the guys and me were going to play cards. I really wanted a strong drink, too, as I was feeling uneasy myself about the strength of the winds.

It was just easier to be in the company of men, ignoring the dangers, having fun until I'd wake with a hangover and a story of adventure about how we all rode out the storm, laughing and drinking.

Some of the orphans had already started to cry and I just couldn't take it. Sister Elizabeth seemed to understand. But I felt bad. Real bad. I'd make it up to her now.

Soon the boy, Blue Eyes and myself rounded a small hill on the way to the orphanage. We stood, stunned.

The boys' dormitory was gone. However, I knew the nuns had planned to take all the children to the top floors of the girls' dormitory. And, while devastated, a partial section of the girls' dormitory still stood. The rest of the building and the ones around it were washed away. Completely.

"Where is everybody? Where are ye?" My voice caught on the wind.

"Sir, maybe they headed back to town," the boy offered.

"Wait here," I said as I went to the bottom of the shaky staircase. I could see the small swinging sling in the rafters.

"Do you think we should go up these stairs?" The boy's voice took me by surprise. He was right behind me and he startled me so I stumbled.

"You're too heavy. Let me go up." He said as he ascended the rickety stairs faster than I would have ever thought possible.

"See that piece of material in the rafters?" I pointed at the swinging sling as I spoke.

"Yes sir, I see it," the boy said as the baby in the sling started to cry. The boy's face registered surprise as he heard the newborn. Cautiously, he moved forward to the top floor and disappeared into what was left of the building.

"I'm coming up. Ye're not tall enough." Next thing I know, I looked up and the lad was crawling across the roof. "Don't!" I yelled. Blue

Eyes gripped my arm hard. I felt her fear coursing through me. Neither of us could take any more tragedy.

"There's a hole. I can reach in and get the baby out," the boy said.

The structure started to give way.

Everything started to sway, and the boards creaked.

"I'm coming up." I yelled.

The boy, flat on his stomach with his hand in the hole, looked at me terrified.

I hurried up the staircase.

The roof collapsed. Dust and debris covered me. I fought my way over the mess, worried my weight would crush the now silent baby, if the timbers hadn't already.

The spirit of Sister Elizabeth hurriedly swept past John. As she pulled the boy and baby up through the rubble, the newborn began to howl.

Miraculously, I saw a hand pop up through the rubble … then I saw the boy's head. Oblivious to the danger, the boy came out of the hole holding the baby in one arm. Relief flooded me as I let out the breath I'd been holding.

"Let's name him Lucky," the boy said smoothing the newborn's hair.

Shaking my head in agreement with his choice of monikers, I pulled out a small flask of clean water I had gotten from the church earlier that morning. Blue Eyes ripped off a clean piece of her slip and wet it as best as she could. Twisting it, she let drops of water fall into the infant's mouth. This seemed to satisfy him.

I watched the boy as he put his hands on his hips and said, "Never dreamed you'd be looking for a baby, Mister." Ignoring his remark, I said, "Remember the story we heard this morning, about the woman giving birth in the storm last night? Go back to the convent and see if they can help ye find her. Ask her if she will feed this baby, too."

The boy didn't question me. He did as I asked and for that I was grateful.

I watched as the boy and Blue Eyes made their way across the debris-filled landscape. Occasionally, Blue Eyes would stop to examine something and the boy would wait patiently by her side. Finally, I could no longer see them and I felt a rush of fear at being left alone.

"John," I whispered on the wind, "your new friend's name is Sarah Michelle. She and the boy and the baby need you." I wanted to tell him I was happy the swinging sling held tight. He wasn't listening, though. I tried to reach out and touch him. Get his attention. I was unaware of what I could and could not do in my interactions with the living, as I had only been dead a few hours—a virtual baby in this new stage of being.

SARAH MICHELLE

I couldn't talk. I could only function. The horror was too much. My head hurt. My body hurt. I was afraid to leave the man named John.

... but, needed to go find food ... for the baby ... and the boy.

What was the miracle of the woman giving birth last night? Someone told us the pregnant woman and a toddler were clinging to a roof across from the convent. The nuns could see them out the top floor window they were looking through.

The woman slipped ... and the toddler slipped ... and the woman fell into a floating washtub ... a floating washtub ... and, they said the wind forced the tub right against the convent window and the nuns pulled her in ... she was in labor. The baby was born as so many were dying.

They also said something about the toddler falling into the water and being pulled out by a man clinging to a nearby tree. He grabbed the toddler by the hair and plucked him out of the rushing water. Then he swam to the window with the nuns. The child he had saved in the darkness of the storm had turned out to be his own nephew ... and the woman he saw pulled in his sister-in-law, but her husband didn't make it. My husband Thomas didn't make it ... my son Tommy didn't make it. I saw them both go down in the water while my hair got tangled in a tree ... holding me ... keeping me from them.

The room I'm in now is filled with blinding sunlight. The beautiful dancing light makes everything appear bright and cheerful even though I'm desperately afraid.

I couldn't help but notice some things were left untouched by the storm, like that delicate statue of a sparkling glass swan. How Tommy would have loved its intricate shape. I would have told him how back in England, when I was a girl, I had seen a similar statue blown by mouth out of a bubble of glass on the end of a straw … oh no, is this how it is going to be now … everything reminding me of Tommy Jr. and Thomas. Surely I will go insane without my dear husband and darling son. I've lost all reason to live.

But then I remembered I needed to do something important. What was it? It was the reason I had come to the convent. I needed to find the new mother who gave birth in the storm … ask if she could feed two babies. The baby we found in the orphanage rafters must survive. Where was the boy? He would find the new mother for me.

Coming here the boy had stayed right by my side … sometimes holding onto me and other times holding me up. Oh, God, the devastation. I couldn't tell which direction to go because the island was a mountain of broken things. Snakes of all kinds were everywhere. Some of them drowned just like the people. Snakes were even in the tree I was caught in last night. I shoved them away as they climbed in the limbs for safety. I saw other people get bitten. I did not to get bitten. Why not? Why did I live?

I remember they built the orphanage away from the middle of town thinking it would protect the children from the yellow fever. But the walk to and from town was long ... a long walk for little ones ... or anyone for that matter. Where are all those orphans? Only the baby was left. Did they leave the baby and walk into town? Why hadn't we crossed paths with at least a few? Did the nuns at this convent know where the nuns from the orphanage went? I must ask them.

I had to help Sarah Michelle and the boy walk the last few steps to the convent. I whispered in the boy's ear, "Take the baby from her." He immediately did as I asked. Then as they approached the door, I let go of Sarah Michelle and she gently slid down to the ground with a soft thump. The convent nuns rushed out to help.

JOHN

Let's name him Lucky." Is that what the lad had said? Is he Lucky though to *still be alive in this mess?* I guessed so. I was glad to be alive. But I couldn't really think. Maybe if the woman would breastfeed him. Or maybe if the nuns could bottle feed him he would live to be an old man. How were we going to take care of a newborn? I wish we could get him off the island and to the mainland. I would carry him myself if I could get hold of a boat that wasn't damaged.

Oh my God, the stench, it just wouldn't let up. It only got stronger as the sun rose in the sky. And why couldn't I find the nuns and the children? Both Blue Eyes and the boy didn't ask why I stayed behind. I think she knew and I think the boy was only thinking of saving Lucky. Good for him for leaving with Lucky. This doesn't bode well—there is no sign of life.

I looked across the sandy beach to where a large pile of storm debris had formed. Lumber, barrels, furniture ... it was all coming back in with the tide. Or maybe it had been pushed out with the tide. Who could tell with the world upside down?

"Halloo there!" A voice called out.

What the hell? I turned and looked in the direction of the voice. It was a man's voice and it was coming from behind or under a large mound of rubble.

"Are ye stuck?"

"No, but I could use some help," the gruff voice answered as an old sailor came from behind the mound. He was as old as any human I had ever seen, but much to me surprise very spry. "Sure glad you happened across me. I heard tell of three boys who weathered the storm in a tree near the orphanage. Came back to look for more survivors."

He nervously paced back and forth before continuing, "Maybe you can help me look?" Then he lifted his face to the heavens as if he saw them there, "Seems like God scooped'em up for safekeeping while this Hell on earth is happening."

My stomach tightened at his words. "Let's look for them along the beach," I suggested. "There's a neighborhood in this direction. Perhaps they're headed there."

As we walked I took a long, hard look at this stranger. He had a big nose. The kind of nose a really old man has—bulbous is what I think they call it. He had silver hair and silver whiskers. He talked like a true Texan.

"I'm Scots-Irish." I said for conversation's sake.

"I'm not." He said. But he offered nothing more and I had to laugh.

Suddenly, we noticed another person up ahead. Out of the sand, he was pulling a body dressed in a white nun's habit. Immediately, I recognized it to be Sister Elizabeth. But before I had a chance to grasp the horror, I realized another body was popping up out of the sand. And another. And another. Nine in all. I couldn't comprehend why they were attached together with clothesline at their wrists.

Was this someone's idea of a cruel joke? Then, I remembered. The sister had tied them together to keep the group of little ones from being separated in the high winds. Her greatest fear was losing one of them. What had Sister Elizabeth said to me as I nailed the little swinging crib in the rafters? "I'll have me hands full with the toddlers. Maybe if I tie us all together no one will get lost during the storm."

I cried. Big billowing sobs. And my nose and throat, already dry, became swollen and congested and I could hardly breathe. And I hurt in a way that I thought I couldn't come back from. I loved Sister Elizabeth in a way that I shouldn't have and I loved her in a way that I should've and she never condemned me for it. She just kept being her perfect self. Seeing only the good in me. Never pointing out the bad. And, I didn't know if I was crying for her dying, or crying for me still living.

The Texan was down on his knees praying and the other man just kept crossing himself. It went on this way for quite some time. Both had tears running down their faces. I thought I would die, as I could not endure this pain. Deep, and searing ... right through my very heart ... piercing me in such a way that I could only twist and endure.

Thank God these two strangers were with me.

Stumbling, I turned to look out across the ocean. Gentle waves rolled slowly ashore toward my feet only to turn back before touching me. A misty sea spray caressed me face and a seagull screamed, bringing yet another sharp pain to my heart.

THE BOY "SEAN"

"Oh, no," the lady who had been walking with us since the storm fainted just as the nuns took baby Lucky out of her arms. "Please sisters, the baby needs to eat," I said frantically to the nuns as I rushed to help the lady.

"Here, help us get your mother to a bed, boy." The nuns assumed she was my mother. Why tell anyone otherwise? To tell the truth, I had already started to form a plan in my head. Maybe this storm was a way out for me, a new start.

"She can't talk. She can hear, I think." The nuns nodded. "And, my baby brother, needs to eat. My mother can't feed him." The nuns looked startled. "Something's wrong with her and I …" Both nuns stopped helping my new mom and focused their attention completely on me. "… I was hoping … we heard about a lady that gave birth in the storm. Maybe she could feed Lucky, too. He's only a few days old."

The nuns conferred in hushed voices. Then one approached me and said they would ask the woman.

I carried Lucky in my arms as they took me to the woman with the newborn in a nearby room. Lucky began to cry and the woman reached out her arms toward us even as the nun was asking her if she would consider feeding two infants. I took Lucky to her and he seemed to know naturally what to do. Who knows? Maybe he was a breast-fed baby.

I bashfully stepped out of the room and headed back to the lady I now referred to as mother. She was starting to rouse and the nun was holding a wet rag on her forehead.

"Mother, mother! You're awake. How do you feel?" I was truly worried.

The nun looked up at me and gave a little smile. Her face was ageless, with soft ivory skin and gentle slate-gray eyes that seemed to sparkle each time she looked at me. Considering all she had been through in the last twenty-four hours, the nun seemed remarkably calm. I drew strength from her inner peace and I was glad she was the one helping my new mother. Together we would bring her back to health.

From underneath the rag, the woman couldn't see that it was me, and she held out her hand to the son she had lost in the storm. I put my hand in hers and she grasped it with much love. Then she quietly went back to sleep.

"She's exhausted." The nun said as she tucked a dry, slightly dirty blanket around her. "Your mother will feel much better when she has slept. Let me get a blanket for you, too."

"No, thank you. I actually slept through part of the storm. Can you believe that?" The nun didn't say anything. I continued, "If you'll excuse me, I must go and inquire about something."

"Please take something to eat." The nun pushed a few biscuits from a tin into my hand. At the sight of her small food offering, my mouth started to water and my stomach churned with hunger. Even though I was ravenous, I made myself slow down to savor each bite as if it were caviar. I would take nothing in this life for granted again.

"Thank you," I said to the nun. "I must go now. I'll return soon."

Then I bent over and gently kissed my new mother's cheek as any dutiful son would and I was on my way.

JOHN

I'm trying to think what happened after we discovered Sister Elizabeth and the orphans on the beach, but my memory leaves me. I know it took us all three quite some time to recover. The other two recovered faster because they did not know Sister Elizabeth and the orphans personally. Or maybe they did, I really don't know.

I remembered the Texan holding a bottle of whiskey near my mouth. I took it, even though I couldn't breathe because I had been crying hard. I choked it down, with some of it running down the front of my shirt. It burned, and I did it again.

"Let's make a plan." It was the other man talking, the one who wasn't the Texan. I recognized him from town. He worked on the docks, too. A barrel-maker. But I hadn't ever formally been introduced to him in the two years I had been living on the island. He was probably like me. There were many people like me who had come here to make money and improve their station in life. Nowhere else in the world was like America, and Galveston was the place to be in America. With more millionaires per capita than any other city in the U.S., Galveston had everything. A world-renown seaport ... a thriving downtown ... homes with all the latest inventions ... and, now, it was all gone. Swept away. Everything reduced to piles of boards and debris ... and it only took a few hours ... maybe even minutes.

Ignoring his attempt to make a plan, I said, "I've seen ye around. I don't think we've ever formally met." I didn't recognize my gravelly voice. The tears and tightness of my throat had changed it.

"I'm Jack. I've seen you and your friends. A fun bunch of fellows you appear to be. Maybe when we've gotten through this hell on earth, we'll all go out for a beer, heh?"

"Me friends are all dead, I think. Maybe some are alive. I was going to go look for them after I checked in on Sister Elizabeth."

"Sister Elizabeth. Is this her?" He looked down at her. "I'm sorry." And I could tell he truly was upset. Finally he started to speak again. "I'm helping to find the dead and take them back to a makeshift morgue. But I don't know what I was thinking? There are so many dead. If we could find a wagon or a boat, maybe we could take their bodies into the morgue in town."

"It makes more sense to bury them here." It was the Texan. A practical man, you could tell. His big bulbous nose was red and more swollen than before, if that was possible.

"I'll go into town and try to find someone with a wagon. I'll tell them what has happened here." Jack ran his fingers through his thick hair as he spoke.

"I don't know what to do," I said. Jack looked at me and shook his head.

"Soon it'll be nightfall. I'll be back by noon tomorrow with a wagon." Then he was off and the Texan and I just sat there, not knowing what to do. We looked out over the ocean and watched a gull swoop down for a fish. Along the shoreline sand crabs scurried back and forth. Mother Nature didn't seem at all concerned by the havoc her fury had wreaked just hours before.

This was the saddest moment in my life and only the stranger beside me would ever understand the depth of my despair. I was thankful once again to have him by me side. Instinctively, I knew I needed to go and find the boy and Blue Eyes. They needed to lean on me just as I had leaned on this crusty old sailor. I couldn't do much for them other than just be there, and, I guess for now that would be enough.

SARAH MICHELLE

It was a glorious day. Gulls were dipping in the ocean. A gentle breeze wafted across the land. The sky was cloudless and so blue. No wonder I had dozed off on the beach on this dreamy day.

Thomas was a ways up the beach beckoning us to him. I heard little Tommy calling, "Mother, mother. You're awake. How do you feel?" He was holding my hand. Thomas motioned for us to come to him again. I couldn't wake up. Was I dreaming? Or was I awake? I had this vague notion of a nightmare. But what was it? And why would I want to remember it when I was here in this marvelous place with the two people I loved. I would concentrate on the here and now. There was much beauty and much love. I wanted to say something back to little Tommy. For some reason, my words wouldn't come out. I channeled my love through my body, through my hands, through my fingertips. I was sure he could feel it.

These were the sweet moments that make life worth living. Your loved ones are your Heaven, my grandmother used to say. Oh, was that Grams leaning over me? The sun was so bright behind her head I couldn't tell if it was her or an angel. The light was getting brighter and brighter, warm and welcoming with all its love. It was flowing over me and through me.

A baby's cry pierced the air. I needed to take care of the baby. The baby needed me. Where was the baby? Where was the baby? But no words came out of my mouth as I frantically thrashed about looking for the baby, my baby.

I hit the ground with quite a thud. Every bone in my aching body hit against each other. And I looked up to see a nun rushing in from the next room. She had a concerned look on her face. I reached my arms out and wordlessly mouthed, "Lucky."

"Bring the baby," the nun called to someone in the other room. "She's calling for the baby."

I had fallen back into the nightmare. I wasn't ready to leave yet.

THE BOY "SEAN"

Slipping in and out of the jumble of furniture, boards, trunks, dishes and anything and everything was harder than it looked. I wasn't even sure if I was headed in the right direction. I just had to check on something before I started my new identity and I had to make certain no one saw me hanging around this part of town.

I rounded a corner of what I thought was the right street, or at least the right area—and saw an unbelievable sight. Apparently the whole neighborhood of houses had buffeted one into another during the storm, creating one long mountain of debris where a once beautiful tree-lined street had been. Gorgeous, well-tended homes now a pile of rubble, shattered to tiny bits and pieces by the relentless strength of the storm. My magnificent Galveston was no more.

Sitting down, I began to weep. I would never find it in this mess. But I didn't get a chance to feel sorry for myself. Voices were headed in my direction. Quickly, I opened the door to a large wardrobe that miraculously had been left standing upright. Inside there were clothes. I moved in behind them. The smell of fine perfume wafted over me, and even though I was holding my breath, the woodsy scent reached my senses by osmosis. Heady from the delightful fragrance, I made a mental note that I should also quit using big words to impress people. Who knows what my new mother's background would be? And, my real mother had warned me before she

31

passed that my extensive vocabulary could be construed as prideful. Therefore, I should use it with caution so more common people would not think me "arrogant"—a term she often used to describe my rich, well-bred father whom I hated.

The voices were drawing nearer.

Barely breathing, trying not to make a sound, I strained to listen as the voices stopped for a moment in front of the wardrobe. Soon they passed and I cracked the door open to let in fresh air.

The fine fabrics hanging in the wardrobe caressed my face—silk and lace. Then it hit me. I knew what to do with these elegant clothes from the better side of town. I slipped the garments over my arm. They were amazingly dry. Outside, I began to run with them back to the convent. I didn't want anyone to see me or ask questions about what I was doing.

Darting this way and that through the debris, my spirits were high and I was able for a moment not to notice the chaos and devastation around me. I know that sounds impossible, but maybe it was because I'm still just a boy. I try to be a man, but it's only an act. That's why I stay close to John and Blue Eyes. I've taken to calling her that too. However, I must remember to call her "mother" if I'm going to pull off my plan. And I'm going to treat her like my mother. Haven't I already found some fine clothes for her? Yes, this is a new start for me.

I noticed a group of men ahead. Something was wrong. One of the men had a gun pointed at the other men's backs and seemed to be forcing them to walk forward. Looters? I hid behind a tangle of wood and watched. When they got to the turn in the road, I stepped out and followed, slipping in and out of hiding as I went.

When I turned the corner the boy inside me began to quake. There was a large pile of stiff dead bodies in front of me. They looked unreal, with their twisted expressions and hard forms. The man with the gun was forcing the other men to load the bodies onto a barge. Up close I could see that he was a policeman.

I ran all the way back to Blue Eyes and the nuns. Only I wasn't in high spirits anymore. Blue Eyes and baby Lucky were sleeping. I showed the nuns that I had brought my mother some of her clothes. "How lucky you are to have found them," one sister said. "Now you must eat something."

The sight I had witnessed was still fresh in my mind and I had no appetite. Then I remembered how John had said he always ate to keep his strength up no matter what. So I pushed my thoughts out of my head and made the food go down. It was hard at first. I choked and coughed and it tried to come back up. But I pushed the bad things I had seen far away in my mind and continued to eat. What was it my real mother used to say? "When one must, one can."

I stayed with the boy Sean and the man John at the same time. This new way of being was a constant surprise. I was only just beginning to understand the whole world. How everything worked. How it came together every day, every minute. For instance, Sean needed to eat and I was able to help him. At the same time, John was devastated by his discovery of my human body along with those of the nine children — all attached together with a clothesline. He needed comfort too. That's why the old Texan appeared for him. The old Texan was like me, except he was more evolved. He didn't die in the storm. He died years ago and was able to take the form of a human in certain circumstances. Not every soul gets to his level.

GALVESTON ISLAND

Monday Afternoon

September 10, 1900

John was recovering from his shock. The grief would stay with him the rest of his life. That's something that I no longer felt. But I could sense need and he needed me right now. Get up John; they are coming with the wagon.

JOHN

I stood to my feet and felt the old Texan's hand on my back bracing me. I could see Jack coming in front of the wagon and it looked like a military-type person was pointing a gun at Jack. The cart was full of the dead. People I knew. Locals I recognized. With the exception of sailors coming in and out of port, there were very few strangers on our small island. All of them gone with a single swipe and now, so bloated and discolored they were almost unrecognizable. I had to turn my head away.

What happened next is a blur. Basically, the military man told us to build funeral pyres for the dead bodies. The thought of setting fire to my Sister Elizabeth was too much. The old Texan was right. We should have buried her and the children right away, not tried to wait for Jack to take them to the morgue.

The old Texan started talking to the military man that had a gun trained on us. Started telling him we ought to bury the nun and the orphans here near the orphanage site. Told him he felt it would be appropriate for us to bury the nun and orphans together … and he went on about how I knew the nun personally. The military man said he would have the others help us dig the grave here on the beach. It didn't take long with so many working together. Then the guns came out again and we were told to build a funeral pyre for the dead on the wagon.

All those bodies and no time to identify them properly for loved ones. Jack and I tried to call out names and faces we recognized to the one policeman in the group. He listened carefully and quickly wrote it all down in a small leather book he was carrying. Occasionally he asked us a question about how to spell a particular name. His voice quivered with emotion at times, other than that he handled himself well.

"The bodies must be disposed of before disease starts to spread," the military man said loudly. Was he reassuring us, his men or himself? He told us how the first day they took the bodies far out to sea for burial, but they came back in with the tide.

After a while the military man in charge started to help us with the work while the other two military-types kept a gun trained on us. If they hadn't, I would have run and never stopped. As it was, I occasionally had to stop and puke.

My mind started to wander … I needed to check on Blue Eyes and the boy and the baby. I felt responsible for the baby since I had helped the Sister save him. Sister Elizabeth's little hammock idea was perfect. Too bad the clothesline didn't work. In a normal storm it would've enabled her to keep tabs on everyone. I couldn't even imagine what they went through … the ten Roman Catholic Sisters of the Incarnate Word and ninety orphans. I know at least three boys had made it back to town. But their story of the buildings being washed away didn't leave much hope.

Argh, I could smell the putrid, vile odor of burning flesh.

The funeral pyre had been lit. I couldn't stop them. I didn't have a better answer.

Words couldn't describe the nightmare of it all. The feel of tight skin on bloated bodies, cold clammy corpses of people who had once been my friends, my neighbors. I told myself I would not relive this over and over. I would do what I had to do to survive. I would love again. I would laugh again. I would go forward. But I knew deep inside something had fundamentally changed. I would carry this.

THE BOY "SEAN"

I thought John had left us to fend for ourselves. A bachelor like him would probably find Blue Eyes, the baby and myself a burden. I checked around for John near what was left of downtown. Then I went out to the St. Mary's orphanage to look for him. Where were all the nuns and orphans? I headed toward the beach.

It was beginning to dawn on me that the aftermath of the storm was going to leave us with some mysteries that would never be solved. With so many people missing, and so many buildings and documents lost, some things would never be traced or tracked down. This gave me a thought — I could pose as one of the orphans to keep people from asking too many questions about my past.

Holy shit! I saw John up ahead. A man was holding a gun on him.

Positioning myself behind a pile of tangled seaweed, I hid myself from the men. Then, I watched in horror the very same scene I had witnessed the day before—bodies being prepared for funeral pyres. The pain it caused me was so great, I hadn't realized tears were washing down my face until I put my hand up to flick a fly from my cheek.

I had wanted a new life, and for some reason, I wanted that life to be with John. Probably because of his confident ways … John was the kind of person who made people feel safe. And I didn't know how to tell Blue Eyes he might not be coming back to us.

Grief overcame me. I sat down and cried into my hands. I was certain my wails could be heard. But no one came. The men were still there but they had a pain of their own and could not hear mine. I must have cried myself to sleep because when I woke the sun was high in the sky and clouds were floating by, promising a better tomorrow.

JOHN

They held a gun on us and made us drink whiskey. But being drunk just made it worse. After the first two swigs, I only held it to my mouth and kept my lips pressed together tight. No one seemed to notice, and while the others got drunk I kept looking for a way to get away.

There weren't just dead human bodies that needed to be taken care of — there were horses and cows and dogs and even fish. I thought the fish were washed up on land from the storm, but apparently, the old Texan told me, they fell from the sky like rain. In some strange way, the fish were caught up in the fierce winds of the storm and taken very high up. Many of them fell to the earth frozen. People were eating the fish. Might as well before they thawed completely. "Here we are in hell and God found a way to feed us with frozen fish from the sky." That's what Sister Elizabeth would say. A sharp pain jabbed inside my chest as I thought of Sister Elizabeth and the way she was always sorting out everything according to God. Right now, I'd be highly interested in how she'd explain this storm. It sure needed some explaining. Why would a loving God take a nun and nine orphans? I stacked another twisted body on the funeral pyre.

Finally my break came when one of the military-types carrying a gun told me to start another pile for the animal bodies. But his companion pointed out they should take care of all the human remains first. They started to argue and since they were a little drunk, it didn't take much to get

40

them into a screaming match. While everyone turned to watch, I slipped off into the darkness. The morning light would be breaking soon and I had to hurry. Town was about three miles away and I had to negotiate everything that the storm had put in my path.

The closer I got to town, the more I slowed down and began to think back on the night of the storm. How we had been playing cards. Laughing in death's face. It sure took me by surprise when that big wave crashed into the side of the upstairs room we were in. Especially when it pulled back and took part of the wall with it. That's when I ran around to look out the door. Why did I do that? Why not look out the wall hole? It was so big we could have all walked right through it. But only Dean did. He saw the next big wave coming in and he took a gamble. I saw him take a deep breath and leap right into it as it crashed against the side of the house. This time taking everything down and under. In the next second, I found myself riding the very door I was holding as the wave bounced the door and me back up in the salty water. It tossed me about on the roaring ocean much like a child at play in the bath. I clung to the door so hard I would notice later that I left indentions.

I was getting close to town. I should stop in and check on Blue Eyes, baby and the boy before I went back to what was left of my house to look for my friends. However, judging by my wild ride across the island that night on the door they could be anywhere. Including on the mainland.

When I was building the funeral pyre, the policeman said he'd heard one young lady was taken that far. She had to sail back with some of the first rescuers into Galveston to tell her family she was alive. "The bridge is out and the railways are a tangle," he had said. "It's going to a while before things are back to normal."

"I must get out of this black hole."

"What are you saying? Did you speak?" The nun who had been helping trim my hair into some kind of presentable shape asked me again. "Did you speak?" She stopped cutting and peered directly into my face.

"Yes." It sounded foreign as if it was coming from another place, but it was my voice only a little weak and squeaky sounding.

"What is your name? Tell me your name." The nun asked in an excited voice.

"All I could do is repeat, "I must get out of this black hole." It seemed to satisfy the nun and she ran calling, "Sean, Sean. Your mother is talking." Something kept me from saying out loud *is the boy's name Sean?*

2 TENT CITY

JOHN

The tents billowing up ahead made quite a pretty picture against the brilliant blue sky. When had they thrown up this city of tents? And how could I get one? I was going to need a place to stay if I was going to rebuild. It would be easier to leave Galveston, but I was determined to stay.

Just like Jack, I was a barrel maker by trade — but I was finding it a lot easier to make a living by other means these last few months. In fact, I had recently won a lot of money at one of the city's finest gambling establishments. "Aye, the luck of the Irish." I said it aloud to no one. My money and my friends had gone under with that big wave, and I had no hope of getting any of them back but Dean. I hoped he had reached safety when he jumped through the hole torn in the wall during the storm.

While not really a friend in the sense of a friend you could completely trust—Dean was an entertaining personality who brought excitement and fun to everything he touched.

I went to where a group of men were pitching yet another tent. "What does a man have to do to get to live in one of these tents?"

"Well it helps to have a family," a sincere looking little man said. "We're trying to get the women and children out of the elements first."

My first thoughts were to go get the boy, Blue Eyes and the baby. But then I thought better of it. Why would they want to live with a bachelor like me? They were better off with the nuns. And, to tell the truth, the responsibility of the three of them made me a little queasy. I would do well to take care of myself. But I did feel a responsibility to check on the baby. Seeing how's I helped make the swinging crib and all. I felt responsibility for him—like he was mine.

It was strange how everyone seemed to enter a new world when we emerged from the storm. Many of our friends and loved ones gone…Blue Eyes and the boy had been a real comfort to me in those first few hours. I somehow felt responsible for them, too. Especially the baby, since I had managed to help do something really good by saving his life. Sister Elizabeth would be proud.

I looked down at my hands. They were blistered. Dirt filled every crease and crevice. I needed to wash my hands—and considering the kind of work I had just done, I needed to wash my whole body. In very hot water preferably.

"Mister."

The small man looked up from his work. I could tell he was kind by looking at his face. I told him about what had happened. How I had been enlisted to work on the funeral pyres and how much I needed a bath. I could see compassion register in his eyes as he nodded and took me to a

45

tent that had been set up for bathing. One tent for men. One tent for women. Clearly this little man was quite the organizer. He should be mayor of the tent village. I could tell without asking that he was in control of the operation. A hero of sorts in his own quiet, dignified way. Already straightening out the chaos. Thinking ahead and making plans when all most of us could do was take another breath.

I watched as he whispered to two women overseeing the bath tents. They looked at me as he spoke. At one point I saw their eyebrows go up in a surprised sort of way and their mouths made a little "o". Then the little man walked back in my direction.

"Go ahead. The men's tent is empty at the moment. All we ask is that you throw out your own bath water and rinse the tub as best you can. If you're feeling strong enough you could also draw up some buckets of water for them to boil for the next person. Then you can sleep in my family's tent over there until you find your own family." The little man turned to leave me to my bath. Suddenly he turned and extended his hand. "By the way, my name is William Clifford."

"John McLaren," I said as I started to take his hand. "Wait. Better take a bath first before I go shaking your hand." He smiled a short little smile and said, "I'll go tell my wife and daughter you're coming. Maybe they can find something for you to eat. A lady nurse has arrived from the mainland with food, medicine and other necessities."

46

I entered the tent to find a steaming tub of water and soap. I took off my clothes and began to soak. There were no towels. No washcloths. So I used my shirt, which also reminded me that I needed to wash all my clothes. After I bathed, I put the rest of my things into soak. Then I got down naked on my hands and knees and scrubbed each piece of clothing as I thought to myself, "God, please don't let anyone walk in and find me in this awkward position."

Actually, a lot of people had lost all or most of their clothes in the storm so it probably wouldn't have shocked anyone. The thought made me sad and I shook a little inside as I remembered those survivors running naked just after the floodwaters had subsided. Many were crying and screaming on the very edge of insanity as they raced around trying to find loved ones.

I was going to have to put my ragged clothes back on wet. Thankfully the afternoon sun was making for an unusually warm September day. I poured out the water and rinsed the tub, but I was too weak to draw up more water.

It was all I could do to get myself across the way to William Clifford's tent. His wife and daughter welcomed me with food. I told them I was grateful. I sat down on the little bed they offered and began to eat. I don't remember falling asleep or how long I slept, but when I woke up I found my world had changed again.

This time it appeared for the better.

I couldn't believe my eyes, my long-lost friend Dean was sitting cross-legged on the floor inches from me. Just staring. Not at me, but rather through me. His left hand and rib cage were bandaged. The bandages were clean and wound very methodically, obviously tied by someone who knew what they were doing.

"Where did you find clean bandages?" I managed to creak. My throat and voice were hoarse from so much crying the day before.

"Good God man, I thought you were dead like the others." Dean's deep baritone filled the tiny tent and made me realize what a miracle it was that we were both alive. "I got the bandages from a lady nurse that has arrived to save all 37,789 of us Galvestonians. Only now I suspect there are a lot less of us by the looks of things," he said as he handed me a newspaper. "Here, take a look for yourself."

"They're able to put a newspaper out already?" My voice was growing stronger.

"Yep, and it's got a long list of the dead and missing." He pointed to a list of names. "Here's our friend Constantine and here's crazy Pete. I found Harry in the morgue of all places. Not too many in the morgue because they decided to burn them where they found them."

I looked at him carefully to judge his reaction to the funeral pyres. He didn't seem to notice as he continued talking. "Seems like the best idea as there must be hundreds of bodies. Some are saying thousands."

I interrupted him. "Dean, how did you find me?"

"Well, I wasn't really looking for you so much as I stumbled across where you was at. A young girl helping the nurse lady, told her about a man who'd just come through to take a bath and get a good night's sleep in her family's tent. She said the man told her father that he had found some of the orphans and a nun dead and buried in the sand. All attached together with clothesline." Dean paused and sucked in his breath before continuing, "I knew it had to be you she was talking about. You were always hanging out around there helping Sister Elizabeth. Hell, ain't that why you were late getting back to our card game that night? You were helping her with the orphans." He settled back into his cross-legged position and started to stare off into the distance again. "I'm glad I found you, John."

"I'm glad you found me too Dean. I need all the friends I can get. Even if they are cheating lying gamblers like yourself."

"Yessiree, I resemble that remark." He moved out of his sitting position and into a fetal one. "Tell me what happens next my friend." His eyes were heavy and he was on the edge of sleep.

"Dean, you know what I heard?" I didn't expect an answer, but to my surprise he responded.

49

"What did you hear? And it better be pleasant because I don't want any bad dreams." Dean was looking at me with one eye open and one eye closed.

"I heard they're going to go through with that plan they were discussing before the storm of building a seawall…and they're contemplating raising the whole island."

"Now how the hell they going to do that? Or better yet why the hell are they going to do that?" Dean was fully awake and sitting upright.

"To restore Galveston to its former glory. To get our lives back," I almost yelled.

"Well I got news for you. Ain't nobody going to get their former lives back the way they was. We all need to move forward now—quit pining about the past and make ourselves a future." He slid back down on his thin blanket and turned on his side with his back toward me. "Hell, I don't even know if I'm going to stay on this glorious island that everyone seems to love so much. It ain't Texas' crown jewel no more…No Ellis Island of the South."

"Where you going to go Dean?" Silence filled the tent. Just when I thought he wasn't going to answer, he did in one of the tiredest voices I've ever heard. "Let me sleep on it. I'll tell you in the morning if you still want to know."

Heaven is where I stay now. It's another dimension of time filled with bright shimmering light and joy. Most humans are not capable of imagining its eternal beauty. I know I wouldn't have been able when I was in my human state. I had no frame of reference. And while it is wonderful here, I do sweep down to check in on my earthly brethren. Today, I'm with the boy and Sarah Michelle on the beach.

SARAH MICHELLE

The boy Sean wanted me to go down to the beach. He said sunshine would lift my spirits. He said he knew a stretch of beach that had already been cleared of debris and dead bodies. It was the first time I had actually seen the funeral pyres. They didn't really bother me as much as I originally thought they would. Lord knows, after what I've witnessed, I may never feel an emotion again.

However, I was glad I had left the baby Lucky with the nuns. Smoke wouldn't be good for a baby.

When we got to the beach, Sean found a shady spot for me to sit on a blanket he'd brought. Then he ran up and down where the sand met the water, leaving footprints for only a moment before they were washed away. Up and down he ran throwing his arms in the air and in general being a silly fool. I wish I could be a silly fool. I wish this heaviness that was sitting on my heart would subside.

I looked down at the sand near the blanket. Some kind of vegetation was trying to grow. As if the world hadn't fallen. As if hundreds, perhaps thousands hadn't died. I looked up in the sky and I knew somewhere in this world it was someone's happiest day ever. Somewhere someone was falling in love at first sight, lifting their newborn up into the air, feeling their deepest wish fulfilled. Experiencing one of the once in a lifetime moments that are so special. And that person probably didn't even know about what had happened here.

How many truly awful things had happened in the world that I didn't know about? How many times had I been laughing or loving or simply spending my time mindlessly as someone else's world was coming apart in a most terrifying or terrible way?

I looked out across the way to check on Sean. He was totally engrossed in his play. Dipping his toes in the chilly water, chasing sand crabs, basking in the sunlight.

How I wished to be normal again. To just simply *be*.

But nothing was normal and I felt discombobulated. Nervous and jittery. Far from myself looking at what was going on in the real world as though I didn't belong to it anymore. My eyes wandered back to the edge of the blanket. A small ant was trying to hoist itself up on it. The last thing I remember thinking before breaking down was, "How did that ant manage to survive such a storm?"

My heart was racing. Panic overcame me and the tears took control. Great heaving silent sobs. How will I go on? How will I cope? There's no one to help me. No one to love me. No one to comfort me. My body was shaking so it hurt my heart. Breaking my heart. I had no kerchief and snot ran down my face. I could taste the salt in my mouth. I tried to wipe it with my hand, but did not dare to soil the beautiful dress that Sean brought to me. Where he found it goodness knows. I had never owned such a fine piece of clothing.

Crying, I laid down in the blanket, using it partly to clean my face and partly to hide from the world. Suddenly I felt Sean's hand on my shoulder, stroking my back. "Don't cry, now. Don't cry," he said over and over as a parent must have done for him at some point in time. Some very kind person who knew how to comfort when there were no words of encouragement to be said. After all, there was nothing to be said. Nature had decided to remind us that she was in control and we were forced to accept it.

Finally my panic subsided and I sat up. My nose and throat were swollen. Sean sat quietly beside me while I tried to recover. My heaving sobs slowly turned into quite hiccup-type sounds—something that would have made me laugh out loud in the past. Neither one of us laughed. We couldn't. We could only sit. We sat that way for quite some time before Sean pointed out to the sky and the clouds hovering over the tranquil water and said, "Just for a second when I was playing, I forgot that the world had changed. Look how beautiful it is."

I felt like that beautiful sky was falling in on me. But a little less so thanks to Sean. I knew at that moment I would not tell the nuns that he was not my child and I would wait for him to tell me why he had told them he was. When he was ready, he would tell me why he was pretending to be someone other than he was. He had hinted to me he was one of the missing orphans. But I didn't believe his story. For one thing, he was too well educated. I could tell it by his manner, the way he held himself. The way he talked. I also knew Sean was not his real name. He didn't respond to it quickly enough when I called out to him.

Knowing all this, I felt there was no real need to rush Sean. The truth would come out a little at a time. It always does. Hadn't I learned that myself? In my heart, I believed Sean was not capable of wrongdoing. His secret persona must exist for a good reason.

A gull flew overhead and gnats buzzed nearby. The little ant had finally made it up the blanket. I started to flick it off, but didn't want to hurt it. Didn't want to take away its hard-earned success of getting what it wanted out of life. Then for some reason, Sean and I both knew it was time to go and we stood and dusted off the blanket. I folded it carefully so that the tear-stained part was on the inside where it would not touch my beautiful dress and we left. I was thankful to Sean for being there. My grandmother had told me even in the roughest times God always gave you something or someone to help you get through.

My thoughts wandered as we walked and I wondered where John was and if we'd ever see him again. For some reason I looked for him in every face we passed on our way back. It had been the same on the way out here, too. Perhaps if I found him he could tell me more about the baby we had saved at the orphanage. The Lord giveth and the Lord taketh away was another thing my grandmother used to say. God, I wonder if you were trying to prove this by letting a helpless baby and a tiny ant survive this storm while many a strong man died.

As if to read my thoughts, Sean started telling me a story of how someone had found a puppy that had survived the storm by riding in a closed dresser drawer. Apparently the lightweight bureau tossed about on the sea like a ship and when its owner found it and opened the drawer, the puppy was inside just as he had been when he put him there before the storm.

"Wonder if the little puppy even knew what happened?" I said out loud. "Aside from being shaken up a bit and hearing lots of commotion, the little animal probably didn't know his life was in danger." Sean looked at me intently as we continued to walk. "I'm glad you started talking," he said with a happy smile.

He started twirling around with his arms outstretched like any ordinary boy on any ordinary day. No worries. No cares. Then he turned to me and said something very strange. "I didn't steal the clothes I brought to you."

The boy was able to release his cares. But Sarah Michelle, Sarah Michelle couldn't put her burdens down.

JOHN

A good stiff drink is what I wanted. But then again, I always wanted a good stiff drink. Problem is getting any kind of alcohol in this mess. Dean was a heavy drinker, too. Yet he didn't seem to be craving it as much as me. Maybe I should cut back.

I looked over at Dean. He was smiling as he said, "Let's go get that lady and them kids. Sooner they're with us, faster they'll give us our tent." Dean pushed back his hair from over his eyes as he said these words to me and anyone else who was in ear shot.

Dean had a lot of hair and the ladies seemed to like it and just about everything else about his caddish self. Which reminded me that maybe Dean wasn't the right person to be putting up a shelter with us. I didn't know if the others would be comfortable with him. His way of life and all the things he'd seen and done. But he was physically strong and I knew he wouldn't hurt anyone or anything. Just does plenty of cussin' and gamblin'. That's all.

"What you thinking so hard about?" Dean poked me in the side. He was smiling and happy this morning. A person like him didn't get too upset over anything.

We walked along to the building where Blue Eyes, the baby and the boy were staying.

I looked straight ahead as I asked Dean a question that had been bothering me. "What happened to all your money you made?"

"You mean the money I won the night of the storm at your house or the money from the fine business establishment I was a partner in?"

"Your business."

He didn't answer at first. Then he stopped and picked up a rock. He examined it closely. "It went out into the ocean. The ocean took it all. Everything. Somewhere out there is a big ole safe with a whole lot of money in it. Good luck trying to find it. Wasn't a stick of lumber left of the building." He put the rock in his pocket. "Ocean took the money I won that night too. But it puked me back up. Guess the ocean doesn't want me to have any money. Don't really need it anyway. Ain't got no one to take care of except me. And, lord knows, I don't need nothing fancy."

"Now that's not true. You're one of the best dressed men in town."

"And I'm one of the most handsome, too." He smiled wide showing all of his perfect teeth and I laughed. He was joking but it was true. My girl had always seemed to notice him. Always ready to flirt with him. Wonder where she is now. Wonder if she'd heard about the storm. Don't guess I could rightly call her my girl anymore. Seeing as she just up and left a few months ago to go pursue her career.

Dean seemed to know what I was thinking. "Do you hear from January?"

"No, she's singing somewhere I guess."

"How'd she get that name January? Was she born that time of year?"

"Actually, she was born in October. Guess they named her January because it sounded better for a girl's name than October. Or maybe it was because she was cold-hearted. Or maybe they just liked the sound of the name."

"Makes a nice stage name." Dean picked up another rock and put it in his pocket. He squinted his eyes against the sun. "Damn, it's hot. I bet them guys burning them bodies are dying. Let's keep out of their line of sight lest they recruit us." From that point on we kept completely silent as we stealthily made our way to Blue Eyes, the boy and the baby. We would do our part to help rebuild, but I had had enough of funeral pyres.

SARAH MICHELLE

I wasn't surprised to see John walking up to the church. And I wasn't surprised to hear him ask if Sean and I would bring the baby and live with him in a tent. Somewhere in my mind it was imprinted that we were family now. A collection of orphans ourselves.

"I need help," tears started to fall down my face, "… with the baby."

Sean started to cry too, which was unusual. He had maintained such a happy façade for the last few days. What was his story? Maybe he was just glad to be alive. If his story of being an orphan were true, he wouldn't be grieving his parents, but he could be grieving his caregivers and his friends.

"We can get your things and leave now." John was very kind. "I'm glad you're talking." He didn't know what to say.

Dean stepped forward and took the baby from me. Sean gathered our little group of belongings and we said goodbye to the refugees at the church. That's all there was to it. That's how simple life was these days.

Walking along to the tents, I saw a trunk that belonged to me. It held my special papers and memories inside. Without stopping, I leaned over and picked it up. No one even questioned if it was mine. John also saw a pipe and picked it up.

Finders keepers. No one on the island had much of anything at all anymore. Thus we all shared everything and no one even fought. Not even siblings. Once that started again I knew we would be normal. But people weren't back to their petty ways. The storm had showed us how insignificant our everyday cares were. My insides shook, as did my legs. And I just walked on one foot in front of the other. To my amazement my body held up even under the weight of my chest of memories.

It's always exciting to move into a new place. Even in these dire circumstances. It would be nice to have an area of our own and a place to cook. A place to stretch out and think. A place to recover whatever I could of myself. Thank goodness that man is carrying the baby and he's doing a good job of keeping it happy.

The man looked up and saw me smiling at the baby. He flashed a smile and his dimples showed prominently. Up until that point I hadn't really looked at him.

"My name's Dean."

I was suddenly aware of what I must look like with my hair chopped off. Was the left side of my face still a purple bruise? My eyes still red in the parts that were supposed to be white?

I nodded. That was all I could muster and it seemed to be enough.

John and Sean were running to a group of men. I could see John pointing back to me and Dean with the baby. Then he pointed at Sean. I could see the men shaking their heads and giving him some paperwork and a pencil.

John took the paper and pencil. I heard him say, "Can anybody read this to me?" Sean said he could. And he could write in the blanks for everyone's name too. We all called out our names and Sean wrote his name down last. I couldn't see what he wrote.

"Now," John was excited. "Let's go get our tent."

We went back to the group of men and one of them told us to come with him. He took us to a white tent with quite a large space inside. It was one of a number of tents set up on a grid system. We would have to do something to distinguish our tent from the others so we could find our way back to it.

Inside there were some blankets and bedrolls. We had at least one pot that Sean had found for us earlier. The man was telling us where to take our baths and get drinking water. I hoped the others were listening because I wasn't. My eyes and thoughts were on a small woman in the doorway of the tent. She had brought us food. Hot steaming soup.

I ate and slept. Later I would discover it was Dean who took care of the baby.

JOHN

Sarah Michelle was asleep and didn't hear the gunshots.

Dean said he didn't want to know what it was all about. So Sean and I left the newborn with him and went toward the sound of the chaos. It didn't take us long to find out it was a couple of men who had been shot for stealing from the dead. Specifically, taking money and valuables off of the dead bodies. There hadn't been too much stealing. Depending on what you referred to as stealing. People's stuff was everywhere, all mixed up together, and honestly we had all been doing a bit of taking here and there. Clothes, pots & pans, dishes, furniture that had survived intact, and the various odd toy or decorative object. Some things were found by those they belonged to but the majority went to new owners, and the way I figured it, it all turned out even for those of us left alive as we took what we could. After all, we were left with nothing, starting anew.

But no one asked my opinion and it was too late to voice it out loud. Here were three more men shot dead and for no good reason. Others would say it established order on the island. Perhaps so, because we all were a lot more careful about what we picked up and took with us from then on.

It made quite an impact on Sean. He said not a word. And I realized this was no place for a kid. I was definitely not used to having a kid around.

"Let's go back." I said aloud as I looked at the disgruntled crowd.

Sean didn't answer; he just took my hand and started walking in the direction of the tent. I was touched. Nobody had ever taken my hand and looked up to me before, and I was sorry that I had been feeling like Sean might be a thorn in my side. He wasn't much trouble and he took care of himself. In a few years, he would be more of a friend and sidekick I suppose than a child. But right now he was a child and the moment was too much for him.

Later that night events seemed to show up in Sean's dreams. He cried out in his sleep and screamed as I had heard some other people do a few days after the storm. I went to him but Sarah Michelle was already there. He was clawing the air and pushing her away. Even when she got him awake he wouldn't quit crying. The baby roused but went back to sleep as Dean picked him up in his arms. I don't know what I would have done if both of them had gone off.

Finally Sean seemed more awake than asleep. Sarah Michelle wrapped her arms around him. He reached out for me and I did the same. It was a strange but comforting feeling. Somehow we all stretched out on the blankets and Sarah Michelle fell asleep.

"John are you awake?" said Sean.

"Yes."

"John I took some jewelry when I was out looking for stuff."

My stomach turned and screwed up hard. From across the room Dean moved a little.

I couldn't tell if Dean was asleep or awake as I whispered, "You haven't done nothing most of us haven't done or thought about. You're just a boy, Sean."

Dean stirred. Now it was evident he was awake. In a quiet voice he said, "Tomorrow Sean, you and I will go take care of things. There's no need for anyone else to know or for us to speak of this again. Tents ain't no place for secrets."

THE BOY "SEAN"

"Oh God! Oh God!"

People and shouts filled our small tent. Someone was twisting my arm and pulling me off my pallet. Someone else clubbed me with something hard. Blood filled my eyes.

"Get up," screamed a man's voice. And just like that I was dragged out into the angry crowd.

"Is this one of the boy's you saw taking jewelry off of corpses?" a deep man's voice said, so low the rowdy crowd was forced to quiet in order to hear.

"Yes. That's him. I think. He's had a bath. His hair is combed." Another voice I didn't recognize.

The man that dragged me outside of our tent gave me a small kick as he said. "Boy, do you know what the punishment is for looting?"

I couldn't answer because he had his foot on the side of my mouth. Twisting, pushing down. My teeth cut against my inner mouth. His boot tasted of sandy mud. My head swam. It hurt so bad . . . so bad. The crowd was crazy. Ugly. Half indignant, half afraid they would get caught for the small crimes they had committed as well. Life as I knew it was no more. We had new rules now and people had done things they had never done before. Me included. Help me God.

A single female scream pierced the crowd. People became stone still and the scream pierced the air again, only one octave higher.

The scream reminded me of the storm. Screams, screams, screams … then quiet, as the person succumbed to the storm … gone from that frightful night of horror, out of this pain-filled world, I told myself, and into heaven.

"This boy did not steal anything." The form of a tall man moved forward through the crowd. "Why would he, he's the son of one of the wealthiest men in Houston."

The tall man reached his hand into his coat pocket and produced a small photo of a family and held it up to the crowd. "Compare his face to the one here in the photo. This child is no thief. He is R. L. Stockton, Junior. As in, son of the railway magnate R. L. Stockton."

The man holding his boot over my face released the pressure and pulled back. He held the stick with a burning rag up close to my face. Then he moved the light back toward the photo. He pulled me to my feet.

"May I remind the crowd that the generous Mr. Stockton has already donated plenty to help the people of this island during this tragedy. Much more than this boy would have taken, if indeed he did take it." My bold rescuer addressed the crowd as he reached down and gently brushed sand from my face. "Now let's get going son. Your Poppa's waiting. And your sisters are worried about you."

67

And just like that I was thrust back into my old life of terror and pain without even a chance to explain things to Sarah Michelle, Dean and John.

SARAH MICHELLE

I don't remember much after I screamed. Dean and John told me the story of how the man came through the crowd with the photo. Sean's gone. I'm so distraught. Can't even think again. How am I going to care for the baby without Sean to help me?

"He gave the jewelry to me." I said to no one in particular. "He brought me all kinds of gifts he had found. It was just his way of showing appreciation. Friendship. Sean didn't understand it was so wrong."

Dean took my hand. "What bothers me more is that he seemed to prefer being in this hell than going back to his family."

"Yes, Sean sure didn't try to leave," John said as he sat on the floor of the tent and sifted sand through his hand. "Told me a cock-a-bull story about being an orphan. I knew all the orphans. He wasn't one."

"I'm going to go after him." Dean stood and started packing a few things. "Just make sure he's alright with where that man's taking him. Houston was it? I think that's what he said."

"It ain't going to be easy with the rail lines down and the bridge out." John countered.

"I don't like doing nothing easy. Besides I would like to get off the island for a while. Get away from all this," he said looking at me as if to ask if I wanted to go with him.

I stared at him blankly and said, "Thanks Dean for going to check on Sean. I don't think I could go on without knowing he's okay."

"I'll be back." And just like that Dean was gone too.

I began to cry again. I curled up on the floor and shook and cried till my tears ran dry. John sat beside me for a while and awkwardly stroked my arm and back. Eventually he stretched out beside me and put his arm around me. Tears ran down his eyes and he shook a little too.

The baby slept, peacefully unaware of all the heartbreak in the world it had entered.

Outside, crickets sang. As I pulled the rough woolen covers up under my chin, I wondered how the crickets had survived the storm.

Because I knew Sarah Michelle would not quit worrying, I prayed God would let her escape into a deep, dreamless sleep. I watched John slip the bottle out of its hiding place when he thought no one could see him. And I watched as he drank himself into oblivion.

JOHN

Sarah Michelle was a very handsome woman even with her ragged short hair and tear-stained face. I tried to remember if I had seen her before the storm. I thought I recognized her a little from the first moment I found her tangled in the debris. For some reason, I could see her with her husband and son. They both had dark hair. Her son looked a lot like her husband. In my mind's eye, they were dressed in church clothes.

Then it hit me. I had seen them at the orphanage. They had come to see Sister Elizabeth. They wanted to adopt one of the orphans. Perhaps even the baby that slept so quietly in its basket now. No wonder Sarah Michelle took Lucky as if he were her own.

I could see the three of them sitting on the front porch in rockers. Drinking lemonade. Enjoying the sunny day. The ocean waves whispering underneath their lively conversation and occasional laughter. Who would have thought the ocean could become so angry and dangerous as to take the lives of two of them and torture the third one so?

Yes, I had seen Sarah Michelle before. It was a small enough island. It would be hard not to have noticed her.

I remember that day—I was happy too. Fixing a clothesline. It was probably the extra line I had left behind that they had used to link the children together the night of the storm. I meant to use it to put up a second clothesline near the girl's dormitory.

Sarah Michelle started to stir. She opened her eyes and wasn't surprised to find me right beside her. Looking back at me. She whispered. "I had a cat once. I took her in after her owner had abandoned her. She was a beautiful cat and she was pregnant. And I was pregnant at the same time. I related to her and I took care of her. Gave her food and fresh water. And she brought me lizards and tiny snakes she had killed. She brought me gifts to show her gratitude to me for taking her in. Just like Sean did."

I brushed the hair out of her eyes. She continued, "I knew he wasn't an orphan. Sean was very refined, very cultured. Did you know he played the piano?"

"No."

"We found one sitting in the middle of a street when we went on a picnic. It still played and he went to town on it. Played some really sprightly songs."

"'Twas surprising how well he could write the day we moved into the tent," I paused before continuing, "I never pushed the issue with Sean, but I knew he was hiding something bigger than a few stolen jewels. I saw scars made by a whip on the lad's back when he changed his shirt the other day. Scars that had been there for years."

We didn't say anything more. We just held each other until sleep came. In the morning Sarah Michelle said her throat was sore from crying.

3 HOUSTON

DEAN

There was a curfew of sorts to keep order. So there weren't many people out meddling around this time of night. It was easy to slip through the darkness, with a little moonlight peeping through the clouds to guide the way. I hoped the man was taking Sean to Houston because that's where I wanted to go.

I wished I had a horse, but that was not going to happen. Most all the horses and cows had been killed in the storm. Not too many of any kind of animal had survived. Even the fish had taken a hit. I wanted to hurry and get to Houston and leave all this behind. Get a room. Have a nice meal. Have a drink. I had a hundred dollar bill, one that I carried on me at all times for luck. It was drenched and dried out, but I reckoned the hotel would take it.

The cemetery was ahead. I had one job to fulfill before crossing to the mainland. Didn't even tell John and Sarah Michelle because I didn't want them to know where the jewelry went in case someone interrogated them.

The cemetery was a disaster. Some of the above ground graves were washed away from their original locations and some of the ones in the ground had been brought to the surface. Damn storm. Even tried to hurt the dead.

At last I found what I was looking for. A dark gray headstone with no ornamentation—nothing to set it apart from the others.

I got down on my hands and knees and started to feel around in the dark. I found the loose stone on the front and moved it out. Everything was just as it should be. I moved the interior stone a bit and felt around inside. I took out three gold coins I had left there years before. My mother had given them to me just before she died. It was all she had. I didn't trust banks, still don't. Three gold coins were a lot of money for me at the time. It felt good to know I had them to fall back on. They were cold and heavy. I slipped them into my pocket and pulled out a small kerchief with the jewelry. It fit in the hole perfectly. I was pushing the last stone back when I felt a sharp piece of metal against my shoulder blade.

"What the hell you doing Dean?"

Clouds were passing over the moon now, but I had just enough light to see his face. It was one of the soldiers that had made us burn the dead bodies. He also had frequented my gambling establishment on more than one occasion. At least it was a familiar face.

"I'm praying for my poor dead Mama that she doesn't worry about me in this devastation." I tried to smile my most charming smile. "How are you this fine night, Seamus?"

I could hear the strike of a match. It flared in the velvet darkness as he lit a lantern. "Better not be stealing anything from the dead like that boy living in your tent." He held the lantern to the tombstone. My mother's name appeared in the light. He didn't look down to see that the stone I was kneeling over wasn't pushed all the way in line with the others.

"You're a strange one. Can't imagine the likes of you even having a mother." He laughed and I could see the glint of his white smile in the darkness. He pulled out a bottle and offered me a swig of whiskey. I didn't really want it, but I took it so he wouldn't be offended.

"Do you still carry a hundred dollar bill on you for luck?" I knew by the way he slurred his words he was drunk and his tone seemed to be less threatening than when I first saw him. I didn't answer and he continued, "You know I didn't like having to push men to burn the dead. You know that don't you?"

"It had to be done." I told the truth.

"Yeah, well I'm not such a bad guy. Just doing my job. Do you need a ride to your tent?"

"No, Seamus. I'm on my way to Houston."

"Dean, you know we need every man available to get this island back in shape."

"You're a good man, Seamus. Let me go, I have business there. It can't wait."

"Then get the hell on my horse and I'll take you as far as the bridge. But you know you can't go over it. You'll have to find your own way from there. And, if anybody stops us, I ain't helping you, you're my prisoner."

I kicked the stone in line with the others. Not that anyone would notice with the cemetery being torn up the way it was after the storm. I hitched up my pants and threw a leg over the back of his horse. A horse was a true treasure now on Galveston.

" Look at that Dean. That there's the new fence they just built around the cemetery. I heared a joke about that fence when I was playing cards back at your place."

"What joke was that, Seamus?"

"Feller says you know why they built a fence around the cemetery? People are just dying to get in."

We both laughed as the horse we were on slipped like a shadow through the night. It was the last noise or bit of conversation we made, as we both knew it would not benefit us to draw attention to ourselves. Seamus nodded to me quietly as he left me off near the bridge. I could hear the water gently lapping nearby. It was so dark I could not tell which direction he had taken. I couldn't even see what was around me. But I needed to get across before sunup. I was going to have to look for a boat.

Or something that floated. Maybe a door like the one John rode on during the storm. I myself preferred a boat.

I heard a voice coming toward me. I stood stock-still.

It was the boy Sean's voice. He was with the man that had saved his life. The man that was taking him back to his family in Houston.

"Who goes there?" I heard myself saying.

Silence.

I waited for what seemed like an eternity before I said, "My name's Dean Johnson. I aim to go to Houston if I can find myself a boat."

A man's voice broke the night air just paces from me. "Well now, I thought all able-bodied men needed to stay on Galveston to help with the rebuilding."

"I have a wife in Houston. She must be scared sick about me." I lied. "I need to go tell her I'm alive."

"Dean Johnson. You didn't tell me you had a wife." I thought it was the boy Sean's voice.

"Who's that?' I said to be certain.

"It's me Sean," the boy answered back.

"Sean. Are you alright, son?"

"This boy's name is Robert," a man's deep voice corrected me. Yet another match lit the night, only this time a small candle illuminated the darkness. "Why did you tell him your name was Sean? Were you afraid he would hold you for ransom?"

Sean addressed the man who had rescued him earlier in a pleading tone, "I told him my name was Sean because I did not want to return home. Dean helped me. He doctored my cut hand with medicine." Sean hesitated. "I lived in a tent with him and three others and we helped each other."

"Let's not linger here. Let's head for the boat," the man's voice softened. "I feared you were truly dead when I found your name listed in the newspaper."

"Yes, I turned my name in myself. Told them I was the servant boy at the Lloyd house and that I had seen Robert Stockton, Jr. dead with my own eyes."

"You need to go back boy. You can't live here in this … this hell on earth." The man's voice paused before continuing. "Your sisters and father are worried."

"And my dear wife must be beside herself." I added in a pleading voice. "I must let her know I'm alive and I have already helped a great deal here."

"My boat's down this way a bit." He blew the candle out. "I'm going to save the candle for when we cast off. Just then the clouds slid completely from the moon and our way was lighted.

I looked down and noticed the man was leading Sean-Robert by a rope tied around his hands. "Why don't you let the boy go? It'll be dangerous to cross the water in a small boat with his hands tied."

"Who said we were crossing in a small boat?" The man said. I could see the flash of a knife blade as he freed Sean's hands.

I moved along the water's edge following the trio in their dark world. Carefully, I watched their every footfall. Only the boy seemed to be aware of me. Dean didn't believe in such nonsense as religion or spirits. There had been a time when he believed he felt God's presence. Specifically, when he was performing a life-saving procedure. But that was his past. Dean rarely thought of anything from his past. He preferred the here and now. I ran my hand over his damp, dark hair and patted his shoulder. I saw him visibly shiver then relax. He could feel me, even though he wouldn't acknowledge it even to himself.

JOHN

At first it was uncomfortable being the only two in the tent together. We had the baby but that only seemed to make us more self-conscious.

We got past things by doing daily tasks. Cooking, cleaning, tidying up. Of course, I went out each day to help put up more tents for others who were now coming to our little village ... a sea of white tents flapping like seagulls in the wind.

Not too many days after Sean and Dean had left there was a rainstorm. It started in the afternoon just like the big storm. Only this time people didn't ignore it. Children started to cry and people got nervous. I didn't wait. I went home to the tent where I found Sarah Michelle sitting on the floor shaking. Head put down on her knees. Arms wrapped tightly around her legs. The baby cooed in the basket beside her.

She looked up when I entered the tent and held out her arms. I sat down beside her and we held each other. *Oh God, 'tis just a rainstorm.* Yet we both cowered.

"Sarah Michelle would you like to dance?" I said to shake our fear.

She looked at me like I was crazy, and she began to laugh. She stood and curtsied. I took her hand. Then we danced. We swept around the almost-empty tent, kicking blankets out of the way and stepping all over the thin pallets we had made.

Sarah Michelle's dress swished above the little one's head as we passed by and I thought I saw a smile form on Lucky's face.

"Look, Lucky is smiling."

Sarah Michelle countered, "An infant Lucky's age cannot smile."

"But he smiled." I insisted. "Look! Will you?"

Sarah Michelle looked in the baby's direction. "I'll be. He is smiling. He has no fear. He remembers not a thing of the storm. It would be nice if we had some music."

I started to hum.

"Now aren't you a talented man." She smiled at me and I noticed how her blue eyes danced. This was a real smile. "You can fix almost anything."

"Even a broken heart." I said as I pulled her closer. Hot blood cursed through my veins at the feel of her full breasts on my chest. Her heart was beating wildly. I could see desire as she boldly looked up at my face. But almost as soon as the lightning occurred between us, Sarah Michelle pulled back. I held her tightly and I felt her body start to melt into mine again. Leaning forward, I let my lips lightly brush against hers.

Brushing her hair back from her forehead, I looked deeply into her eyes and saw confusion and fear. She was not ready for what was happening between us.

Quickly, I released my hold and held her at arm's length as I said, "It's been so long since I smiled, the sides of my face hurt." The tension drained from her body.

I began dancing with her again, as I continued. "My face muscles aren't used to moving in the up direction." As I whirled her around, we both laughed, and she said, "My face hurts too."

And for a moment we were happy.

DEAN

The boat was so large it was manned with four sailors to help us across. A few strangers were also in the boat. A couple needed to carry their teen-aged son across in hopes of getting medical help at a Houston hospital. He was lying on a stretcher they had fashioned. Bloody rags wrapped around his head.

Sean's rescuer spoke with the sailors before turning to us. "Let us go. The sun is coming up. We will use the injured boy as an excuse if we are stopped for any reason." Then he turned, extended his hand and introduced himself to me. "My name is Hansen."

I shook his hand and said, "My name is Dean." Then I turned to Sean and said, "I guess you would like me to call you Robert."

"Yes, that would be best." Sean grimaced as he said it. Then looking at the injured boy who was about his age, he said. "Do you think he'll be alright?"

"A hospital will give him the best chance. I'm surprised there are not more injuries going to the Houston hospital..."

Sean interrupted me, "A lady named Clara Barton and eleven volunteers were sent to bring medical supplies and help with the injured on the island. She was also helping the orphaned children. Someone told me to go there. But I didn't want to."

Hansen looked hurt, but he only said, "There must be a lot of orphans after the storm."

"No," Robert-Sean replied. "Surprisingly not." He glanced at the injured boy and said to me. "Let's talk of finding this wife of yours. What's her name?"

"January. Her name is January." I said aloud more to myself more than anyone else.

"Before you go to your wife, I would like you to meet Robert's parents so they may reward you." Hansen was digging around in some boxes. He brought out some food. "There's cups in that box if you don't mind getting them out."

The sun was starting to break over the horizon. Shots of colored light filled the sky. Seagulls flew near the big, billowing sails of our boat. It was a magnificent view. The woman with the injured son looked up. It seemed like a sign for all of us. "Mother Nature isn't mad at us anymore," Robert stated flatly as he stared at the morning sky.

"I don't know that she ever was. That's just her way." The injured boy's mother said to Robert. "You know what they say, change is in the wind."

"I have an ambulance standing by on the shore." Hansen volunteered. "You and your family may use it. I don't believe Robert will be needing it."

"Did you expect him to be hurt? Did someone contact you?" She questioned.

"I didn't know. The telegraph lines were down. We didn't know how bad things were." He stopped for a moment. "The last official word was casualties are to be expected. I, ah, I didn't know exactly what to expect so I came prepared for the worst."

The woman looked down at her own son before continuing, "And how is it you were in Galveston, Robert?" The woman asked politely to change the serious nature of the conversation.

"I was visiting my Aunt Tulia Lloyd's house. I was only supposed to stay a day and a half on this particular visit. Even though I visit often, this was my first time to travel by myself."

"The Lloyd house is one of the grandest mansions in Galveston," the woman commented. "May I inquire if your Aunt and the rest of her family survived the storm?" She didn't try to mince words, as almost everyone had lost someone. It would have been more impolite not to ask.

"No. Just me ... and one servant boy. We went to the attic to watch. When things got real bad, we chopped a hole in the roof with an ax he found there. We stayed on the roof for the better part of the storm. He went to look for his family as soon as he could. I didn't see his family's last name listed in the newspapers so I'm hoping for the best for him."

"I'm sorry your news is not as good. I'm happy this man has found you and is bringing you home."

Hansen came over and said, "Robert, after I get you home, I'll need to go back for your relative's bodies so we can give them a proper funeral."

"No, they've already been burned. I'm certain I saw my aunt and uncle in one of the funeral pyres before it was lit." Robert turned and looked out over the water. "If I had been braver, I would have taken their bodies out and claimed them. But they were near the bottom, you understand," Robert's voice trailed off.

"You don't have to talk…" I intervened.

"I did take my Aunt's jewelry from what was left of her house and I gave it to a lady that helped me survive."

I cocked an eyebrow at Robert's last words. Of course, the boy wasn't a thief.

SARAH MICHELLE

John surprised me when he came into the tent in the early afternoon. He was waving a small piece of paper. "Sarah Michelle, I've been to where my house used to be and there is nothing left." He waved the paper again. "But a crew is working on this street that I believe you may have lived near." He held out the small piece of paper to me.

"I thought you couldn't read John." I said as I took the paper from him.

"I've been learning. I can read and write some. I wrote the address down of the area they're at now."

"It's my street. The house number is near my house." I put my fist to my mouth and bit down hard on my knuckles. "What did you see?"

"I think you should come. Some of the houses are not completely destroyed." He took my arm and pulled me to the door of the tent. "Get the baby."

When we got to my old house, my stomach turned inside out. The neighborhood was almost unrecognizable. I knew there were other parts of the island that were worse.

John had nothing but the door he rode during the storm. He was keeping it, he said, to put on a new house if he decided to rebuild.

Then I saw the tree that was in our front yard. It still had leaves on it—green leaves—and I went and sat underneath it. I looked out toward the water in the distance and for a moment pretended nothing had changed. I took in the salt air. I felt the sandy soil. Any minute now the children would be coming home from school.

I turned around to my shell of a house. John wanted me to come inside. I gingerly walked through the front door. "Careful" he said. "Careful." I gave the baby to him.

Once past the front foyer of my dining room, I discovered my kitchen was fairly intact. China, silver, some furniture could be saved. Our bedrooms were not there and I remembered where I found my trunk earlier with Sean. It was a mile or more on the other side of the island.

"I've got a friend coming with a cart. Let's save everything we can, Sarah Michelle, and take it back to our tent." John went outside and motioned for a man coming down the road with a cart. He had another man with him.

And just like that John and the two men loaded up what was left of my life and pushed it down the rubble-strewn street back to our tent. I sat under the tree and watched, thankful to have these men help me. I noticed little beetles running over the sand, busy doing whatever beetles do. How did they ever survive the storm? Did they ride on top of the water? Cling to a branch? I guess every single man, woman, child, animal, bird, fish and bug had its own special story about surviving the storm. I wish I could know every story, but not right now. In the future, I would find and gather the stories. Now I needed to just get by moment to moment. I told myself that's all I need do.

"Now how could fine delicate china like this survive such a wicked storm?" John was gently loading the china between two soft pillows. He stuck pillows all around the dishes to keep them from breaking. He even put a few pieces in the basket I was carrying the baby in. Then he stopped and looked out over the ocean from my tree. "This would be a good place to rebuild, Sarah Michelle."

"Are you going to rebuild, John?"

"Not until they put in the new seawall they've been talking about and fill dirt. That gives me lots of time to think if I'll rebuild or not. Don't know if I could go through the same thing twice."

"But this is nice and it did withstand the storm better than some areas. Do you have people to go live with?" John put the question that had been on both of our minds out in the open.

"No." I'm going to stay here. "Going to try to adopt this baby by myself."

"They'll never let you adopt a baby without a husband and an income, Sarah Michelle."

"I know. But maybe…"

He looked at me with a questioning fear in his dark eyes. The thought just crossed my mind. Did he think I was going to ask him to marry me?

"I had hoped you could see your way clear to not telling anyone this is not my baby. Sean never told anyone and if you don't …." she paused before continuing, "all the other orphans except the three boys in the tree were lost … I think this would be best, John."

"But there are people here who know you didn't have a baby before the storm."

"Yes, but many also know we were looking to adopt a child. I'll tell them it went through."

"Okay, okay."

"Look how far your friends have gotten up the road with the cart. Let's catch up and help them."

"You mean I'll help them." John said. "You'll carry Lucky."

"If you'll carry Lucky, I'll show you I'm as strong as an ox. And yes, I'm going to rebuild here."

What I didn't tell John is that I could never go back to England.

The return of Sarah Michelle's material possessions served to remind her of a life long gone. She took the dishes and other items back to the white tent more out of necessity than desire. Life with Thomas and Tommy was over. Nothing held any real value compared to her love for them. I was pleased to see she was beginning to let go and merge into the flow of her new life.

DEAN

Fancy. Fancy. Fancy. That was the only way to describe Robert Stockton, Jr.'s life. Fancy house. Fancy clothes. Fancy furniture. Fancy family. It made me very uncomfortable at first, but then I started to enjoy it. Plus, I could report back to Sarah Michelle that everything was fine. No reason for Sean not to want to be at home with his folks.

Sean's—I mean Robert's—father, was very colorful. Making jokes and having fun all evening, he even had Hansen laughing. But I wasn't born yesterday and I knew there had to be a reason for Robert to report his own death. Maybe it was related to some of the old scars and bruises I had noticed on his arms. They didn't come from the storm.

"I must reward you for looking after the safety of my boy," the elder Stockton said in an inebriated state.

"I can't accept a reward. If you must reward anyone, reward a woman named Sarah Michelle." I knew she really would need help. "I'll get by on my good looks alone." I cast what I hoped was a winning smile toward Robert's two older sisters. It appeared to be working its magic when Hansen said, "But what about your wife? Surely she would appreciate the luxuries a reward might bring."

"Yes, let's reward Dean's wife with a new jewel. And give this Sarah Michelle whatever her heart desires." Robert, Sr. reached into his pocket and jingled the change. He turned his gaze toward Robert, Jr. "Son, do you know where to tell Hansen to find her?"

"I think I can find her. Galveston is not that large." Hansen stroked his chin and squinted his eyes. "I bet I can tell you what her heart desires too."

"What's that?" Robert Sr. replied.

"The same thing everyone on Galveston wants right now — a place to live." Everyone smiled at his obvious answer.

"Then a new house it is. A fine one for saving my only son's life."

Suddenly, I was sorry I had not taken him up on his offer. But what would I do with a house? I would be tied down to one place. Even if it is a tropical paradise, I didn't want anything tying me down—at least for more than a few years.

"Excuse me, my lovely wife still doesn't know I'm alive. While I've enjoyed the food and the company, I must be on my way now." I stood and turned toward Robert, Sr.

"Please take one of my horses. You can bring it by tomorrow with your wife and I will present her with your reward."

"That would be lovely. What time shall we call?"

"This same time tomorrow. It'll give you time to catch up, and time for her to rejoice over your salvation from the storm." This time it was

Robert, Jr.'s mother who had spoken. By her age, I guessed her to be his stepmother and not his real mother.

I turned as I left to see Robert, Jr. surrounded by his two sisters. Obviously, they were delighted to have their brother back, even if he had been living in unwashed clothes and had mud in his hair. "How did you cut your lip?" I heard one of them say.

A groomsman appeared with a beautiful black horse. One like I had always dreamed of but never imagined owning. Well, I didn't own it this night either, but it would appear to others I did and that was good enough.

Now if I could find January and get her to repay the same favor I had done her not so long ago. We were two of a kind and my first guess was to go to the Rice Hotel on Texas Avenue. They had a bar she could sing in for money and some of the nicest rooms around. She would want to make herself comfortable. After all she had given birth only a month or so before. She never did write me to tell me how things went. But that was January, a person only heard from her when she needed money or help.

JOHN

I was floating on a door. My front door. And it was gently rocking back and forth as it settled on what seemed like a mile high pile of debris. I looked down at the seemingly endless pile of boards, bricks and all the things that make a house, a community. They were piled so high I couldn't see the land beneath them. I got off the door and started to climb down, but the mountain of rubble started to sway, started to fall away.

I was slipping, falling through mid-air. I woke before I hit ground.

Now I knew I would be awake for the rest of the night. Heart pounding. Ears buzzing. Another attack was coming on. I was so glad to have Sarah Michelle sleeping nearby. Yet afraid at the same time that she might think me less of a man, less of a person because I kept panicking. I don't understand, I don't even remember panicking the night of the storm. Now almost a month later it's started happening. Already I could feel the cold sweat on my body. My mind racing much too fast. It's hard to breathe … hard to be with people … hard to be alone.

Maybe if I get up and walk around. What scares me even more is that I'm starting to cling to Sarah Michelle. Maybe I should have a drink. Where did I put that bottle? I found it and went outside to sit in the dark. Just outside the tent. What was I afraid of? My unknown future? How much I had lost?

Houses can be rebuilt, everyone says, but what about the money? I worked so hard, so many hours to get that house and I still owe on it. It's all gone and I still owe on it. Maybe I should just disappear.

I wish I were a boy again, when my most important things in life were playing stickball and marbles. Fishing. Running around barefoot and dreaming of coming to America. My dreams are crushed and I'm far from home without enough money to get back to Ireland. My plans to make something of myself are gone. Sadness and fear weigh heavy on me. I want to be brave, but inside I must be very cowardly. It seems even gentle Sarah Michelle is stronger than me. Who I want to be and who I am are far apart and I'm so overwhelmed I can't even get up and try.

The only good thing is there should be plenty of work for a man with my skills once the real building gets started. If I can rest my shoulder and not hurt it again maybe it will feel normal. Or maybe this is a pain that I will take with me throughout the rest of my life. The vague memory of a large window frame popping up in the water and coming down on my right shoulder and upper torso flashed in my mind.

I'm so far behind what I expected for myself at this point in life. No wife. No children. But if I'm honest with myself, I'm very afraid of the responsibility. My girlfriend January didn't seem to want a family life. She preferred her singing. Called it her career. She was a very modern woman. Unlike any I had met before, and I loved her.

My mind went on like this running randomly…my heart still pulsating at times. I sort of felt dizzy and wondered if the window frame that hit my shoulder might also have hit my head too. I wasn't right in the head anymore.

DEAN

Ah, the Rice Hotel. It doesn't get any better than this. No wonder January had selected it as her new place of residence. I looked around at the lavish surroundings. Ruby-colored silk draperies. Plush carpeting. Giant potted palms.

I went to the front desk to inquire about a room. The gentleman ahead of me had just finished checking-in. I could tell by his well-worn leather wallet that he was a man who had seen the world. As I glanced around the lobby, I felt out of place among the sophisticated clientele dressed in the latest fashions. Tomorrow I would get new clothes to replace my storm-damaged attire.

"May I help you sir?" It was the same desk clerk as a few months ago. He pretended not to notice my less than stellar appearance. Or my long absence.

"Yes, I would like a room near my wife January Johnson."

"Would you like the adjoining room to your wife, sir? It's open."

"Yes, that would be fine. I'm planning on surprising her with my return. I've come from the Galveston storm. I was unable to get word out to her that I'm even alive."

"Mrs. January had told me you were on an extended trip to Galveston for urgent business. She has been very distraught, what with losing the baby and all." He gave me a disapproving look before handing

me the key. "Here...I'm certain you want to hurry to her side."

I ran up the stairs...this is the first I had heard of January losing

the baby she was carrying. But then again, I wasn't aware of anything that

was going on outside of my little world. The storm had left us in a bubble

of our own and I had forgotten there were others facing obstacles as well.

I opened the door and threw down my meager belongings. The

door between our rooms was locked. I went outside and knocked. This

wasn't how I had planned our meeting. I wanted to shower and shave.

Bring fresh flowers.

The door opened and January stuck her face out. "What are you

doing here?"

"I came to tell you I lived through the storm."

"Only the good die young. I imagine you lived through with hardly

a scratch."

Understanding her anger at my absence, I softened my voice, "The

hotel clerk told me the news, I'm so sorry...."

Just then a man's voice could be heard in the background. "January

dear, is that your brother?"

January slammed the door in my face. I turned around and went

back into my rented room next door and proceeded to shower and shave. It

felt really good what with the warm meal still in my belly courtesy of the

Stockton's. I let the hot water run down over my head and face and

thanked God for the wonderful convenience of a modern shower. If you let

it, life just seems to work its own self out. Or that's the way it seemed to me

at that particular moment.

THE BOY "ROBERT/SEAN"

Without a doubt, it would not be long before I received punishment of some kind. I know Hansen would never tell my father about how he found me in Galveston, but I could sense my father was mad at me for not returning home as soon as possible.

My father slammed the front door before ascending the large oak staircase. His heavy footfalls echoed down the long marble hallway lined with my ancestor's portraits. Throwing open the heavy oak door to my private chambers, he jerked me from my warm bed. Before his arrival, I had been in a sound sleep—one of the first I'd had since the storm. Before I knew it he was kicking me and throwing me against the wall.

I headed out the door and toward the top of the stair landing. They were grand stairs, wide and high. I felt his heavy hand grab my shoulder. As my sisters watched in horror from the other end of the hallway, he threw me down the steps.

I woke in the hospital. Bright white lights and soft white sheets. My head bandaged. I could sort of see out of one eye. I had a broken arm. Or, so the nurses told me. It hurt, and they gave me pain medicine.

I stood at the boy's bed. Three of his long-deceased relatives, two of whom had portraits hanging on the wall of his home, joined me. Like sentinels we stood guard at each corner. Swords poised ready to fight the war of good and evil. Once the battle commenced, it raged through the night while the humans moved in and out among us,

oblivious to the history that was taking place in their broken world.

DEAN

What to do now but go get a new suit? I saw a gentleman's store nearby. I looked around at the new woolen suits. Eight dollars and ninety-five cents for the one I wanted. More than most men make in a week. But I had to look good for the ladies. I also picked a couple of cotton linen shirts for the island. Hmm, I guess I've decided to go back to the island. In that case, I'll pick an extra one for John. Luckily the boy found all the fine women's clothes for Sarah Michelle. I suppose they were his Aunt's. Sarah Michelle told me he said he didn't steal those either. Sarah Michelle would be happy to know the jewelry was his Aunt's too. He had some rights to them being a surviving relative. I like that little Sean, I mean Robert. He's a spunky kid. Sarah Michelle will be happy he has such a nice home. Perhaps he will reconcile his argument with his father just as I did mine right before he died, I should have done it much sooner for my poor mother's sake.

My thoughts were running along in this order while I tried on all the clothes. I needed work pants too. The store clerk told me I would need to go down the street for those.

I remembered I had the Stockton's black horse stabled at the hotel. I would need to send it back, but first maybe I would take it for a ride. Just because it was such a beautiful fall day.

"I'll wear the suit and hat." I said as I handed him my old clothes to wrap in a package. "You know what? You can throw those clothes away."

"As you wish sir. Shall I send the other packages to the Rice Hotel?"

"No I'll carry them."

I left the packages off at the front desk of the hotel and started for the stable. One day I would have an automobile. I did so enjoy new inventions. But a horse was always a welcome mode of transportation. If I had an automobile, I would probably long for a horse. That's the kind of never-satisfied person I am. More, more, more when less is probably better. I heard piano music coming out of the bar. It was happy and uplifting and quite frankly I had never heard a song like it.

Intrigued, I entered the smoky interior and watched the man play. His long-fingered hands moved so fast. It was music to be danced too. "What is the name of this song? I've never heard anything like it before."

The experienced musician didn't miss a beat. "It's ragtime. The name is 'Maple Leaf Rag.'" He continued playing before adding, "You can buy the sheet music at Caroline's Music Manor near the hospital."

Now, I couldn't play the piano but I knew someone who could — January. Maybe it would be a good way to get back into her good graces if I decided to do so.

"Thank you very much for the information." I started out toward the stable to get my horse. It was a lovely ride to Caroline's Music Manor and I had the pleasure of meeting Miss Caroline herself. Her dress was more of a costume than a dress and she had on stage makeup. "Sweet Mother of Pearl! Everyone in the world wants that new piece by Scott Joplin. I keep it right up front," Miss Caroline said in a high sweet voice.

She also asked me if I wanted a harmonica and for some reason I did. "Say do you want to donate to the Galveston Victim's Fund for the hospital next door?" She motioned to a jar of money she was collecting with a handwritten paper sign on it. I dropped a few coins in the jar. I still had a pocket full of change and dollar bills from when I had used one of my mother's gold coins at the clothing shop.

The Victim's Fund started me thinking about the wounded boy on the boat crossing. On impulse I went into the hospital to see if I could find out any information about his condition. I saw a nurse. Someone I used to know. She looked surprised to see me. And well she should have been, because I had quit practicing medicine over five years ago.

"Doctor, how nice to see you," she recovered from her initial shock quite nicely. I guess nurses are good at recovering from shocking things quickly.

"Hello Dottie, I'm here to check on a young storm victim with a head injury."

"Are you… are you…" she stammered nervously.

"No, I'm merely here to visit. No more doctoring for me."

"I believe the boy you are referring to is in the children's ward on three. Check in at the desk and they'll give you the room number.

Once on the third floor I saw a boy with his head wrapped lying in a bed. I started toward the open door when I heard a soft female voice say, "Mr. Johnson, is that you?"

It was the injured boy's mother. I recognized her from watching her so closely on the boat. Only this time there was no fear and sadness in her face. In fact, she seemed rather chipper. "Yes, I was in the area and decided to come by and check on the boy."

"I'm proud to say he's recovering better than expected," she looked inside the boy's room and whispered to me. "The first doctor that saw him right after the accident said the hit to his head might leave him different." She looked into the room again, and mouthed, "Not the same personality."

"So he's better than expected."

"Yes, he's our Joe. So much the same he can still play the piano. We've had him up and at it on a paper keyboard." She went inside the room as she spoke. "Joe, this is Mr. Johnson. He was on the boat crossing with us."

"How are you? I don't remember the boat crossing." He spoke with a strong voice. "I'm happy to have a visitor though. The hospital is boring. Tomorrow, at least, they've agreed to let me go next door to see if I could still play a real piano."

"I hope that works out well for you."

"As soon as this headache's gone I 'spect I'll be as good as new all over."

I reached out and handed him the sheet music I had purchased. "I got this next door for someone else, but I think it might make a better gift for you."

"Maple Leaf Rag" he slowly read the title and studied the music. "I can read music. Someone taught me how for free. Well, not exactly free. I had to do work around the house in return."

"It looks like it'll be a challenge," I commented.

"I like a challenge and I like the new ragtime. I really wanted this. How did you decide to give this to me instead of the original intended recipient?"

"Don't know, took a gamble, I guess." There was an awkward silence, as we didn't know each other and had nothing to say. Still I was happy I came. For lack of conversation, I inquired about the other person in the room nearby. "What happened?" I gestured across the hallway.

"He fell down a very long flight of stairs. Cracked his head and broke an arm." The mother leaned in and started to whisper to me again. "When they brought him in he kept saying his drunk of a father pushed him. They have him medicated now."

"What kind of person would do a thing like that?" Joe looked past me at the figure lying still and quiet in the bed. "He's close to my age."

"Nurses say he's been in here before with other accidents." Joe's mother started to say more and stopped. "I guess we should mind our own business. I don't usually gossip."

"It's a frightening story. I understand your concern," I offered. We all felt awkward again. "I must be going now. It was just on a whim that I dropped in to see if I could find out more about your condition."

"Thank you so much, and thanks for the song." He said as he held up the sheet music. "Do you know where they found our piano after the storm? Out in the middle of the street."

"It still works. It still works. We've got a lot ahead of us but we'll make it." I could tell by the look on his mother's face as she said it she believed it, and that was good enough for me.

"Good day then." I said as our visit ended. "I hope our paths meet again."

"Yes, I hope they do indeed." Joe said from his sick bed.

I stopped at the door of the other boy's room and looked in at him. You could barely see the tip of his nose under the head bandages. His skin was very pale and his chest barely moved up and down as he slept on his back with his broken, bandaged arm high up on his chest. He looked in bad shape, but I knew he was in one of the best hospitals in the state.

A nurse walked up behind me. "May I help you?"

I pointed at the unknown boy's broken arm. "I was just walking by and noticed. I wondered if you could position his broken arm a little more comfortably."

"Yes, of course, Doctor. How could I have overlooked that earlier? I'm certain he didn't move it into that uncomfortable position by himself, he's highly sedated."

I watched as she gently moved his arm up and over resting it on top of the blankets. Then she put the back of her hand on his forehead checking for fever. Turning to me, she said, "I'm going to get a cool rag to put on his forehead. Excuse me, Doctor."

It was no coincidence that Dean stopped in on the boy. I called to him to come. For all his resistance, he still is very attuned to the spirit world. Robert needed Dean's help. A plan was in the making. Robert's fall was the start of his rise.

THE BOY "ROBERT/SEAN"

They wouldn't listen to me. They didn't believe me when I told them how my injury happened. They poked with needles … gave me medicine. Now I can hardly move. The bandage blocks my vision. I'm so out of it, I thought I heard Dean's voice right outside my room. It must have been a doctor, because I heard the nurse address him as such. He told her to move my broken arm into a more comfortable position. It made all the difference in the world. If they didn't have me so full of pain medicine, I could've moved it myself. Keep thinking…keep thinking…don't let yourself sleep.

SARAH MICHELLE

In some ways it was very freeing to not have a planned-out life and to only own a few things. This way of living was so different for me. I was used to nice things and having everything I wanted—more than I could ever possibly need. I never realized how it weighed on me taking care of all my pretty things. Dusting, arranging, keeping them safe.

John and his two helpers had found and brought back the last few pieces of my old life. They reminded me of my husband and my son. I had not had time to grieve yet. I had only been trying to survive. Now that things had calmed down a bit I could think. But I didn't want to think. Not yet. So I got up and started tidying the already immaculate tent. There's not much to clean in a tent. I went outside.

The island was total devastation, but the sky was beautiful. Chock-full of streaks of blues, grays, pinks and purples. The last of the funeral pyres were burning and the stench of death was not so strong in the air. I went inside and got the baby so we could go for a walk. It was hard to have a baby around, especially considering the circumstances. I don't think the little one has slept through a night yet and he's a good baby.

John was working with the crews to clear the storm debris. He told me how they are using it as landfill to raise the level of the island and he described to me how they were going to build a seawall. Too bad they hadn't built the seawall before the storm. So many new innovations in this day and age it's hard to believe the things they can do. My mind whirls at the progress.

I hear the rest of the country is now sending aid. It took a while for the word to get out. Who would believe it's so bad here, especially when they didn't expect Galveston to take a direct hit from the cyclone? I was never one to pay much attention to the weather and I remember how I actually had a sense of excitement at the very start of the storm. The charge in the air, the rush of the wind. I paid it little attention, like so many others, I was unaware of the true horror approaching.

I could see this denial in other areas of my life too. Not paying attention when I should have been. Not really seeing because I didn't want to see. Not hearing correctly because I didn't want to know. I vowed to change my ways. This was my start. This was my beginning.

Even as I thought the thought, a little tug pulled at my heart for the people I had lost. At least they were together and I was alone. Not really alone because I had John in my life and the new baby Lucky, but it still felt strange. Sometimes when Dean and Sean were still with John and myself, I would look around the tent and feel as if I weren't there. As if I was watching a dream or a play. Who were these people? I didn't feel a part of the scene. I felt dizzy and strange. Sometimes I felt I was watching it from above.

Strange thoughts filled my head and they still do. What if I were dead and this is hell? What if I'm condemned to go through this for eternity? Why wouldn't I go to heaven? Did I need to do more works? I thought of a Bible passage that said salvation was based on faith and not of works lest any man should boast. I've known that verse since I was a little girl and for the first time it was meaningful to me. I think it means you only have to have faith. But John might argue, as he believes differently.

There was a large rock ahead. I went and got up on it. Not in a very ladylike manner. But I was tired of being ladylike. From now on I would do as I pleased. I could see a lot from the top of the rock and I was glad I had taken the effort to climb it.

My thoughts turned dark and my stomach felt sick. Images of things that happened during the storm flooded over me. I felt dark and uncomfortable. I wanted to get away from it all. Wanted to quit reliving it or thinking about it and I hated the fact that it always came back to me.

I sat still and contemplated things. It occurred to me that I had been so scared I hadn't really let my muscles relax. My whole body was still a knot and here it was weeks after the actual event. Sean, I mean Robert, had nightmares. I had no dreams. John told me he felt panicked at times to the point where he thought he might die right on the spot. We had more than physical cuts and bruises. Our very souls, and really our very essence had been wounded.

I didn't like having to deal with my dark thoughts or the situation. I wanted to just have a day again where I wasn't feeling anything in particular. One of the many non-descript days I had wasted in my life doing mundane and ordinary things without even a second thought. I just didn't want to feel like I was going to come unwound, but I did feel that way and I couldn't make it go away.

I hurt inside and I wanted to make the pain stop. People all around me were hurting and I couldn't help them anymore than they could help me. But a moment ago the pain and fear left. I was hopeful it would get better with time. What I wanted was to wake without the immediate remembrance of what had happened crushing down on my chest and causing heartache. I had a hope that this would one day happen.

And I don't know why I did this, but I turned my head to the brilliantly colored sky and prayed aloud for the safety of Sean. I know the man said his name was Robert, but to me he would always be Sean. How had the boy picked John and me of all the people to follow? I couldn't even speak to him at the time. And, it was not lost on me that the name he had picked for his new identity was the Irish version of John. He must admire John's strength and character as much as I did. Yes, John was a special one, indeed.

I could feel the warm sun on my upturned face and my spirits lifted in the balmy breeze. It was an incredibly beautiful day. I plucked a single rose from a nearby bush. Its fragrance reminded me of my Aunt Claire's gardens in Edinburgh. My trips to visit her in Scotland were some of my favorite memories.

JOHN

Sarah Michelle was different from most women I had known. She didn't need a lot of attention or expect me to take care of everything. She was a little like Sister Elizabeth, to tell the truth. She was very independent. Take, for example, the fact that she wanted to keep the baby Lucky and raise him alone. Or even the fact she intended to stay on the island and rebuild. No one would fault her for going to the mainland like most other women did.

She wasn't physically very strong, but she managed to get things done. When we were gathering her belongings, she lifted several big pieces of timber to get to things. I saw her looking at a locket she found in her trunk. Inside were two pictures. Tiny little pictures of her son and her husband. It made me think, I would like to have a photograph of myself taken someday. Now that I had realized my life could end so easily, I wanted a photograph taken for the world to remember me by.

I had seen two men near where the orphanage buildings used to stand. They had a box on a tripod and were taking photography of the devastation. I would find them again and bargain with them in some way to take a photograph of me.

Sarah Michelle came back into the tent with the baby. "I had the most lovely walk. The world is still beautiful, is it not?"

"I'm still glad to be in it." She smiled at my words. "Sarah Michelle, I saw two men taking photographs at the orphanage earlier this week. I'm going to find them tomorrow and ask them to take a photograph of me."

"A photograph. Oh, I would love to have a photograph of the baby." She almost jumped with glee at the thought of the baby's photograph.

"Then come with me."

"I will. I'm going to pick out what to dress Lucky in right now."

"Why don't you get your photograph taken, too? Then the world will always know what you looked like." She had a strange look on her face at my words. "I mean you will be able to remember one day what you looked like when you were young and beautiful."

She immediately put her hand to her short-cropped hair and a little pain pierced my heart.

"Your hair looks nice. The nun did a good job of trimming it."

"I'll wear a hat," she said with a smile.

I couldn't help but smile back.

DEAN

I stood in front of the Stockton's mansion before knocking. The groomsman was taking the horse I had returned to the stable and I watched him from the front entryway. This house was an architectural work of art; each exterior detail was exceptional.

A servant opened the door. I told her I was returning the horse as planned and she invited me inside. Sean-Robert's two sisters greeted me warmly. "Please have dinner with us again tonight," the elder one spoke. "Our father has been called away on emergency business so it will be our stepmother and ourselves."

"What about Robert, Jr.? I've brought him a small gift." I took the harmonica out of my pocket.

"He's gone back to boarding school." She looked uncomfortable.

"Already? I thought he might want to spend time at home after what he's been through."

"He didn't want to get too far behind on his lessons." It was the young stepmother. She didn't look evil, but she didn't look kind either.

"Here," the younger sister took the harmonica. "I'm going to visit him soon. I'll see that he gets it."

"And we've got something for you," the elder sister chimed in with a twinkle in her eye. "Was your wife not able to come with you?"

"No, my wife was feeling ill tonight. She asked me to send her regrets."

With that she went to a tiny desk and unlocked a drawer. She pulled out a velvet box and brought it to me. She was rather tall and thin. I noticed she sashayed ever so slightly like a dancer as she crossed the room. Stopping right in front of me she held the box up at chest level with both hands. "Just as promised, a reward for you that will please your wife."

I flipped open the box. Inside an impressive dark stone ring flanked by diamonds sparkled. She looked at me with anticipation to see my reaction. "I selected it myself. It's very stylish," she said. "And the stone is a garnet for the month of January."

I smiled a seductive smile I had practiced on many a young woman with successful results. It was not lost on her. "You do like it, don't you?" she said flirtatiously.

"It's beautiful. Far too expensive." I wished I hadn't lied about being married. Most men lie the other way and say they are single. Not me, I must be crazy. Now I would have to act like a respectful husband.

Dinner was wonderful—the best of everything, including food, wine and conversation. After dinner the girls surprised me by asking if I would come look at the new table game their father had brought them back from Britain.

"It's called ping pong," the youngest girl said laughing.

"I think you're pulling my leg. Ping pong is not a word, it's a sound."

The elder sister named Jane said, "It really is ping pong."

"And I'm to tell people tomorrow that I spent last evening playing ping pong. They'll think me daft." We were headed toward a game room in the back of the mansion. "I'm going to call it table ball." The opulence around me evoked a sharp stab of envy. Why would Sean ever want to leave?

"Does Sean play Ping Pong?" I said out loud.

"Who's Sean?" said the younger sister named Jeannie.

"Did I say Sean? I meant to say Robert, Jr.," I blundered on, "apparently someone has had too much wine tonight."

The next morning I found myself in my hotel room waking with a bit of a headache. What a wonderful evening! What wonderful sisters Robert-Sean has. I managed to sit on the side of my bed and rub my blood-shot eyes.

The memories of that awful storm were fading and I wanted to do everything I could to make them a distant memory, but still I found myself thinking of Sarah Michelle—the lady with the beautiful eyes that watched me when she thought I wasn't watching her. Even her name was beautiful. Could she ever love the likes of me? Sarah Michelle was a deep down thinker and that only made her more beautiful to me.

And now that her bruises were healing and her hair coming back in, I knew it would only be a matter of time before John noticed her beauty, too. In fact, I think he was already secretly smitten with her. Maybe I should take January back with me. No, no conniving. I would win Sarah Michelle's heart the honest way.

No I wouldn't. Who was I kidding? I was a gambler and a liar. I would win Sarah Michelle's heart anyway I could. The way I had come to figure things, most respectable people lie too. They're just not honest enough to admit it to themselves like I do.

So now the only thing left to do was to get up, get dressed and get on my way back to Galveston and Sarah Michelle. Wonder if the electricity was back up yet?

I could hear January laughing through the thin walls between our rooms. Still entertaining the same man I bet. Possibly the one with the well-worn wallet I had spotted in the lobby. His cigar smoke smelled the same.

I smiled as I picked up the small velvet box holding the ring. I would need it when I asked Sarah Michelle to marry me one day. It was going to take a while; I could tell she didn't like my sort of man. Maybe my tracking down Robert-Sean will mean something to her, though I did it as much for myself as for Sarah Michelle. I had come to be fond of the boy.

It occurred to me as I walked past the hospital on my way out of town that I should check in on Joe and his mother. He wouldn't be going home anytime soon and his mother might want to send word to the folks back on the island. I had decided to take the train as far as I could to Galveston before it reached the area where the tracks were damaged. There was time for a visit to the hospital, the train didn't leave for an hour.

It was a good thing I did stop in because the woman had written letters to mail back home. I assured her I would track down the intended recipients and hand-deliver them. The sheet music was a good call. They had created a paper piano keyboard and the boy had already started practicing his new song. He played for me on his paper keyboard and it was clear he could hear the notes in his mind. The bouncing of his fingers on the paper made a musical sound enough so I could tell he already had a good feel for the intricate, fast-paced melody.

On my way out, I glanced into the room of the boy who fell down the stairs. I noticed a harmonica beside his bed. It looked like… no, but it had the same initials engraved on top…why would the sisters give it to a stranger. Just then a figure stepped forward from a corner of the room and said, "Dean, is that you?"

"Jane?"

4 WEST TEXAS

THE BOY "ROBERT/SEAN"

"Come in Dean," I said from my hospital bed. "So pleased to see you. What are you doing here? I thought I heard your voice the other day."

Dean appeared to be in shock. He was still staring at Jane. "Please explain," was all he could utter.

I watched Jane look away from Dean in shame.

"Robert, Jr. is obviously not away at school. He fell down the stairs." She kept her eyes on the ground.

"I did not fall down the stairs, I was pushed. Only no one will do anything because my Poppa has made large donations to the hospital." A nurse passing in the hall looked in and gave a stern look as if to say keep your voice down.

Just then Hansen walked into the sterile room. He was obviously surprised to see Dean. "Young Master," he said to me. "Did you call Dean to escort you?"

"No, he just showed up. But he is the sort of man that is up for adventure." I grinned from ear to ear under the bandages. "What do you say Dean, want to run away with me to West Texas and be a cowboy?"

DEAN

The thought of being a cowboy had its appeal, and I sensed that Robert wouldn't live to adulthood in the Stockton family home if this treatment continued much longer. Jane explained to me their father had not physically hurt her or Jeannie...only Robert, and he did nothing to provoke the majority of the outbursts.

Even though I wanted to see Sarah Michelle again, I knew my absence would be of no concern to her. She would appreciate me more for going with the boy Robert. And I had always wanted to see the West ... without too much more thinking, I accepted the job of being Robert's escort to West Texas.

Seems Hansen was a kinder soul than he originally appeared back at the boat crossing. The last incident on the stairs had made him take matters in his own hands. He was sending Robert to his cousin's place way out in West Texas where there would be no chance of anyone recognizing him. Only Jane, and now myself, knew of the plan. The rest of the family would be told Robert had run away again. Only this time, not to a relative's house where he could be easily tracked down.

I contemplated going back through Galveston to report back to Sarah Michelle and John, but I decided to write them instead. Then I remembered the letters I had promised to deliver for Joe's mother. "Hansen, would you be opposed to making one more trip to Galveston to deliver some letters? I know the mail is up and running, but I gave a lady my word I would hand-deliver them when I got back on the island."

"I'm already planning a trip there to reward the lady Sarah Michelle with cash for a new house. I'm certain Mr. Stockton will want to honor his word and she did take care of Robert, Jr. in the most dire of situations." He reached his hand out, "I'll be happy to deliver the letters."

"Good, I'll feel better knowing the woman's letters are in your capable hands. Also one letter is for Sarah Michelle herself from me." I stammered a little. It was not a love letter, but parts of it were of a personal nature.

Hansen put the letters in his coat. "Galveston is a small island, I'll deliver them as promised." He took out two pieces of paper. One had an address and the other a map. He handed them both to Sean.

A female voice behind me said, "I feel much better knowing you're traveling with my little brother." I had forgotten Jane was still in the room. I turned to look at her lovely face. Her blue eyes had a purple tint and dark curls framed her pale skin perfectly. She knew I found her attractive and she gave me a smile as she said, "He's much too young to travel so far by himself."

One side of me wanted to run back to Galveston, but there wasn't a thing for me there. Who was I kidding? I knew John was a better man for

Sarah Michelle than I could be at the moment. Besides I was married to January.

"Heck yeah, Sean! Let's go ride the range. Ain't nothing holding me here."

Jane's pensive face showed visible relief, but there was a note of sadness in her voice when she said, "Hansen's arranged for Robert, I mean Sean, to go soon. I hope it won't inconvenience you too much. I'll reward you handsomely for this, Dean Johnson. You're a true life-saver." Then she did something very strange. She took my hand, looked straight into my eyes and said it again. "A true life-saver. You understand me."

Thank you Dean. You will be rewarded in this life and the next.

JOHN

Aye, it was a fine day. Someone had told me earlier the photographer and his assistant were staying near what was left of downtown. They were documenting the storm for people to understand what had happened here. I had my doubts that anyone who hadn't witnessed the storm for themselves would ever fully comprehend it. Even seeing the actual aftermath of the devastation would never tell the whole story. The stench. The horror. The heartbreak. All were elements that could never be conveyed through visual or verbal means alone and I wouldn't wish living through an actual storm of this caliber on another human being—but really that would be the only way to understand.

People who had been through bad times were different. I knew I had seen people like that and now I was one of them. Hopefully, it would one day make me a better person to other people. But right now it was doing the opposite. The bad feelings that seemed to suck me down would mysteriously leave and come back at the strangest times. I had gotten into a way of dealing with them. I would just work through them. If I were with the cleaning and rebuilding crews, I would stop for a water break and take a walk around, in circles if I had to. Maybe sit down until my heart stopped racing. I knew others were having the same problems and it didn't help any to find a body underneath the debris we were moving. Would we ever quit finding bodies?

These were my thoughts as Sarah Michelle and I walked silently toward the ruined downtown buildings. Before we got there, we saw the photographer and his assistant coming our way. "Hullo," I said as they hurriedly passed us. "Wait!" I called out. "Would you take our picture? I have money."

They stopped and turned. They looked at us in what was left of our finery. Sarah Michelle looking very beautiful in the clothes Sean had found for her. Her hair swept up. Myself, clean and in a suit I had borrowed, holding the baby in a basket.

"You," the photographer said to Sarah Michelle, "Stay exactly where you are." Then he motioned to his assistant, "Roman… put the barrel over here… take it and position it by the woman for the man to sit on." Next he addressed me. "Now sit the baby on your lap, sir."

After arranging our little group against a backdrop of total devastation, the assistant pulled out a tripod for his camera. The photographer checked and aligned his instruments. "The lighting is perfect." He took one photograph of us. "I do not have much film. I can only take one." He talked as he worked. "You are a handsome couple. The people of Galveston's strong spirit shows in your faces."

"The baby is a newborn." It was the photographer's assistant Roman talking now. "Is it the baby born during the storm?"

"No, he was born a few days before the storm." I volunteered before Sarah Michelle had to say anything.

"Too bad." The photographer's assistant was now taking his camera off the tripod. "It would make for a good story in the newspaper."

"Yes, get their names Roman and let's go." And just like that they were finished and we were dismissed. He turned as he walked away. "Come with us if you like and watch our new photographic experiment. We are taking some of the first moving pictures."

Sarah Michelle and I looked at each other and laughed. We had ourselves documented with a photograph. Not the single images we had planned but a family type photograph. I was surprised it didn't bother me. The only thing I could think of is how pleased I was to be documented. Our images would prove we existed on this earth. For some reason it was important.

"Yes, we would love to watch your experiment." Sarah Michelle was following him with the baby basket in her arms. "I can't imagine how a picture will move. It doesn't seem possible."

"It is possible and..." the photographer glanced at Sarah Michelle and the baby. He must have realized how important the photograph would be to her. "Roman make an extra print tonight for these fine people and deliver it to them."

"We live in a tent," I said. "It will be hard to find us in the sea of tents."

"Then meet us tomorrow evening in what used to be the weather station. Part of it is left standing and the people who own it are letting us use a room for our work. Tomorrow evening will give Roman more time to make a nice print." He squinted into the sun. "Wouldn't want to rush him. Great work takes time."

The photographer was racing against the light trying to document this historic event with his new moving pictures camera. Sarah Michelle, the baby and myself were only a tiny pinprick of what was happening in the world...only a small part of the big storm that had taken over and changed our entire lives. The photographer wanted to get the big picture. Small wonder that he would even waste one bit of film on the likes of us.

THE BOY "ROBERT/SEAN"

Every bump of the carriage ride to the train hurt even though Hansen had put pillows all around me. Hansen was more like a real father to me than an employee. I would miss him and my sisters terribly. But I had left once and I could do it again.

"Hansen says his cousin's husband is a doctor. Do you think he'll take my cast off soon?" I said it to Dean, but I didn't expect an answer. He was gazing in a daydream out the carriage window.

"No, it will be at least two months." Dean reached over and took my good arm and felt of my pulse. "How do you feel? We shouldn't be moving you yet."

"I feel some pain."

"Where?"

"All over."

Dean reached into his coat pocket. "Doctor said to give you one of these once we got on the train. I think we're close enough. You can take one now and it'll lessen the hurt when we move you to the train. Then you can sleep all the way to Abilene."

"I can't take a pill without water." I said eyeing the little white thing.

"Yes you can." He didn't even look at me when I took it.

I started choking a little. He pulled out a flask and handed it to me. I took a swallow and waited for the burn of hard liquor in my throat, but there was none—it was water. I took another drink and put the top back on. I could hear the whistle of the train as we approached the station. "Hats down Sean, we don't want anyone recognizing us." Dean opened the carriage door and started getting things out.

I don't remember the first part of the train ride except for the fact I was in a little bed that seemed to rock with the wheels. Soon I drifted off into blissful sleep, dreaming of miles of gleaming white sand and blue sky with puffy clouds. Being near water always makes me feel better and in my dream I felt better.

When I woke, Dean was staring at the map and address Hansen had given us. His brow was furrowed and he was deep in thought. He was one of those people that dreamed a lot and you could often find him staring off into space. And though his grammar didn't always make him sound like an educated man, the thoughts that came out of his head did. I didn't know what to make of Dean. He wasn't an obvious upfront sort of individual, but I knew I could trust him with my very life.

"What about your wife, Dean? Is she going to meet with us?" My mouth was dry and tasted like metal.

"I don't have a wife. I lied to get myself across the waterway." Dean smiled and paused for a moment before adding, "Oh what a tangled web we weave, when first we practice to deceive."

"Sir Walter Scott," I said.

"I tell you what, boy! You must have got your learning from some fancy schools. That knowledge is going to go a long way toward impressing the ladies some day." Dean leaned back along the bench-like chair across the aisle from me and stretched out. "The rocking of the train feels nice, I hope it ain't hurtin' you too much."

"Not too much," I lied. There it was again, Dean's improper use of grammar. Either he was reverting to a way he had grown up talking or he was affecting it to hide something of himself. You never knew with Dean, maybe he just liked the way the words rolled off his tongue.

I wasn't going to make him explain himself. I was coming out to West Texas to hide and I suspected he was too.

Dean's mind had strayed a million miles away again. "What you thinking of Dean?"

"All my money at the bottom of the ocean."

"Yep, I bet old Neptune made quite a haul the night of the hurricane."

Dean smiled at my newly affected western accent.

JOHN

There was a man in town asking about Sarah Michelle and the baby. I told one of my tent neighbors to find out what he wanted. The need I had to protect her felt odd. I was continually drawn to her even though she kept me at arm's length. Just as well. I didn't want to take on a wife and child before I made my fortune.

Soon my tent neighbor reported back.

"He wants to reward her for taking care of Robert Stockton, Jr. after the storm. I think he's the man that rescued Sean from getting shot over the stolen jewelry."

I felt I should go to the man and see what this was all about. I didn't want him asking too many questions seeing as Lucky wasn't exactly Sarah Michelle's. It would kill her to give the baby up. The way I figured it, the world had given Sarah Michelle the newborn. She was a wonderful mother and for some reason I felt responsible for Lucky, too. Not just helping Sister Elizabeth save his life. I felt like we were a family now that we had been through this thing and survived. Sarah Michelle and I knew why we did the things we did now. We didn't have to explain ourselves to each other.

But the island being so small, it didn't take long to track down Sarah Michelle. Soon the man arrived at the door of our tent before I got a chance to go to him. He had a newspaper with the photo of the three of us in it. "Excuse me, may I come in," he said. "I have some news I would like to discuss with you."

"Yes, of course," I said warily as I took the newspaper from him and looked at our photograph. The newspaper listed our names as John, Sarah Michelle and Lucky McLaren. I was a little shocked and I knew Sarah Michelle would be too.

"John, our photo is in the Houston newspaper," Sarah Michelle said as she took the paper from me. "Now the world will know you existed long after you're gone."

The stranger had stepped inside our tent. "The word 'world' is most appropriate. Just about every newspaper in the country has picked up this image. The devastation is hard to comprehend even with the statistics and photographs."

I turned and looked the man right in the eye.

He stuck out his hand in greeting and said with a friendly-enough voice, "My name is Hansen and I work for Robert Stockton in Houston. " It was the same man who had rescued the boy from being shot over the jewelry.

"I'm John McLaren and this is ... this is Sarah Michelle and baby Lucky." I wanted to get right to the point of his visit. "How may we help you?"

"No, the question is how may I help you? Specifically you, Sarah Michelle. My employer wants to reward you for caring for his son Robert Stockton, Jr. Your friend Dean suggested to Mr. Stockton financial help with rebuilding your family home would be most appropriate.

"I don't know a Robert Stockton, Jr." Sarah Michelle grasped the baby to her as if someone would take it away. "Our baby's name is Lucky."

The man named Hansen looked confused momentarily, "Robert Stockton, Jr. is the boy ... how should I say this ... is the boy that was about to be shot for stealing jewelry." He continued on as Sarah Michelle stared at him with a wild look. "Just outside your tent. About a month ago, right here," he pointed to the place outside the tent door. "Surely you must remember."

"We knew that boy as Sean," I said weakly. "He never told us he was Robert Stockton, Jr."

Sarah Michelle sat down limply.

"Yes, I'm certain Robert, Jr. disguised his identity as it would not have been safe for the railroad heir in the chaos surrounding the storm." Hansen rattled on in an attempt to explain Sean's alias.

"Is Sean alright?" Sarah Michelle seemed desperate for news. She literally grabbed at Hansen's arm with one hand while holding the baby in the other.

"Why yes, I have a letter from Dean for you to prove it so," he handed the letter to Sarah Michelle. "Please don't read it until I'm gone and never tell anyone I gave it to you. The contents of the letter will explain Robert Jr.'s whereabouts."

With that he pulled out his checkbook and produced a receipt of deposit from a bank in Houston. "Mr. Stockton took the liberty of opening a joint account in your names in Houston for the reward money. You may use it as you see fit," he said matter-of-factly as we stared at the large sum. "We had heard the bank in Galveston was totally destroyed and we felt it would be best to deposit it in Houston rather than send cash to the island."

With that he stood and bid us farewell. "I must be on my way now so I won't have trouble crossing the waterway in the dark. Thank you. Thank you both very much. Robert, Jr. means so much to us and we feel we owe you his very life." And just as quickly as he came he was gone.

We both sat down on the tent floor and looked at each other. "I guess we're married now," was all I could say.

Sarah Michelle laughed and said, "Didn't you say no one reads the newspapers?"

Well, at least one person in the world did.

***

Early the next morning, January Buchanan was at our tent door holding a Houston newspaper with our picture in it in her hand. Rage

137

shown in her green cat-like eyes as she flailed at me over and over again. I tried to protect myself with my arms. Sarah Michelle watched in amazement from her nearby pallet. I knew she was concerned about how it would look to January that she found us sleeping so closely together.

The baby woke and started to howl.

Sarah Michelle ran to Lucky and January turned her focus toward to him.

"What is this baby's name?" she demanded.

"Lucky," I said.

"Lucky what?"

"Lucky he made it through the storm being born only a few days before," I offered. My joke fell flat under January's hateful stare.

"That's not what I meant. I meant what's his last name?"

"Lucky McLaren." As I said it, I meant it. Sarah Michelle gave me a wondrous look.

"And what is your name," Sarah Michelle said to January in a most polite manner considering the circumstances.

"My name is January. January Cola Buchanan," January smoothed her dress and patted her auburn hair, "You must be Sarah Michelle. You look like your photo." She held up the photo of the three of us in the newspaper.

"Yes, that's me. Do you have business with me?" Sarah Michelle held the baby close as she soothed it. She kept the baby's face away from January. "Why do you want to know the baby's name?"

"I wanted to know if you and the baby were a family with John." She sniffed in an affected way to show her sadness. "I'm afraid he lied to me and told me he was a single man. John has courted me for at least two years."

An awkward silence filled the air as Sarah Michelle's questioning eyes locked on mine. I could see tears brimming. My gut heaved.

"I'm afraid we were lovers even as you were pregnant with this child. Probably before." She looked away. "I'm a fallen woman. My life is over."

"January, you left me for your acting career." I said with anger in my voice. "You left me months ago."

"But not over nine months ago. You conceived this child with your wife and let me believe you were eligible." She had now produced a few very realistic tears. "You are no better than your gambling friends."

"My gambling friends are dead."

"Dean is not."

"Dean was merely my acquaintance until after the storm." I replied. "How do you know Dean is not dead? Did he come looking for you?" Now it was my turn to be jealous.

"Dean was in Houston and I saw him for only a few moments in passing. He told me you were alive. He did not tell me anything of your secret life." Her voice had a self-righteous tone. "Why are you staying in this mess? You should come to Houston."

"We have no money." It was a lie, but not really. I had lost everything in the storm and the reward money from Robert Stockton belonged to Sarah Michelle.

"Get up," January grabbed my ear like a small child. "Come with me." She turned to Sarah Michelle. "I deserve a few moments of privacy to tell this scoundrel what I think. Then you can have him back if you want him."

"No, I don't want him back." I could see real tears falling down Sarah Michelle's face. "You can have him. Now get out of this tent—both of you!" Her shouting made the baby cry harder, which incited her to start pushing me forcefully outside.

Outside the drizzly gray morning fog hit me full in the face.

January whined. "It was very dangerous for me to travel through this fog. But I felt I must let you have it for abusing me."

"You weren't abused," I couldn't control my volume. "You don't want me. You just don't want anyone else to want me."

"I do so want you," she looked somewhat sincere. "I love you. I want you back."

"But you can't have me back. Besides, I wasn't lying when I said I was broke." She looked hurt, but I continued. "The storm took my house and I still owe on it. And obviously I don't have a job."

"You'll get you a new job," January pouted. "I have money from my singing."

From the corner of my eye, I saw Sarah Michelle marching by with the baby in one arm and a bucket over the other. She was on her way to get water. I reached out to help her. "Don't you touch me, bastard!" Her voice held so much anger it ripped a hole in my heart. Each breath now brought stabbing chest pains. The crying baby looked over her shoulder at me as she marched off into the fog hanging over the sea of white tents.

I turned back to see January watching me watch Sarah Michelle. She actually looked hurt for real. I tried to go to her, but January ran to a little rise near our tent. The fog was clearing now and she looked out over the total devastation. Her face registered the horror of what she saw.

As soon as she took in the view, real tears surfaced in her eyes. She cried so hard I felt compelled to go sit by her and put by arm around her. People came out of their tents to watch. After all, they'd already heard everything. Their faces appeared a little blank as they watched January go through the same shock and emotional pain they had experienced over a month ago—an eternity ago. Her crying brought tears and fresh pain to everyone who heard. She struggled as she spoke through her tears, "It's

gone. All gone. Oh my God, Galveston's gone."

SARAH MICHELLE

I was coming back with the pail of water, balancing it and the baby, thinking about the few conversations I had overheard between Dean and John about this January Cola Buchanan. Dean didn't seem to think very highly of her and John did say she left him. I could tell he pined away for someone but I wasn't sure if it was January or Sister Elizabeth. What am I thinking? Of course, John grieved his friend Sister Elizabeth.

That January. She's a piece of work. Bursting into our tent. Waking the baby. Questioning the baby's birth. Was she suspicious it was not John's real son? Only three people knew Lucky was found at the orphanage. It was highly unlikely she talked to Sean, but Sean could have told Dean. If so, did Dean tell January? And would she use it against us to hurt John? It was almost humorous that she thought we were married and that John had betrayed her. He wasn't that kind of man. It was hard to imagine him with the likes of her. January Cola Buchanan. It couldn't be her real name.

It was all too much to think about. And now as I rounded the tent near ours, I could see her sobbing in John's arms. A twinge of jealousy hit me; I had hoped John would be Lucky's father in the back of my mind. And January's abrupt arrival had only brought it to the very front of my mind that this unacknowledged wish of mine would never happen now.

Holding the now calm baby, I sat the water bucket down and leaned against a tree—one of the few on the island not damaged by the storm. I comforted myself as I had recently learned to do very well and reminded myself of the money from Sean's father. I could live without anyone else. I would start a boarding house. I would rebuild where my former house stood.

It was fear that was driving me to care for John. I had never been alone before. I had married young before both my parents died. I had a baby shortly thereafter. Now I had Lucky—even though John had discussed with me turning him over to the nurse Clara Barton who had come to take care of the orphans. He didn't want me to feel obligated, he said. Well, I didn't feel obligated. I felt attached. Lucky was my lifeline and purpose for being. I wouldn't let him go. They would have to kill me to take him from me. I would do anything to keep him. Anything.

Let John go back to January. I could tell he cared for her by the look on his face when she burst into our tent. His eyes held hope that she loved him back even as she was hitting him with the newspaper. "Show people," I muttered out loud. It wasn't enough to have to perform drama for a job. They had to have it in their everyday life, too. Maybe she should have ridden out the storm. That would have given her a lifetime of drama.

Even as I thought it, I really didn't mean it. She was lucky to have left Galveston just a few months before. She didn't have a scar on her body or a bruise to be seen. She wasn't crazy like the rest of us. She wouldn't jump at every clap of thunder, every crash of lightning. She wouldn't have nightmares of maritime hell. Her dreams would not be filled with swirling

black water made blacker by the night sky, howling wind, screams of the

dying. If January didn't live through it, she would never understand. It

wasn't something easily verbalized. I sat on my knees in the tent rocking the

baby back and forth in a way that gently rocked me too. I could be strong. I

would be strong. I didn't die in the storm. I had a reason for living.

I peeped out the opening of the tent. John was still holding January

and the people in the neighboring tents thought they knew why. After all

everyone knows everything when you live in a tent city. I could see how

they looked at John now—and worse yet, how they looked at January—

with pity. I knew they would look at me with pity, too.

Not that I cared what people said anymore. That was one of the

good things about facing death squarely in the eye and winning. You didn't

care about what others thought, and since all my tent city neighbors were in

the same state of mind, I knew that they really didn't care to talk too much

about the situation John and I found ourselves in now.

January had brought her particular brand of trouble to us in early

November…she was the storm after the storm so to speak.

All things are working together for good, Sarah Michelle, I whispered slowly on

the wind. I know she heard because she was already laying this new trouble down—

something she would not have done a month ago.

DEAN

The land out the window was flat as far as the eye could see, but there was a beauty to it. The sky stretched out forever reminding me of what heaven must be like. I cocked my head to the side and looked up. This time of day, the sky was spun with strands of gold and orange-red. The sun was descending in the sky and the show was spectacular.

The train stopped in what you could really call a one-horse town. There appeared to be only the depot and one other structure as we pulled into the station with a loud whistle. Several passengers stood to get off and I decided to take a walk around myself. Sean was sleeping thanks to the medicine. Hansen was one of those men who thought of everything. I wondered if he developed the trait after he started working for Robert Stockton, or if he was born with the ability to anticipate every need and that's why he landed the job he did.

The wind was dry and hot. Soon, it would turn cold. That's what someone had told me once about this area of the country. I didn't know a lot about West Texas except that everything in it was supposed to be wild and untamed. Not a bad reason to choose a land for a new start. I would find a way to make another fortune here and hope Mother Nature would not see fit to take it from me again. That reminded me, I wanted to check on the weather. I never used to check on the weather until the storm. Now I noticed the slightest change.

I stepped onto the platform. Smoke from the train was pouring into the air. A few people were waiting to get onboard, going to the big city of Abilene. There was a man and a woman that appeared to be married and another single man beside them. Probably, the three of them composed half the population of this small community. I looked them over out of the corner of my eye. But they were all three looking directly at me in a most unusual open, honest sort of way. They wore plain homemade clothes, but they carried themselves with an air of dignity. So much so it made me envy them and their sureness of the world around them. One of them was carrying a newspaper. He saw me looking at it and offered it to me. He said he had already read it.

"Yes, thank you very much," I said as I took the newsprint from him. It was a weekly paper instead of a daily one like Galveston's, but it was a newspaper and frankly I was surprised to see one in this small town.

The man nodded and they went on their way up the train steps. I tucked the newspaper under my arm and took a stroll around the platform. Storm clouds were rolling in from the east. I hadn't noticed them on the train because they were behind us. I tugged at my hair and took my handkerchief out of my pocket to wipe the dusty sweat on my forehead. Then I headed back to the safety of the train. I didn't want Sean to wake and not find me there.

Sean was still asleep when I took my bench seat again. I was looking forward to reading the news. Imagine my surprise when I unfolded it and there on the front page were photos of the wreckage after the Galveston storm. I took it all in very slowly. It had done me a world of good to move out of the area. To be concerned with other things than the bad things that had happened there. It had been a godsend to get out and to reenter the world as I had known it before it was turned upside down. To just have a shower and shave in the Rice Hotel seemed to save my soul from the despair of it all.

I didn't want to look at the photos now. If I shut my eyes and tried really hard, I could almost believe it was a dream. But I couldn't keep my eyes shut and when I turned the page, I saw a series of photographs taken of the storm survivors. One in particular caught my attention as I read the caption, "John and Sarah Michelle McLaren with baby." My heart felt a sharp pain. An imaginary knife went in through my left ventricle. I felt like I was being stabbed in the same place repeatedly.

"What do you see Dean?" It was Sean. He was struggling to sit up on his little cot-like stationary bed. The sway of the train seemed to hurt him as he moved himself around. "Ouch, ouch, ouch. Damn." I couldn't help but laugh at the comical way the cuss words came out of his mouth. He was hardly in West Texas and here he was cussing like an old weathered ranch hand with a rich boy accent. I handed him the newspaper, "There are some pictures of Galveston in here."

"Before or after the storm?" he asked.

"After."

"Because before might be too sad to look at." Sean managed to stand and come over by me.

I handed him the paper. It was opened to the page with the McLaren family photo. "Look here," I said, "Here's one cheery picture. Looks like our friend John went and married Sarah Michelle. Probably wanted to help her with her newborn now that she was a widow. John's a good man that way."

Sean looked at the photo and smiled. "Now doesn't Sarah Michelle look pretty in the clothes I brought her…," his voice trailed off and his eyes clouded over. "I hope she kept the jewelry, too."

"Sean, Sarah Michelle gave me the jewelry and I put it in a safe place. A secret place." He looked at me as if to say, "Why?' I continued, "John and I thought it would be dangerous for them to find the jewelry if they came looking in our tent…" Sean continued staring at me. "I put it in a very safe, secret place." Then I just blurted it out how I had hidden it in the headstone of my dear mother's grave. I told him all the details of the secret compartment at the bottom border of stones.

Finally he quit glaring at me as if I had done something wrong. I realized he wanted to say something to me, too. He looked at the photo in the newspaper. "Do you realize Sarah Michelle is living for baby Lucky?"

"Yes." I had realized it was what seemed to occupy her every thought.

"I think John married her because she was afraid she couldn't adopt Lucky without a husband."

"Why would Sarah Michelle need to adopt Lucky?" I was baffled.

He leaned forward conspiratorially. I could tell he needed to tell someone his secret. "Now I'm going to tell you something I ain't never told no one before." I noticed he had slipped into my pattern of speech. Sean took a deep breath, then proceeded to tell me the whole story about how they had rescued baby Lucky in the swinging sling the morning after the storm. No wonder Sarah Michelle was unnerved whenever anyone asked questions or paid too much attention to Lucky.

"The way John and I see it the good Lord gave Lucky to Sarah Michelle because they needed each other," the boy rationalized.

And I thought to myself, that was very good of the Lord, but what about the part of taking away her husband and son? But I didn't say it out loud. It didn't seem right to blame the Lord for everything. After all it was the devil's world. Maybe God was in there trying to undo the devil's work by making it where we could always get by, even if it was just a little something holding us on inside. A baby nailed up in a swinging hammock of cloth in the rafters of a shaky old building surviving one of the worst hurricanes ever. Well, that would be the good Lord's doing.

5 PUMPS, SLUDGE & CANALS

JOHN

Fear seized my body, but I didn't dare tell January. She wouldn't understand and would probably laugh at me. It started slowly while I was holding her as she cried. At first just a few heart palpitations, then they became stronger and more frequent. I couldn't breathe. My heart was exploding. My ears thudded with the rhythm of my pulse. It didn't last long. I had found that if I just waited it would pass. But it left me dizzy and shaky. No one noticed, because as usual all eyes were on January.

A woman I recognized as our tent city neighbor came with a small white rag. Another woman came with a cup of tea to calm January's nerves. No one offered me tea or a rag. No one noticed I was falling apart. But that's the way it is in life—people don't know what's going on inside other people's head and if you keep quiet they don't know you need help. Suffice it to say, for the first time in my life I realized there are probably a lot of people hurting in the world in ways that I could not even imagine. It was one of the few good things that had happened because of the storm. I now looked at the world and the people in it with a deeper, clearer understanding.

The women surrounded January and took her to see the nurse, Clara Barton. How could a nurse help her emotional pain? A nurse could only help with physical ailments. I didn't try to stop them, because I wanted to be far away from January and the responsibility of taking care of her.

After they hustled her away in a flurry of skirts and loving kindness, I looked up to see Sarah Michelle coming toward me. Why didn't the women surround Sarah Michelle? She needed their attention more than January.

Sarah Michelle came and sat beside me. I hoped I had not hurt her deeply, but I knew I had. I felt guilty even though she tried to make me feel anything but that. She took my hand and held it to her face. Some people were still watching our morning spectacle from behind the privacy of their tents. I suppose people didn't make a thing of it not being proper for us to live together because Sarah Michelle had lost her family and circumstances were anything but normal.

Women and children got first call on the tents and that's originally why I went to get Sarah Michelle and Sean. So Dean and I could have one of the first tents. But I knew inside myself there was another reason. I brought them to live with me because I wanted them near me. How strange that they had decided to follow me in the first hours after the storm. They had seen something in me that I wanted to see in myself. Destiny had brought us together and I was letting these good connections in life go by the wayside without a second thought.

Sean was gone. Dean went after him to make certain he was okay. But I hadn't lifted a finger other than to read Dean's letter—and my name was on the reward money check right along with Sarah Michelle's.

"Sarah Michelle, we need to go to the bank in Houston. We need to put the reward money into an account in your real name." She didn't respond. "I know January, she'll want the money and I don't want her to think it's mine in any way. Besides you took care of Sean, the money should be all yours."

"Okay." That was all she said. And I thought back to the first days when she couldn't talk at all. She smiled and put her arm around me. "I know you love January."

The funny thing was I did love her before the storm. She had been my every thought, but now I saw her differently. I could see her for what she was...

Sarah Michelle interrupted my thoughts. "What's that?"

A group of people were surrounding a few men on a makeshift stage of wooden boxes. The newspaper had mentioned a public city council meeting this morning concerning issues of the most importance. I reminded Sarah Michelle of what I had told her earlier. Without another word, we both walked hurriedly to the group to hear the future of Galveston.

One of the newly appointed Central Relief Committee leaders was addressing the crowd. His voice was deep and resounding as he listed the accomplishments the city had made so far.

"Ladies and Gentlemen," he began. "Before I describe our plans for the future of the great city of Galveston, let me begin by recounting the many phenomenal ways the storm survivors have already begun rebuilding. For starters, The Galveston Daily News never missed an issue as September ninth and tenth were published together on a single sheet. One side listed the dead and the other side recounted the devastation of the storm. Within days after the storm, telegraph and water service were restored. Even as I speak, lines for a new telephone system are being laid." He paused for effect and a rustle of approval went through the crowd at his words.

He continued, "Houston relief groups offered major help in the days following the disaster in the form of food, supplies and putting up U.S. army tents for the more than eight thousand left homeless. In the third week of recovery, most of the Houston relief groups were on their way home leaving us to start again. And start again we have, with electric trolley service operating and freight moving through our harbors. Now it's time to face the largest of our rebuilding obstacles." He stopped and looked out over the crowd to make certain the right amount of tension was building in his speech. People strained forward in anticipation of his next words. "Ladies and gentlemen, after much consultation with experts of the day, our civil engineering project leaders have a proposal for this great city and its people's future. Without further ado, I give you Alfred Noble, Henry M. Robert and H.C. Ripley."

One of three men stepped forward to address the crowd. He was a tall, thin, intelligent-looking sort who spoke with a confident air. "There are two extensive projects we have decided to pursue to protect Galveston and its residents in the future against hurricanes of the magnitude seen two months ago. They will both take years to complete and cost major amounts, but we believe it is the best course of action."

As if on cue, another man stepped forward. "Building a seventeen-foot seawall from Sixth Street to Thirty-ninth Street." The crowd rumbled and swayed together as if they were an ocean wave. The third speaker raised his hand to quiet the crowd as he added, "and the second project needed to ensure Galveston never sees devastation on this level again is to raise the island's elevation." The crowd became slightly unruly, the man brought them under control again and continued, "I know you cannot imagine how these lofty projects could even be brought about, but believe me we have specific plans which my partners will share with you now."

Over the next half hour the three men presented their vision of how the work would proceed. The city would be raised first by getting more than sixteen million cubic yards of sand to the island. They explained how the sand would be dredged from Galveston's ship channel. They demonstrated a process by which it would be pumped through pipes into quarter-square-mile sections of the city that would be walled off with dikes. When the water drained away—the sand would remain. It sounded simple enough, but before pumping could begin they went on to detail how every structure, along with water and gas lines, would need to be raised. They explained to us how manual jackscrews would be used in this involved procedure.

They also went into details of their seawall recommendation. It would be seventeen feet high and slope downward at a pitch of one foot for every fifteen hundred feet to the bay. You could tell the three engineers believed their plans were the best they had to offer and everyone, myself included, wanted to move forward right away.

Thus it was decided that the pump structure would be put into place and dredging would officially begin possibly as early as the new year. And just like that our city began to be covered with pumps, canals and miles of catwalks.

It was hard to think about the fact it would take years to recover from what the winds and water had done in just a few hours. Once again, I marveled at man's fragile existence. But as a group we were incredibly strong that night as we made a decision to move forward and overcome. It was a good day.

SARAH MICHELLE

Heaven sakes alive! I wasn't expecting January's head to pop through the tent entrance. She came in head first in a manner that reminded me of a bull charging. No greeting. No pleasantries. She just blurted out, "Sarah Michelle, what are you doing here?"

"I live here."

"You did live here, but now that you've left John, you need to get out of his tent," she said to me as if I were taking advantage of John in some way. As if I were the one doing something wrong.

"I'm not leaving the tent." I said it in a firm, yet non-threatening tone.

"You mean we're all three going to live here? Without fighting?" She whisked her fine skirt around to remind me that I would have to contend with her and her selfish ways on a continual basis.

"No, not three of us. Four of us." I pointed to the baby on a nearby pallet I had just made for him. "Of course, you and John could live somewhere else."

January ignored my last comment. She was eyeing the baby. She got down on her hands and knees and looked at the baby in awe as if she had never seen an infant before.

"He has John's eyes, don't you think?" She tenderly smoothed the child's hair. "He's beautiful."

I was touched by her words, but then instantly wondered if this were some tactic of hers. I had met other women like her that were kind in front of you, but very unkind behind your back. I felt uncomfortable around January's beauty. My hand went immediately to my hair and I touched what was left of my long beautiful tresses. My husband used to call it my finest asset. Who would be jealous of me now? Definitely not this person before me. A beautiful, well-traveled woman such as January would only pity me, the way I looked now.

I couldn't even imagine her so much as sleeping a night in our tent. Even though we kept it tidy, the floors were made of dirt. Community showers and carrying buckets of water for cooking didn't seem like January's style.

A shaft of sunlight came through the tent door spotlighting January and the baby. She was still observing Lucky as if he were the most special infant in the world.

My skin began to crawl.

"They do resemble John's eyes, but they're not his," I heard myself saying. As soon as the words escaped my mouth I wish I hadn't said anything. I would safeguard my words from this moment forward. Somehow I knew instinctively anything said to January might later be used against me.

"They're not your eyes," January said looking directly at me.

"They're my husband's eyes." I lied. "John is not his father." There I had told January half the truth and I felt better. "John helped me with Lucky after the storm. You could imagine the horrors of caring for a few-days-old infant…"

"Your baby was only a few days old at the time of the storm?" She sat up and rested her hands on her knees. Her face went dark.

"What is it that troubles you, January?" I faked a caring tone.

"I knew of a baby born a few days before the storm. But things went wrong. I …," she paused before continuing, "We lost it. It was my sister's."

I felt pain. "I know what it's like to lose a child. I lost my son … in the storm."

January jumped up and came to me. As she put her arm around me, she said, "Please tell me his name." This time I knew her words and actions were heartfelt.

Just then the tent door flapped open and in came John. He had been on the work crews building the pump structure and he was absolutely covered in a brown sludge-like substance. With a weary eye, he took in the situation—January with her arm around me, giving me a comforting look. John's eyes locked on mine in disbelief.

"I've told January we're not married, that the baby is my deceased husband's."

"John darling, I want Sarah Michelle and the baby to continue to stay in our tent and live with us" January said in a honey sweet voice. "You agree, don't you?"

John shook his head. "I should've showered before I even stepped foot in this tent. Excuse me, ladies." He turned and stomped out the same way he'd come in.

Looking back at January in her finery, I smoothed my dress and remembered my proper upbringing. "May I make you a cup of tea?"

She accepted as graciously as if she were the Queen of England.

I swept in for just a moment. My presence was not needed. The truth would come to light soon enough. Back in heaven, I became part of a loving bright light vibrating with hundreds of singing voices.

DEAN

We arrived at the Kalo's ranch after a long wagon ride from the station. Just like Hansen, his female relative Kitty Kalo thought of everything, she had padded the wagon with blankets and pillows and even brought a gentle, slow-moving mare. We took the long ride extra slow and although she was kind, she was not a talker.

Once when she saw me looking her way, she said as much, "I've always been shy. Don't expect much conversation from my direction." She glanced quickly away and out over the flat land before her. "Besides, I'm alone much of the time out here. I forget to talk when I'm around people. You ever been alone so much that's happened to you?"

"Yes." I smiled and she smiled back.

"My husband's a doctor. One of the only ones out this way." She must have felt like talking now that she remembered she had two new people in her life sitting right here in the wagon with her. "Can't argue with him working all the time when he's saving lives. Just wished we lived in closer to Abilene proper."

"My mother used to tell me to be a doctor. Dean, she'd say, a doctor's always going to have work." I stopped, not wanting to give too much of my history.

"What you got there?" she gestured to my rolled up paper.

I spread it out and showed her some of the photographs after the hurricane. She told me about the storms that followed as the hurricane moved inland. Then she asked me if I knew that about two thousand people across the mainland had lost their lives as the cyclone tracked clear across America, spreading sorrow in its wake.

I had to confess this was new information to me. Living in the moment, in the aftermath of the storm, I hadn't thought past my little bubble of existence and my fight to survive. Of course, the storm took a toll as it raged its way across the U.S.

To tell the truth, no one had been able to discuss the hurricane with me at length in Houston because I constantly changed the subject whenever it surfaced.

"Who would have thought that the cyclone that was brewing that day would be one of the worst ever?" She cocked her head to one side as she talked like a delicate bird. I found it interesting she referred to the storm as a cyclone instead of a hurricane, as did Sarah. Well ... whatever, one called it, I agreed it was one of the worst ever.

"It caught most of us completely unaware. I'm telling you I went to the beach to watch the waves with a lot of other people that afternoon. And I decided to ride out the storm with a group of friends playing poker that evening. I decided to play poker on what could've been my last night."

"Now that's something, ain't it? How life-changing events just sneak up on you like that," she adjusted her sunbonnet as she said it.

"Yes, a few months ago I would have never even dreamed of getting a new start in West Texas."

"Uh-huh." That's all she said before suddenly going quiet again. I guess she had grown tired of talking.

Finally, we arrived at a rather large frame house. It was simple in design and the yard was bare but tidy. Not too far away from it stood another much smaller house, a barn, and a vegetable garden. Several dogs stopped what they were doing and ran to us, barking a happy greeting. Tails wagging. Eyes sparkling.

Kitty bent down to chastise one dog with what looked to be a red ball in his mouth. "Now Duke, quit eatin' my 'maters." I realized the dog was carrying a big ripe tomato. Kitty took the tomato from Duke and ran her fingers over the dog's teeth marks. Tomato juice was running out. "Might as well keep it now. It's no good." She threw it like a ball and Duke ran after it.

I heard Sean laugh. Turning I saw he was sitting up in the wagon, smiling.

Two farmhands came out of the smaller house with a stretcher they'd made. Together they got Sean inside with hardly any discomfort. But the ride had worn him out and he couldn't keep his eyes open as Kitty settled him into his crisp clean bed. "We'll get him washed up tomorrow. He's had enough for today."

Downstairs a cook had prepared dinner. Like the house, it too was simple and plain but in a good way. I ate and ate. I noticed the two farmhands and Kitty did too. The cook seemed very satisfied.

Afterwards I went out on the wrap-around porch to smoke. I sat in one of several rockers and thought of the photograph of Sarah Michelle and John. I took the newsprint out of my jacket and spread it out. The baby Lucky looked like a cherub sitting in John's lap. There was no trace in the babe's eyes of the horror he had witnessed in the first few days of his life. Maybe he just assumed chaos was normal, how the world worked.

My heart seized up. I felt a lump form in my throat. Love was not for the likes of me. I didn't understand why I had such strong feelings for Sarah Michelle. I think I first noticed it when I was watching her being so tender with the baby and Sean. But love was a mysterious thing. Some of it was chemistry, like what attracts animals out in the wild, and I knew it was more that than anything else. I just liked the way she looked. The way she smelled.

How had my life gone so astray? I had gotten off to a rough start, but had turned it around. I had even been respectable at one time—a catch for any young woman, I had been told repeatedly. But that was in another time and place, even before Galveston.

165

I guess you have to keep watching the flow of things very carefully to make certain you don't find yourself in some sort of trouble.

That's how I should live my life like John. He'd told me right before the storm how he has spent most of his days just trying to keep things stable, on an even keel. But if that were true, he wouldn't have been involved with January. I never understood those two as a couple. They didn't seem like they had a thing in common.

I looked down at the paper again. Something was nagging me. I wanted to write Sarah Michelle a letter telling her I knew they had married. As if to show her it didn't bother me.

I decided I'd write the letter in the morning. Tonight I would go in, take a good warm bath, and sleep. As soon as I got settled in this new life, I'm sure I would forget all about Galveston and the people there.

SARAH MICHELLE

When I received Dean's letter I decided to keep it to myself, no small task in our living quarters. January snooped into everything. Often, I would find things just a little out of order. My jewelry, the things in my trunk, my silverware and, strange as it may seem, my clothes and underwear had all been ruffled through just a little bit. I wasn't sure at first and had taken to putting things just so to make certain. Noting how each piece of clothing was folded or how a particular item was turned. She also engaged in conversation with many people, gathering as much gossip as she could so she could spread it on to others.

Thank God, January was gone today. She was helping with the wounded. The baby was asleep and I took the opportunity to write Dean a letter back. I wrote two actually. One for Sean and Dean to read … and one for Dean's eyes-only.

The first letter to Sean and Dean asked benign questions such as did they like the West Texas landscape? How was Sean's recovery coming along? Was Sean back in school yet? and so on. I also gave a short report on Baby Lucky and then, for some reason, I went into detail about the reconstruction process and the raising of the island. I even told them about how I intended to try to raise the tree on my property to keep it alive. And I mentioned how others intended to dig up graves and headstones and raise them to the new level. I guess these were things that had been weighing heavily on my mind. The sheer magnitude of everything that would have to be moved or raised was beyond my brain's comprehension. How would we ever accomplish it all?

I ended on what I thought to be a humorous note. I told them not to believe everything they read in the newspapers—John and I weren't married. The photographer merely had one last piece of film for a photograph and we all wanted our picture taken. The photographer's assistant assumed we were a family when he took down our contact information and discovered us living in one tent. I didn't correct the assistant as I didn't want him to think me improper under the circumstances.

"Never dreamed we'd be front page news." I wrote and closed by saying, "Didn't they think it was marvelous Lucky would have a baby photo to reflect back on in later years. He truly is a very lucky child."

My second letter, for Dean's eyes only, was short and concise. I told him how John's ex-fiancé January had also seen our picture in the newspaper. I went on to explain that even though she had left him months before the storm, she felt betrayed believing that John had been married all along. In as few words as possible, I told of her bursting into our tent in a rage casting accusations at John and me. Just writing the words brought a flush of anger to my cheeks.

Then I disclosed that January was now living in the tent with us, and that I needed a place to get away to allow them privacy. Of course, there were places to get away to on the island, but I didn't go into this in the letter. I only told Dean I wanted to get far away.

I asked him to advise if West Texas would be a good place to build a boarding house and start my life anew. Perhaps he could even look at prices of land for sale or maybe existing structures. I signed off by saying the West didn't seem quite so wild to me anymore after having lived through the cyclone and I would love to start over in a place where I knew at least two people. Having been a somewhat newly arrived immigrant before the storm, I found myself with few ties in America. I hoped he would understand my need to move.

It made me sad inside to see John and January together. This I had not disclosed to anyone.

Next, I carefully hand-addressed the two letters and went to the makeshift post office. After I had mailed them, I considered trying to get the letter to Dean back, but the postman said the mail had just been picked up and was already in route to its final destination.

I stopped by the building with the nurse Clara Barton. Many volunteers were helping her as she looked after the wounded and distributed medicine. But to tell the truth, aside from people with fevers and many, many minor injuries involving cuts and scrapes, there weren't many major injuries because most of those people had died soon after the storm. And there weren't many children orphaned from the storm either. Most of the young ones had been casualties. I imagined their parents desperately trying to save them as Thomas and I had with our son.

However, a nurse was definitely needed, for without the proper medicines in this tropical climate, a small cut could soon become a festering wound.

Inside I found two or three volunteers wrapping bandages and sorting relief supplies. The nurse herself was in a small room talking with someone. I had come for more medicine for my cuts and to see if I could get more bottles for Baby Lucky. I had left him back at the tent with the neighbor girl, Lucy. She was very good with him.

A volunteer helper gestured for me to take a seat on a bench in the waiting area. She told me the nurse would see me when her present patient left. I sat down on the bench and soon discovered I could hear snippets of the conversation. I recognized the visitor's voice. It was January.

She was weeping. I moved forward a little and I could see her back. She was sitting in a chair turned toward the nurse whom I could not see. January's back shook with her heavy sobs. I thought of leaving. I was embarrassed with myself for trying to eavesdrop. But then, I thought of January and her snooping and I stayed. I was genuinely concerned.

The nurse's voice was very soft, but I caught, "only the three boys that were clinging to the tree survived."

January said, "I'm being punished for not keeping him. For putting my career first."

Hmm, January was really remorseful about leaving John for her singing career. I couldn't make out what she said next, but then I heard, "every time I look at little Lucky, I think of my child."

Oh! It was January herself that lost the child born near the same time as Lucky. Her lie about her sister having a baby should've been transparent to me. No wonder she was emotional. It must have been John's child and that's the real reason she left in the months before the storm.

Pieces of the puzzle were starting to fall in place. It was all I could do to act like I wasn't listening. I glanced at the volunteers. They were all busy with their jobs. Not even looking my way. I got up and moved to the window where I could hear even better. I vowed to myself I would treat January much better now that I understood. One of the volunteers behind me dropped some metal trays. They clanged and clattered and I almost put my finger to my lips to hush them. But they went on about their business oblivious to the important conversation inside.

I could hear the nurse saying, "Sister Elizabeth and the others took such good care of the children…you were right to go to her."

Gasping, I held to the back of the chair. She left her newborn with Sister Elizabeth.

The nurse continued. I strained to hear. "Consider God has a plan for each life. No one lives or dies unless it is in his plan."

It occurred to me January would be exiting the door soon and I didn't want her to find me. I turned and started walking back past the volunteers. One of them looked up startled as if she had forgotten I was there.

"Are you sure you can't wait?" The volunteer helper put down the supplies she was carrying.

"I'll come back," I said hurriedly.

My head was spinning at the sound of Sister Elizabeth's name. Of course, January had been so obsessed with the orphanage being destroyed. She had been preoccupied with going over the names in the paper. However, the orphan tragedy was enough to overcome anyone with grief. Only a callous person would not have deep feelings about what had happened there during the storm. But she had left her baby there with the nuns. There was a distinct possibility Lucky was her child.

And I could not, would not lose Lucky.

I wish I could cry and cry and cry. But even when I sit down and try to cry, no tears come. I'm too afraid to feel. Afraid I might not be able to get back to even this state I'm in now. I'm afraid I might perish under the weight of my grief.

I went home and found the next-door neighbor girl playing with Lucky. She had fashioned a small sock doll that she wiggled above him. He seemed completely fascinated and not at all concerned I had been gone for more than two hours.

I watched his eyes following the brightly colored sock doll. They sparkled and danced as she tickled him under the chin with it.

Oh my dear Lord, Lucky did have John's eyes. How could we not have seen it before? Because we refused to see? Or, because January never let on to John that she was going to have his child. She left them both in pursuit of her singing career.

Perhaps fame would lure her again. And my fragile world would remain intact.

DEAN

The letters arrived on a Tuesday. One was addressed only to me, but I got Sean and we opened them both together. We went outside to read in the midday sun on a little table that was used for a variety of chores.

After I read the first letter addressed to me, I realized it was probably not meant for Sean's ears. It told about January coming back and living in their tent. The second letter told about the dredging, the constant mud, and how everything including John was dirt brown. It described catwalks and the jacking of every single thing in the city to raise the island above sea level. It even told about the new seawall itself. And then, toward the end, it said Sarah Michelle wanted to leave. She wanted to come to West Texas.

After we read them, Sean and I sat in awkward silence. A smile broke over his face. It would be great if Sarah Michelle and Lucky were back in our lives. This is the best news ever.

Sean threw the letter up in the air and actually said, "Yippee!" Duke the dog came running with another tomato in his mouth. Sean took the tomato and threw it hard. "Go get it boy! Go get it!" Then the pain in his leg stopped Sean's fun and he sat back down. A grimace replaced the smile on his face, but only for an instant.

It was just about that time Kitty came to the back door, "What you hollerin' about child? You hurt yourself." She came out the door and started toward us just to satisfy herself everything was fine. "Why is he flailing about?"

"He's happy for the first time in a long time," I smiled.

I was happy, too. But I was concerned about the raising of the island. I knew I only had a short time to get back to Galveston and move my mother's headstone myself. Didn't want anyone finding the jewelry I hid there. People would put two and two together, seeing as Sean lived in the tent with us. They wouldn't listen to the fact that most of the jewelry belonged to Sean's aunt—especially when he wasn't going by his real name of Robert Stockton, Jr.

Kitty picked up the letter addressed to me and read it to herself. "I know of a boarding house this Sarah Michelle might want to look into buying." She pointed north. "Just a little outside of town."

"Let's go look at it now," Sean practically shouted in his excitement. Duke came running back with the squishy tomato and Sean threw it again.

Kitty started untying her apron strings. "Let's go before someone else buys it. It's been sittin' empty nigh a year." She looked at me. "Go get the wagon. I'll get some pillars and blankets for Sean to ride on."

The house wasn't far from town, but it was far from the Kalo spread. It was a pleasant day with blue sky and warm breezes. Kitty had reminded us to take a coat because once the sun went down, it gets cold fast. I'm glad she did because I wasn't used to such volatile weather. I laughed to myself at that last thought. Good thing I hadn't uttered it out loud.

I turned to look back at Sean in the wagon. Duke had gotten in beside him and was riding like a king on the pile of blankets and pillows, or "pillars" as Kitty called them. It was always interesting to me how just a few miles one way or another could influence people's dialects. I liked Kitty's very much and thought of adding a few of her more interesting words to my own vocabulary when the occasion was right.

Duke turned on the blankets so he could be even more comfortable. Never mind that it gave Sean less room. "Move over Duke or you get out and walk." Sean poked him in the back with his finger and Duke gave him a look like, "What'd you do that for?"

Soon we were at the house and I have to admit it was nice. "It shouldn't be locked," Kitty said. "Best to leave it unlocked so passersby won't break one of the expensive glass windows to get inside," She went up to the front door. We followed right behind her. "Get out of here Duke, dogs ain't allowed in the house." Kitty let us inside first and shooed Duke away with her open hand. The large hound's eyes looked at her, pleading. Then he just gave up and went around her into the house and straight up the stairs. We all chased Duke, and so it was that we started our tour on the top floor instead of the bottom floor, as a normal person would have expected.

"This was a boardinghouse in the past," Kitty gestured down the hallway. "See the set-up of the rooms…and there's even a bath at the end of the hall." Each of the rooms still had furniture in them. Many of the better pieces were draped with sheets of cloth. This fancy room had a full-length dressing mirror. The couple that owned it had money back East and shipped all this stuff out here.

"Why did they leave?" I expected her to tell me the woman found this environment too rough for her fragile disposition. But instead Kitty replied, "Do you really want to know? Or would you be satisfied just to buy the place without any history."

I looked at Sean. He was busy running up and down the hall looking in the rooms. I had learned that sometimes ignorance is bliss. Kitty continued, "People say there's a lady ghost in this house, but she's the friendly sort. Shouldn't be a problem if it's true."

"Don't tell me anymore." I knew how these ghost tales could make an otherwise normal person crazy—always on the lookout for something strange rather than perceiving everything to be normal. If we didn't tell Sean and Sarah Michelle about the lady ghost, probabilities were good they would never think they saw one.

"Lady that owned it last said she actually saw the ghost once when it passed her on the stairs," Kitty's eyes gleamed as she whispered the ghostly tale.

"Don't tell me anymore please." I laughed as I said it, but I meant it.

We went downstairs and saw the living room parlor and kitchen. "How much does a fine house like this cost?" I wanted to be able to give Sarah Michelle all the specifics.

"Not as much as one in a major city like Galveston… I mean, Houston." Kitty corrected herself. "I guess houses aren't worth as much as they were in Galveston. Such a shame. Such a gorgeous city. All that wealth and splendor washed away."

I thought of my own gambling establishment. No hope of recovery. "Is there someone in town that Sarah Michelle can deal with on this?"

"Yes, the town banker can give us some hard numbers. We can stop by before going back and get some information you can mail out to Sarah Michelle."

"I think I'll take them to her myself," I said.

"I'll go too." Sean chimed in.

Kitty's smooth brow wrinkled. "That might not be such a good idea Sean. I got a letter from my cousin Hansen. Seems the whole city of Houston and thereabouts is looking for Robert Stockton, Jr."

Sean stuck out his chest and stood tall, "If anyone recognizes me, I'll run." We all knew he wouldn't be running anytime soon.

"I'll tell you what Sean. Let me go to Galveston by myself and I'll try to get your sister Jane to come back with me for a visit."

Sean's face brightened and so did mine. Somewhere off in the distance I heard a twinkling sound. I looked around for the source and was distracted by a tumbleweed rolling across the lawn. Gentle puffs of wind lifted my hair from my forehead and offered relief from the heat of the day.

Things were being set in motion. Circumstances were being arranged. And the humans made plans as if they were in control. This thought made me laugh, and the silvery sound of my laughter surprised me. It sounded like music. And, just for the record, I didn't see a ghost lady in the house.

Dean and Sean would be getting the letter any day now and I suppose it would take them days if not weeks to respond, but I began making plans in my head for how to proceed.

It was almost the first of December. What a time for me to decide to leave the sunny isle of Galveston. Had it really been almost three months since the storm? One look at little Lucky and I knew it to be true. He was rolling over and raising his head. I could swear he even smiled occasionally.

I looked at him in his basket, stretched out on his back and waving his arms and legs in the air. It was peculiar how much he favored John now that January had mentioned the similarity of their eyes.

Just then January blew in bringing a gush of cold wind with her. "It's going to rain," she said. "Going to be a bad storm."

My stomach tightened at her words. I stopped folding the freshly washed blankets and stood with my hands on my waist as if making a stand. I hoped John would come home soon from working. He was raising a building. It was hard work, but better than working on the pumps, which covered every inch of him in mud.

January was down on the floor of the tent playing with Lucky in his basket. She tenderly touched the soles of his feet and made little baby-like cooing sounds. Lucky smiled and jerked his feet around. Clearly he thought January was as exquisite as everyone else did and I noticed her beauty seemed to make them forgive her anything. Take John for example. It's a wonder he took her back in so easily. But he's not himself. Maybe she brings him more comfort than heartache.

I felt a little guilty around January because of my listening in on her conversation with the nurse, but I must say it did clear up a few things for me. Not tonight, but when the time was right, I would discuss with her how she must tell John about the baby they lost. He deserved to know and I thought of how he must have felt when she left.

"I'm going to West Texas." I hadn't meant to say that out loud. January turned toward me. Her naturally red lips turned up. "Are you now? That's just perfect." She turned back to the baby. "But why so far away, I won't get to see Lucky very often. Maybe never."

Nothing was said for a few minutes. Then January took me by surprise with the following, "Sarah Michelle, I know how hard it is on you. Would you consider John and myself…" the look on my face stopped her cold.

I didn't know what she was going to say, but I suspected it involved my giving Lucky to her and John to raise as a couple. As if January would make a better mother than me. I didn't run off leaving the man I loved for a singing career. But then again, now I knew that she hadn't either.

What she had just mentioned was not preposterous. After all, I was keeping it a secret that we'd rescued Lucky. I was afraid they'd take him away from me and give him to a family, probably in Houston where people didn't live in white tents or lean-to homes build out of lumber from the storm wreckage. Maybe I was being selfish to keep Lucky.

We could hear John talking to another man outside. The thick material of our tent whipped in the rising wind and made popping sounds. John stuck his head inside and said. "Ladies, we need to secure the ties of the tent. Tis' going to be a hell of a storm."

THE BOY "ROBERT/SEAN"

Dean was preparing to leave and go back to Galveston. I knew that he liked Sarah Michelle, though her tried to hide it. But his happy mood betrayed him. He was even humming a little. Said he wanted to bring her back himself. It was dangerous for a woman and a baby to make the trip alone. Plus, he wanted to raise his mother's headstone up with the rest of the island.

"Wouldn't want to lose the place where she was buried," he had said in front of Kitty and her doctor husband that just happened to be home one night in time for dinner.

They nodded their heads in agreement.

"Burial site of a loved one is a precious thing," Kitty said quietly. "You do what you need to do, Dean. We'll take care of Sean." At that she got up and checked on dessert. The cook had left it chilling in the icebox and it was just right for serving.

Later, we privately discussed how Dean would bring the jewelry back and we would put it in a safety deposit box at the bank. It would be easy to get to if Sarah Michelle or I should ever need it. It was funny that Sarah Michelle was building the boarding house with the reward money for taking care of me, because she really would be taking care of me as I intended to move in and help her run the place.

I sat on the ground and looked as far as I could see in the distance. Not a hill in sight. The wild desert grasses and shrubs had turned brown and dry. We had already had deep snow twice. Up to Duke's ears. Kitty had taken to putting all the dogs in the back workroom off the porch at night. *Boy, West Texas sure could get cold.*

A lifetime had passed since the storm, but it would always be with me. Always define me. Maybe that's why I passed through it alive.

I tried to remember how Galveston looked before the storm. When I couldn't, I tried to remember how it looked afterward. A few vivid images popped up, but I couldn't remember much. Really I couldn't even remember much of the days afterward. I looked back toward town and thought of what it would be like at the school I was going to start attending soon. It would be fun to meet some people my age.

You could tell Dean was a man who liked to travel, who liked to be in motion. He walked toward me across the dirt yard. Red dust kicking up from his boots. "Want to escort me to the train?" He was still some distance away, but I could hear him plainly. It was so quiet out here. I moved toward him. I could see the farmhands helping Kitty hook up the wagon. "Hurry," Dean said as he turned and walked away from me toward the wagon. I kind of hopped to move forward. I was getting better. Things were getting better. Soon Dean would return with Sarah Michelle and Lucky and I could hardly wait.

JOHN

Sarah Michelle helped me while January held the basket with Lucky. I had found some good rope on one of my work sites. I knew it would come in handy in our pieced-together world. We reinforced the existing tent ropes by going over them with the new rope. While the white Army tents were shelter, they had their problems. Water leaked in and they often smelled of mildew. Not that the whole island didn't smell from the funeral pyres, which were followed abruptly by the stink of dredging.

We were lucky to have a tent to ourselves. It was Dean's quick thinking to secure one early on when everyone else was discombobulated. Many of the survivors were still staying at the church or other half-destroyed, half-standing structures that kept them out of the elements. But we had this nice tent.

I had to stop. My heart was pounding in my ears. Blood rushing through my head made me weak and dizzy. "Aye, it's good enough," I said as the first blast of really hard rain fell. "Get inside, lasses, before ye're both soaked to the core."

We decided to take shifts sleeping with one alert person for a lookout. January volunteered to be first. Sarah Michelle and I bedded down on either side of the tent while January took a sitting position by the door where she could look out occasionally. I rolled over and faced the tent wall.

The wind blew it in so hard it almost touched my face. Wind whipped up and strained the ropes; maybe we'll be okay.

I could hear the baby gurgling happily in his basket beside Sarah Michelle's bedroll. The infant was, once again, oblivious to the danger of the coming storm.

The rain drove harder and the lightnin' started to flash. I felt we were very vulnerable to the elements in the tent. I should have found us a sturdier place. I could hear other frightened voices from the nearby tents. One man observed to his wife that we were lucky we hadn't had a really bad storm since the hurricane. I agreed with him in my mind, since he didn't realize I was listening to him, as were so many others.

A loud clap of thunder struck. Lightnin' flashed again. The tree up on the small hill nearby was struck and was now on fire—even in this driving rain. We had felt the electric spark traveling through the ground. *Thanks be to God we weren't close to it.*

I closed my eyes and I was back in the hurricane. I opened them again and January was kneeling beside me, her head in her hands, crying hard. I could barely hear her as she said, "John I can't die not telling you I was pregnant with your baby when I left Galveston." I could see her outline with every flash of lightnin' as she confessed. "I gave him to Sister Elizabeth. She had a good family in mind for him … he was just days old

186

when the hurricane hit ... I fear he was lost during the storm with Sister Elizabeth."

The storm intensified and the unrelenting wind howled around and through our tent. Sarah Michelle sat straight up in bed and grabbed Lucky to her, just as the swaying tent gave way. I screamed out as our home came down upon us.

SARAH MICHELLE

I could feel the sandy soil and wet grass beneath my feet. It was hard to run through the driving rain and not fall with a baby in my arms. When the tent fell on us, I just kept pushing and moving until I found an opening. Now I wanted to find shelter. Real shelter—not another tent.

My skin was chilled. What must the baby be feeling? Young infants can get pneumonia easily. Run ... run ... run. If I'm running in the right direction there is a small, wooden, box-type house that two families fashioned together out of scrap lumber from the storm. It's not pretty, but it looked strong the other day when I passed by it. It would be a good place to ride out the storm.

There it was up ahead. I knocked on the door and screamed, "Please ... please, I have a baby." The door opened quickly and someone pulled us inside. It was already packed with people. Children sitting two-deep on parents' laps and others standing with their arms close to their sides trying to take up as little room as possible. I would have to stand and hold Lucky. It was hard to breath with so many people in such a small place. Outside the thunder and lightning roared. Someone had put a lantern on a barrel near the right front corner. It cast a strange glow and dark shadows in the tiny box house. Hardly any rain leaked in and I immediately warmed up in spite of my soaking clothes. The people near me tried to keep themselves dry by not touching me, which thankfully gave me a bit more room than most.

Judging by the little conversation, more tents than ours had fallen victim to the savage winds. Every once in a while the person by the door cracked it to let in new air. With it came a blast of rain, but it couldn't be helped. Already they said one woman had fainted and had to be revived. I saw her still recovering near the open window. There were two windows in the box. Both had wooden, hinged covers. One was propped open slightly. The faint woman rested her head near it while sitting on one of a few crates. The other window was closed now, but they cracked it open every so often.

"Half-past midnight," a silver-haired man announced as he looked at his fine pocket watch. I recognized him as one of the wealthier Galvestonians. There had been many wealthy people in this thriving metropolis. "The New York of the South," some called it. I looked around at the others; many like me in clothes that had once been fine, but now could not be properly cared for in our living conditions. Women who used to pride themselves on their appearance now couldn't even check their hair. Almost every mirror had been broken. "Seven years of bad luck times a thousand," Sean had observed as he pointed to one of many broken mirrors near where the barbershop had been.

My heart felt a twinge of pain. First Sean had to leave. Now I would be expected to give Lucky to January. My mind started racing with plans of leaving the island with Lucky. January had given up her child for adoption and our family was planning to adopt a new baby. How did I know Lucky wasn't the baby destined for Thomas and myself? I couldn't give him up. I'd die. January didn't want a child holding her career back.

But then I remembered her in the nurse's office. She did regret her decision. But what was a single woman to do in her position? Perhaps she didn't want to live a life feeling like she'd forced John to marry her.

"I'll hold that child for you if you want." It was a slim teen-age girl perched on the corner edge of an already crowded wooden crate. I handed Lucky to her. Then I surprised myself by taking a nap standing up. Well, you never know what you're capable of until you're challenged. When I woke, I turned to the young girl's mother who was now holding Lucky and he was fast asleep. The woman looked at me and mouthed, "Let's don't wake a sleeping baby." I nodded, "yes". Others had fallen asleep and a few were gently snoring. The savage rain had stopped and the two windows were propped open. I wondered what kind of scene we would encounter when we stepped out of our makeshift shelter.

It wasn't too bad outside. The rain had actually cleansed the air a bit and everything felt fresh and new. I took the baby and went to look out for our tent, praying John and January had survived. I could see the tent had blown down completely, as well as several others. But there were many in the sea of tents still standing strong. Just as some houses had somewhat weathered the cyclone with only a roof torn up while others had completely imploded or washed away. It seemed a random pick of location, rather than how well the house had been built. Some people talked of how they axed or drilled holes in the floor before the cyclone to make suction when the water rose so the house wouldn't float away. I don't know how they thought of such a thing. In all my years, I would never have thought of making holes in the floor.

I went to where a group of people had gathered near a cistern. Several of the cisterns had weathered the hurricane but gotten salt spray in them. Others had not been contaminated and were a source of water for entire neighborhoods in the days following the cyclone. Now we gathered around this one. Nearby a woman passed out biscuits from a basket covered with a cloth. She would reach her hand in and offer one to everyone she passed. I went and stood where she was headed so I would be sure to get one. I needed a bottle for the baby. I needed to leave here before John and January discovered me.

My mind made a plan. First, a visit to the nurse's station, or 'infirmary' as they had called it when I was there the other day, to get baby bottles. Then to Houston. I had a few coins in my apron pocket. I put my hand in and jingled them, just to make certain they were there. Someone handed me a cup of water and I thought of how my wedding china had survived and now I would be leaving it behind again. I walked over and looked toward the ocean.

In the background, I listened in as a group of men discussed the island renovations. "Seems their plan is to dredge a channel coming in from the bay near abouts 6th and Boulevard," one said. Another described how they were going to put up commissary houses—small ones and two-bedrooms, shotgun type structures. They would be for the workers and for the people whose houses were being razed to live in.

I knew many workers were coming to help and it would provide good jobs for them. The city commission had already brought in horses to clear the debris. Most of them were brought to pull the carts which transported the dead to the funeral pyres. What a job that was. On and on for weeks and weeks, the horses carried the carts the men had loaded heavy with the dead.

John had never talked about any of it, but I could tell his sadness by the way he looked whenever the funeral pyres were mentioned in conversation. He had also taken to cleaning his hands over and over those first few days. It was an odd habit, but it seemed to help him. I didn't mention it because I didn't want him to feel self-conscious. I didn't know him before. Perhaps he always washed his hands over and over.

A butterfly appeared near me. It was big and brightly colored. The baby reached out for it and it flitted by, as if to play. Up and down it bobbed through the air. So beautiful. So delicate. Only one more of countless extraordinary things about this island paradise that had attracted so many influential and wealthy people. I remember how impressed I had been by the big tropical flowers when we first arrived from Europe. Their exotic blooms delighted me as the warm island breezes wafted their smell everywhere. Surely by the spring they'd be back in their full glory and cover the stink of the dredging.

The butterfly lit on a pink oleander bush. Its huge wings slowly opened and closed, revealing a spot of turquoise. This is the same type of butterfly I had admired once long ago at a dance at Woolsen's lake. It had flown around us as Thomas and I danced under the twinkling lights on the pavilion. Time stood still as we twirled in the company of the butterfly. I sighed and took in a deep breath. Shortly thereafter, I had found out I was pregnant.

I looked down at Lucky in my arms. I could not take another person's child. I would find John—but first, to the infirmary to get the baby bottles. Lucky would be screaming for food soon. I returned the cup to the woman who gave it to me and started picking my way toward downtown.

A thought occurred to me on the way. January had talked openly to the nurse. Perhaps I would explain the circumstances to her and leave

Lucky in her care. She could see that he was returned to John and January, and then I wouldn't have to go through the pain of handing him over for good. I would simply leave from the nurse's office to Houston. I hadn't heard back from Dean and Sean, even though I had it on good authority the mail was running on time these days.

Everything was back up and running again, even the many Chinese laundries that kept the men's shirts starched stiff. The laundry workers were again going around with bags collecting the shirts. I had always found the stiff celluloid collars interesting. I wondered if they hurt the wearer's neck. Probably so, that's the way it is with high fashion and Galveston was definitely a high fashion town.

I passed a saloon and it was certainly back in business. Laughter and music floated out and down the street.

Finally at the infirmary, I found the same volunteers as before. In a very efficient manner, one found bottles and milk while another pulled the top off of a donation barrel. Inside were new clothes sent down from the North. "Would you like to add something to your wardrobe?" the volunteer said. "It's for the survivors,"

"How generous," I was surprised someone had donated these items. I ran my fingers across the fine fabrics, "How luxurious."

"They're not all new, but they are in excellent shape," he brought out a beautiful turquoise silk. "You could use this for fancy outings or a trip into Houston."

"How did you know I planned to go into Houston?"

"Lots of the women-folk have been going onto the mainland to stay until this place is more livable." He was rummaging through another barrel. "Here's a bonnet. You'll need this, I'm sure." When I told him about the tent and the loss, he started filling a basket with food. "You fared better than the lady in there," he gestured to a room down the hallway. "Tent pole knocked her out and cut her head," he leaned in and very, very quietly said, "I'm afraid it's going to leave an ugly scar on her forehead. Such a pity."

Another female volunteer standing near us moved close and whispered, "I hear she's a singer, and an actress." She gave a knowing look

The male volunteer said, "I wouldn't be a bit surprised with that gorgeous face."

"Is she famous? What's her name?" I said caught up in the moment. Lucky was now feeding on his new bottle. The female helper had also wrapped him in a quilt and put dry clothes on him. She handed me his old ones in a sack.

"January. Isn't it an unusual name?" she said as she tucked a stack of clean cloth diapers in my basket of food.

"I know her," I said as I hurried toward January's sickroom, holding the baby close to my chest. The nurse was coming out, "Are you family?" she asked. I rushed past. I could hear her repeat, "Are you family?"

The scene was one of death. January's pale skin was almost translucent. A jagged gash was on the right side of her temple. Her body was limp and lifeless. The nurse escorted me out into the hall. "I'm calling for a doctor to come. She's gravely ill. She's not responding and she's had two seizures." I glanced at the nurse inside the room. John was coming out of the room. I hadn't even noticed him. He took my arm and said to the nurse, "This is Sarah Michelle." Taking the baby from me, he said, "And this is Lucky."

"We've organized a search party for the two of you," the nurse paused and glanced back to January in the room. "I'll call it off immediately." She swished past us and I could see her saying something to the male volunteer that had helped me earlier.

"Were they searching for us because you thought I had stolen Lucky?" I asked John bluntly. He seemed surprised, as if he would never have thought I'd do such a thing.

"We were searching for you because you disappeared in the storm after the tent fell." His eyes searched mine. "Where did you go?"

"I was disoriented and didn't know where to go. A small tree fell in my way and I turned and ran the other way right in the direction of that small, wooden, box-like house."

"I've seen that house. I wish I had taken January there. I carried her to the first tent standing and I went inside. The people helped us all they could. Even got a cart to bring us to the infirmary at sunup." He put his hand in his pockets and pulled out a watch. Not as expensive as the older gentlemen's in the wooden box shelter, but nice for a barrel-maker. "We've been here for hours and no change."

He looked down at Lucky and I held out my arms, "May I take him?" I didn't move as John bent forward and gently put Lucky in my waiting arms.

I held the baby close and swayed a little from side to side.

John stepped close and stroked Lucky's face with his finger. "Me, a father. What would Sister Elizabeth say? Would she be proud? Or disappointed that I was a sinner? Everyone's a sinner, she told me once. What would Sister Elizabeth think?"

He didn't wait for me to answer, he softly answered himself as he looked down at Lucky, "and I think she'd be happy for me to be reunited with him in such a miraculous way." He looked at me and said in wonderment, "Sarah Michelle, I saved my own son."

6 TRYING TO GET BY

Don't be frightened, I whispered. But Sarah Michelle ran without listening, the baby in her arms. Panic consumed her. I redirected her toward the sturdy shelter by pushing the tree down in her path. I'd never intervened in such a physical way before. But I've learned that at times it's best to put obstacles in the way to keep people from hurting themselves. I had also visited John that night as he knelt in the tent beside January. I could feel the tangle of his emotions. I prayed to God to come be with him and soothe him. I hadn't known Lucky was his child until after I came into my new consciousness. January had told me the father was Dean Johnson.

JOHN

When our tent blew down, I reacted by instinct. Pulling and grabbing, I cut wildly at the heavy fabric with my knife. I quickly slashed it back more to reveal January beside me. A pool of blood soaked the heavy white canvas of the tent. At first I feared I had cut her. But I saw a heavy tent pole falling when lightning flashed and as I looked at the gash on her forehead, I knew immediately what had happened.

I grasped her limp body to me and ran screaming toward the closest tent. The people took us in and together we knelt over January and tried to help her in the light of a lantern. I feared the wind might blow this tent down too and cause a fire, but my fear for January's welfare was far

worse. After we had done everything possible, I sat beside her and waited

for the first rays of dawn so I could get her medical help.

"Wake up," I would gently say every so often. "January, please

wake up." My mind went wild as I discovered Sarah Michelle and Lucky

were nowhere to be found. Perhaps they ran into a different tent. It was

unthinkable that I would lose Lucky as soon as I found out he was my son.

Strange feelings overcame me as I thought of January leaving me and giving

him up to the orphanage. Sister Elizabeth hadn't told me a thing.

The storm raged on outside the tent and in my head. I was unable

to verbalize even in my own brain what I thought of the situation I found

myself in. Aye, sometimes it's best not to think too hard. Sometimes it's

best to let events unfold. Isn't that what Sister Elizabeth said when I had

been perplexed by something small and insignificant. I would never fret

over the small things again, I vowed.

Suddenly I felt in my heart Lucky was safe with Sarah Michelle and

I was able to stretch out in a peaceful position. Since the storm my muscles

hurt in odd ways because I kept them tensed. I rarely relaxed. I

remembered how bruised Sarah Michelle had been—hardly any of her skin

had been untouched by the purplish-blue welts. For weeks afterwards small

splinters of glass would come to the surface of her skin, she told me. I had

a few scrapes and bruises, but not like Sarah Michelle.

Then when I least expected it, the sun started to peek up over the island. I started to move around and get things ready. One of the men got a little cart with a donkey and we started heading toward the infirmary. I looked at the cart and hoped it had not been used to transport the thousands upon thousands of dead bodies. Maybe not.

The man that owned the little cart said he was a farmer. I envisioned fresh produce filling it, but my memory quickly filled the cart again with scenes of the dead shortly after the storm. My mind refused to let go. Images of the dead stiffened in the positions they were in when they met their demise. One in particular stands out. A man with his hands clasped and held upward. "You could see that two ways," the man working with me that day had said, "God didn't answer his prayer ... or God did answer his prayer." That day as I piled bodies on a cart, I thought God did answer his prayer. Or at least that's the way I felt about it at the time. Later, I would change my mind on this subject.

One of the stranger sights another person told me they saw right after the storm was a man on a bicycle stuck firmly in the mud. He was still in an upright position, his hat on his head. By the expression on his face, he clearly did not see his impending death. Probably the large wave of water that came in with the storm crashed down on him from above with a fast and terrible fury. He never even had time to let go of his handlebars.

The nurse came out and was running toward us. She had seen us coming in the cart with January through the window. "Please take her around back to the room just off the hallway," she directed us after examining her head wound.

"Her name is January," it was all I could think to say to the nurse. And the sound of January's name reminded me it was already December. Christmas would be here soon.

SARAH MICHELLE

John asked me if I would hold Lucky so he could go back in to the room and wipe January's face with a wet rag. I watched through the doorway as he lovingly took care of the trollop. *Oh my God, I know I shouldn't judge. Lord, please let her live.*

"Does she still have a fever?" I called to him from the hallway. He nodded his head "yes" without looking up from his task.

"Ma'am." It was the female volunteer helper. She took me by the arm and led me toward the nurse, Clara Barton. "Ma'am, earlier when I dressed the baby I noticed he was hot. The nurse should have a look. Sit right here and she'll see you right after this man."

A man was sitting quietly outside of the nurse's office reading the newspaper. He looked up and said, "The baby can go first. I'm in no hurry. Just wanted to get some pain medicine for my back."

He told me he was a soldier from Fort Crockett. When I asked his story, he said, "Made it through the storm without any major mishaps, then the following afternoon our barracks caved in on us. Hurt my back something awful, but I haven't missed a day's work."

"You should go first, I'm going to be here awhile. Please go first, you soldiers have done so much for us." I sat across from him and could see pain in his heavily hooded eyes. "I hope it won't be an injury that plagues you for the rest of your days."

"Even if it does, I count myself grateful to have survived. No one ever promises a soldier an easy job," he smiled and I noticed he had nice straight teeth and a dimple like Dean's. Then I remembered I still hadn't heard back from Dean and Sean, I should check again at the post office today.

"You look like someone I know named Dean Johnson."

"Dean's my cousin, ma'am," he laughed heartily. "Dean seems to know all the pretty ladies in town." My face fell in shock. "Not that I mean anything disrespectful by that last remark. Just that Dean makes it a point to introduce himself." He stopped and looked down at the floor. "Ma'am…" he readjusted in his seat. "Ma'am, have you seen Dean since the storm?"

"Yes," he lived in the same tent as myself and the gentlemen in the other room.

I could see his body relax as I said the words. A smile crossed his lips and his face lit up, "I can't believe it. I can't believe it … I can't hardly believe the good news." He shook his head with a big silly grin. But the light left his eyes as quickly as it came and he said, "I saw a man wrapped in barbed wire in the debris that looked a lot like Dean, thought it might be him. Wasn't certain so I didn't put his name on the list of dead." His smile returned, "I'm so happy. You've made me so happy." The nurse appeared at her office door. "Now you go ahead on in with the baby. My back doesn't hurt no more."

I thanked him and headed to the next room. The nurse put Lucky on a table as I explained to her how we'd also been in the tent that had caved in last night. I talked on about how the baby had gotten chilled and spent the night in a somewhat wet blanket.

"He's got fever all right." She turned to me. "Are you still without shelter? You can stay here. I've got one more room."

"I'd appreciate that," I said and I meant it sincerely. It never ceased to amaze me how everyone helped everyone else after the storm. The donations, the relief operations, and how each individual on the island looked after each other. Strangers taking in strangers during the storm, and ever since then, all the survivors seemed to treat each other as family. With Galveston being a major port, there were people of every background, income level and race living here. Now we blended together as one—much wiser now after the horror we had lived through. An experience like this reminds people we're really all the same. Humans, just trying to get by. Not one of us better than the other. Not one of us really owning anything except the bodies we were born in at birth.

The little room was tidy and clean with a sturdy little cot and washbowl. I put the baby on a pallet on the floor and lay down on the cot. Every muscle had some special pain of its own. I tensed my feet muscles and let them go. Then I moved to my ankles, then my calves, tensing and releasing. My grandmother had taught me this to put me to sleep. It worked. I was asleep before I got to my knees.

I awoke before dawn. Twice I had checked on the baby in the night. His fever was light and he seemed better. Now he twitched and moved in his sleep, then he settled back into a peaceful breathing pattern. Thank goodness he was finally sleeping seven and eight hours at a time. John could take care of him easier, I thought as I gathered my things. I looked out the window. It was twilight. Living out in the open in a tent, I had taken notice of the cycles of each day and I had renewed appreciation for sunrises and sunsets.

Leaving the door open to my room, I tiptoed across the tiny hallway and peered in on the patient. John's cot was pushed beside January's bed. She still remained unresponsive. A doctor had come to visit. He spent quite a bit of time checking her wound. He said he would return tomorrow, which is really today. I best leave now before anyone wakes.

Creeping down the small hallway toward the door, I tried not to make a sound. A volunteer helper slept on a cot in the nurse's office, ready to go get the nurse for any emergency. I reminded myself not to call them volunteers as they actually had real jobs here now. I should refer to them as nurse's assistants, or maybe medical helpers. I smiled to myself at my silly thoughts. Chances are I would never see these people again, it didn't matter how I referred to them.

Still half asleep, I turned the knob and opened the front door. It made a soft pop when I let go of the knob and the lock clicked into place. My heart leapt, but no one stirred.

Like a fugitive on the run, I snuck up the side of the building and looked in the window to check on Lucky one last time. He looked like an angel. I used to sing to him, "You're an angel, where are your wings, are you hiding them from me?" No more baby songs, no more baby smell, no more soft baby skin and hair. Tiny feet. Tiny toes.

This was a good place to leave Lucky—with John and January. They would all be together and safe. My being here felt awkward and I was ashamed that I had considered taking Lucky and running away. Even if they hadn't suspected, I felt bad knowing I had considered it.

I waited on the porch of the post office. A policeman came down the street, but he didn't see me in the shadows. Even when the sun rose and the postmaster came to open the door, he didn't notice me. I had to stand up to get his attention and he almost jumped ten feet in the air. "I haven't got any money," he yelled.

"It's me, Sarah Michelle." I giggled like a schoolgirl playing a prank. "Just checking to see if my return letter is here yet."

"Come inside, I'll check yesterday's evening mail delivery." We went inside and he started checking. "New mail will come within the … wait, here's a letter for you. Look it didn't have a full address." I eagerly took it. It was a letter from a friend back in Europe checking on my safety. News of the cyclone had reached the four corners of the Earth, it seemed. And for once none of the journalists had exaggerated a word. In fact, most hadn't grasped the true horror.

"Are you disappointed?" The postmaster started setting up for the day.

"I was hoping for another letter, but this is nice. It shows at least someone cares about me." I tucked it in my apron pocket with my coins and went back to the porch. The sun was starting to rise in the sky and I didn't want to take a chance of anyone finding me in town. I turned and headed toward the mainland. I would go to Houston and take half of the reward money. I had my new clothes, a basket of food, and a small amount of coins. I would need to stop by our downed tent to get the banking account papers out of my trunk. I would leave some of the checks so John could find them easily in his things.

***

Before I knew it, my task had been completed and I was in Houston. First a trip to the bank and then I would select a hotel until I made my complete plans. I felt excited and free. And it surprised me, this uprising of excitement happening to my being.

Inside the bank, I immediately became aware of my clothes. They were tattered and dirty. I must have looked awful from the storm the previous night. My raggedy hair, I tried to comb it with my fingers in front of the glass teller window. I had to have money before I could bathe in a hotel room.

I took the bank papers out of my small trunk I had picked up at the tent. The trunk was filled with all my memories and the clothes Sean had found for me. I actually was acquiring a wardrobe again with the new clothes I had received yesterday. I bent down and touched the fine turquoise material of my new dress. I could hardly wait to try it on after my bath. Dinner in the hotel restaurant would be the perfect place to show it off. Maybe I would even come back here to the bank to show them what a lady I really am. The teller came back with my money.

He was kind and pretended not to notice my disarray. "Now, you put this in the safe at the hotel. A woman shouldn't be traveling alone with this much money." He said very discreetly. "In fact, I will escort you to the hotel for safety reasons," he got his coat. "Are you staying at the Rice Hotel nearby? It's very nice."

I didn't have a clue where I wanted to stay, so I said yes and off we went. He put my money in his front jacket pocket and carried my trunk in front of him to hide the bulge it was making. I took the basket with my clothes and food.

Once inside my hotel room, I felt strange. Several times throughout the day I had reached out for the baby or wanted to check on him. I reassured myself I had done the right thing. Never in my life had I been alone like this. No one to wait on or worry about. No one to tell me what to do next.

I considered the fact that I needed a bath and I started the water. Incredibly, this luxurious room had its own bathtub.

The warm water soothed me. I had put some of the bread and cheese from my basket on top of a kerchief near the tub. Like royalty, I soaked and ate a snack as I anticipated the real feast to come in the restaurant below. I dried my hands and reached down to my dirty clothes beside the tub and retrieved my friend's letter. She was a girl that had gone to school with me before I married. She had been a dear friend. And as real friends often do, she had timed her letter perfectly to reach me at a time when I needed to know someone cared for me, even if she were half a world away.

Basically, the letter inquired as to my safety. She then told me a little bit about her life. She had married, had two children. They lived in a small brownstone in central London. She described her gay urban life in a few short sentences. And, of course, she apologized for not having written in the past few years. But isn't that the way it goes? We get involved in our lives and let our dearest friends drift from us. No one has time, it seems, to cultivate friendship when the worries of the world press upon us in adulthood.

I closed my eyes and imagined London. Her description had been brief, but it made me want to go there. I had no close relatives in America. In Europe I had cousins in London, France and Italy. What would my parents advise me to do if they were alive? My mother would say, "follow your heart dear," and my father would say, "follow your heart," too, but he would add "you can correct almost any mistake you make later."

Sarah Michelle. You are not alone.

DEAN

Instead of writing Sarah Michelle, I decided to surprise her by coming in person to escort her to West Texas. I hoped the harsh environment would suit her and not send her running back to Europe. Abilene was a larger town than most. I had been particularly impressed with the hospital where Kitty's husband worked, or should I say lived?

The idea of going back into medicine appealed to me. It had been so difficult when the lawsuit happened; I swore I would never practice medicine again. I was much more successful as a gambler and it was the kind of occupation people showed their true colors around. No use hiding your drinking or cussing from a gambler. This was the exact opposite of how I was treated as a doctor. People were always cautious of their behavior around me. They were courteous and polite, and a few even appeared to be frightened of me, as if I might pull out a needle or scissors at any moment and go to work on them right there on the sidewalk while we were exchanging pleasantries.

Oh, this was enjoyable. Riding on the train in my fine new clothes. I had gotten used to everything being dirty in Galveston after the storm. The ocean had covered it with a layer of slime that dreadful night and the recovery efforts left everyone in shambles. Pitiful souls we all were. Now I'm not afraid of dirt and grime, I'm just sayin' it is nice to be clean, with a shave and a haircut.

I thought I would get off the train in Houston and spend the night. Next stop, the cemetery to inspect my mother's grave and retrieve the jewelry. Then I'd meet with Sarah Michelle, John and January in Tent City. I didn't want to stay around any longer than I had to because it might bring back bad memories. Just the thought of going made me nervous. Maybe Sarah Michelle and baby Lucky would be ready to leave immediately. From the sound of her letter she would be more than glad to get on with the journey. January could be a bit much to take. Her words, poised like sharp weapons, were intended to wound those victims unfortunate enough to be in her near vicinity.

Funny how a normal day or a normal experience was important to me these days. Suddenly, I'm not the cocky one with all the answers looking for a wild adventure. I'm just me: a simple man enjoying simple things, trying to get by. Yes, the world does humble a person.

The city of Houston was preparing for the holidays ahead. Wreaths and decorations adorned the storefronts. A poster advertised a Christmas parade. Another advertised a New Year's service for the dead in Galveston, a proper memorial for all those lost in the storm. It took me aback as I read the details of the event.

The thing that bothers me to this day was the way we had disposed of the dead so quickly. True, there hadn't been any other way. Disease would have been rampant if we hadn't found such a quick manner. So many dead. But each one was an individual, someone's special someone. They needed a proper memorial service like this one and I determined right then and there I would attend it.

Even with the devastation and reconstruction going on nearby, the city of Houston was still pretty much business as usual. Not that they didn't care; they had done much in the relief efforts and were still helping in many ways. But life goes on and as I looked around me I was infinitely grateful it did. The pretty storefronts caught my eye. One had a rocking horse and another children's toys. Ah, the perfect Christmas gift for Lucky. Maybe he couldn't ride it yet, but we could hold him on it. Soon he'd be running around and climbing all over it. Babies grow so fast.

A strange thought occurred to me. What if we adults kept growing and changing as fast as children? How tall and strong we'd be! An eighty year old might be fifteen feet 300 hundred pounds. How would we be able to determine what heights to make ceilings and door openings?

Too bad we only grow mentally, and some of us never even do much of that. We have to be prodded. We have to be pushed to achieve wisdom. Was it worth the price? How fun to stay a child and have parents attend our every whim.

The Rice Hotel was up ahead. *Please have a vacant room.* I was hungry and tired, which led me to another odd thought: What if we didn't have to eat or sleep? How would we spend all those hours? Good thing we did have to eat. It slowed us down and gave us something to look forward to at least three times a day. A great meal would be such a treat right now.

Here's something else I was looking forward to at the moment: reuniting with Sarah Michelle and Lucky. One day I would tell her about January and how she'd made me marry her. I was sorry we lost the baby. I would like to have a child of my own in my life. Lucky and Sean were godsends. I had no one before the storm and now I had Lucky, Sean and Sarah Michelle. I didn't even know how much I wanted people in my life until they suddenly appeared there.

SARAH MICHELLE

Eating alone is something I had never done before, but I better start getting used to doing things alone. I would be fine myself. Hadn't I been adventuresome before I got married? Spending summers in France, attending classes at the university ... Marriage had made me timid, made me lose my edge. Well, I would find it again. I looked around the dining room and I noticed several people eating alone.

Where was the waiter? Ahh, there he comes with my plate now.

The smells were so delightful, I thought I'd faint with sheer joy. Plump, succulent roast beef and mashed potatoes with gravy, green beans and corn. I let each bite linger in my mouth. Delicious.

On the table they had a small red candle with a tiny holiday bell tied to it at the base. Christmas would be here soon. Maybe I wouldn't celebrate, just ignore it.

If I sent a telegram to my childhood friend tomorrow, I could be in London with her family for the holidays. But would I be lonelier than ever as her children opened their gifts? I had already bought a few gifts and stashed them around in places Tom Jr. would never look.

I stopped myself from thinking on the past. I was glad I had indulged him in his short life, but now I must look forward if I was going to make it.

A man that looked like Dean walked out of the bar. What was wrong with me, did I think everyone looked like Dean? However, the soldier that resembled Dean at the nurse's office did turn out to be his cousin. Perhaps this was the same soldier out of uniform?

The man I was watching entered the dining room and looked around when he saw me. He stopped. His face broke out in a smile. I could see his dimples were more prominent than ever as his eyes danced.

Then, as if in a dream, Dean was back by my side. "Please say I can join you for dinner. It would be most appropriate, as I've come to escort you to West Texas."

My heart soared at his words and my ears roared. It was hard to focus on his story about a boarding house he and Sean had found for me to purchase. In a moment life had changed its course again and I felt a keen anticipation. London could wait. I would write my friend a letter instead and fill her in on why I was moving to West Texas.

As we talked about Sean and West Texas, I realized Dean was much more refined than I remembered him. He didn't use the slang and his table manners were impeccable. He had always been handsome, but he really cleaned up well. I shared with him the story of meeting his cousin at the nurse's office. He looked incredibly relieved Jim was alive. I knew it was only a matter of time before he would start to ask questions about John and January.

"Sarah Michelle, where is Lucky?" his words broke my thoughts.

"I left Lucky with John and January." I could tell this information upset him so I continued, "Do you have time for a long story?"

We had finished dinner at this point in our conversation. Dean insisted on paying for mine. When the waiter left, he said, "Why don't we take a walk and you can tell me everything? It sounds like it may take a while."

Outside the weather was beautiful. The streets were more crowded than usual because of holiday shoppers, but it only added to the festive atmosphere. We walked, and when the time was right, I started to talk. Dean listened without comment, asking a question here and there. Otherwise he was completely quiet. He did not share with me a word about his relationship with January. That he would tell me later. Much later.

Sarah Michelle, there is no such thing as coincidence. God actively works within the circumstances of your life in both adversity and prosperity. There is a reason. There is a reason, I whispered as I turned back to the light.

THE BOY "ROBERT/SEAN"

Dean's letter arrived after my first week of school. It went into much detail about a Galveston memorial service on New Year's Day. He asked if I thought I could ride the train by myself if he and Sarah Michelle met me at the station. Of course, I would need something of a disguise as many people were still looking for me. The plan then would be to slip unnoticed into Galveston where we would celebrate New Year's.

He also mentioned it would be better for my sister Jane to visit with me in Galveston. It would be less suspicious for her to visit there than to travel all the way to West Texas. And possibly both of my sisters could come to Galveston.

His letter went on to explain after we attended the memorial service that he, Sarah and myself would all make the train ride back to Abilene together.

The adventure of riding the train by myself while wearing a disguise thrilled me. I longed to see Jane, Sarah Michelle, John and Lucky again. What would Galveston look like now? I had read about the plans to raise the island and add the seawall. It would take years, people estimated—best get started right away, they'd written.

I'd overheard a group of men in downtown Abilene talking about how they'd heard Hofphaur Dredging from Germany was going to come to Galveston and pump the sand filling the city. There would be a lot of good jobs for men with strong backs and the will to work. One told of how he was going to apply that week. After the first of the year everything would be getting underway and he wanted to get his name on the list first.

How would I stand the anticipation for another two weeks' time? At least I had school and a few new friends. School was held in a building near the train station and the bank. It wasn't as difficult as my boy's school back home so the teacher moved me up a grade. Each day Kitty sent me off with a lunch pail and my book satchel. She said I could run home and eat if I wanted, some kids do, but I would literally have to run to make it back in time. I told her I wasn't up to running yet.

I held my pencil with my left hand as my right arm was still in a sling. It was surprising how well I wrote with my left hand. Soon Kitty's husband George Kalo, or G.K. as I had taken to calling him, said he would cut my cast off. Every day he took a look at what he called my injuries, just to make certain everything was healing as it should. I hadn't thought of anything not healing right until he said something. Now, I watched like a hawk for any changes such as swelling or redness. G. K. had said the hot dry climate of Abilene was better for healing than the tropical one I left. G.K. sure knew a lot of things.

There was a girl in my class named Penny. She had long brown hair and green eyes. I liked her and was fairly certain she liked me back. However we had not exchanged a word between us. When we did talk, I had determined I would tell her about living through the hurricane, but not who I really was. Leaving that part out would be deceptive, but I couldn't risk it. G.K. told me, "don't tell a soul, even the people you trust, because they'll feel like they need to tell at least one person they trust—and before you know it word will accidentally get back to your father in Houston." And there's no telling what he would do to me then. It was hard to leave the home and lifestyle I had grown up in, but all the money in the world wasn't worth the abuse.

My father was born mean-spirited, my grandfather had told me one day. Then my grandfather told me that's why my father was able to make such a fortune—this mean streak in him. My grandfather died not too long after that and I've often wished he were still alive. Perhaps I could have spent more time with him. He was a gentle person who lived in a rather plain house with meager belongings. The only picture in the house was one of my long-dead grandmother I would never know.

But I contend no one is born mean-spirited, and my grandparents certainly didn't raise my father to fight. I believe he made himself the way he is and I don't know why he would do that, but he did. I think it's because people would always let him have his way because they feared him. Grandfather was right about one thing: the mean-spiritedness did give him a leg up in business.

Please God don't let me follow in my father's footsteps.

Ever since the storm, I found myself talking directly to God several times a day. But I hadn't really talked out the details of the night I spent trying not to die. One day I would when I was far enough away from the experience.

I thought of Sarah Michelle after the storm and how she didn't speak for days. John had been so tender with her and the baby. I hoped to grow up like John. He was not a wealthy man, but a man to be admired. Everyone who knew him had nothing but good things to say about him.

Everyone liked Dean, too, but in a different way. He was charming and fun and made you feel good about yourself. But John was one of those men people looked up to and were proud to say they knew.

JOHN

Ah, Mother of God, the doctor said we needed to move January to the hospital in Houston. Easier said than done. We gathered a small group to help load her into a carriage. Then I got in with the baby. On the way out, we stopped by the tent city and I looked inside our fallen tent, collecting what few things I could: January's traveling bag and my few belongings—so few I stuck them in the bag with January's things. I noticed Sarah Michelle had put the bank account information inside my hat. I left it there and put my hat on my head.

One thing was for certain about my new life; I didn't spend a lot of time cleaning. There was nothing to clean except a few pieces of clothes. I hoped Sarah Michelle had taken the money; she's the one who took care of Sean. I would have left him at the church with the other people. I liked the kid, but I'm not the type who would have thought of looking after him myself. I might have thought of finding someone to look after him, but I wouldn't have done it myself.

At one point, I leaned my head over January's mouth to listen if she was still breathing. I couldn't tell so I put two fingers over her heart. I could feel her chest rise.

Poor Sarah Michelle, overhearing January's confession … it must have killed her inside to give Lucky up. I put my head in my hands and leaned against the inside of the carriage.

A few months back, I would have given anything to marry January. She was the first woman who had ever made me feel this way. Of course, I cared deeply for Sister Elizabeth, but in another way entirely. "Oh January, why didn't you confide in me about our baby?" I said aloud. But I knew why she didn't. I wasn't the smartest guy ever, but I was smart about knowing why people did the things they do. *Fame held more appeal for the lass than being a wife and mother.*

Only the storm brought her back to Galveston. She wanted to know the fate of her baby. From the first day of her arrival, I remembered how she told me she had heard of the total destruction of the orphanage buildings. She had also spent quite a bit of time with the nurse in town going over the list of dead.

Truly, January was no saint, but in my heart I knew she had wanted the best for our child. If she couldn't give it to him in the normal way most parents do, she'd find better parents than herself for him. Now in her unresponsive state, I might not even get a chance to tell her I was certain Lucky was the baby she left at the orphanage with Sister Elizabeth. See, that's what I get for not telling everyone the miracle of Lucky. Sarah Michelle's intentions had been good, but the truth should have been told. Then when January had learned the truth, I'd have known immediately I had a son.

I looked at Lucky. He looked back at me. He did have my eyes, just as January had noted when she first saw him. I shook my head as if I could clear the thoughts beginning to crowd my mind. If I had been married to January this never would have happened. But as it was, it took her away from Galveston that night of the storm. But fate stepped in and played her hand out anyway by taking January another way. I mustn't think she's not going to make it. The doctor had said there's always a chance.

The waves were lapping at the shore as we pulled alongside a small sailing vessel. The water would be choppy and the sailing would not be smooth. Lucky cried the whole way. His fever was down, but it might come back if I didn't get him inside. I picked him up and pointed to January. "Look little guy, there's your mama." He cried again and I knew he wanted Sarah Michelle. She had been attentive to his every need.

Now that I think back on it, Sarah Michelle had been good with Sean and Lucky. They were a family that actually liked each other, as opposed to the many blood families that didn't. I would look for Sarah Michelle when I was certain January was well. I would tell Sarah Michelle I wanted her to be a part of Lucky's life. I didn't have such a good feeling about her being out there all alone, with only relatives in Europe. That was one of the downsides to venturing far from home—there was no safety net when you needed it.

I don't really remember getting to the hospital in Houston. However, I do remember being there and the doctor wanting to keep Lucky because of his recent fever. He had said Lucky would do better with a nurse watching him tonight and that I really needed to get a room at the nearby hotel and rest. I had gone to the hotel, but instead of going straight to my room like I should have done, I went to the bar. I drank until I passed out sitting upright in an uncomfortable position.

7 WAY PAST CARING

DEAN

Sarah Michelle waved to me as I started on my journey to Galveston. I watched her as long as I could, then I turned my attention to the road.

I thought of the horse Mr. Stockton had let me ride the night we brought Sean home. It was one of the most handsome horses I'd ever seen. My cousin Jim would know where I could find a good horse. Thank God he was alive. Couldn't believe Sarah Michelle had run across him at the clinic.

My thoughts turned to the first couple of hours after the storm. Cows and horses ran up to everyone with panicked, pleading eyes looking for someone to take care of them—looking perhaps for their master. The horses were soon confiscated for the soldiers of Battery O who began immediately to patrol.

Eventually, I caught a ride to the island on a small sailing vessel. My first stop was by the cemetery to retrieve Sean's jewelry. The island wasn't as heavily patrolled as it was in the weeks after the storm. In the first few days, police officers and soldiers were told to investigate anyone even kneeling by a body and if they found them stealing they were to shoot. They were strict orders, too. But they apparently worked very well. Few people had to be shot. Many were arrested, but later released. If they were going to raise the entire island, I couldn't risk leaving the jewelry in the headstone for eternity as I had planned. Once they moved the headstone and saw the bag in the hidden compartment underneath, they would come looking for me. And for once I didn't do anything.

Back in Houston, I had bought a bouquet of flowers to put on Mama's grave and now I used it to hide what my hands were doing. Quickly my fingers wrapped around the velvet bag hidden behind the headstone block. It pulled free easily. Still holding the flowers strategically, I put the block back into place. Then with a slight readjustment, I put the bag in my jacket pocket. Finally, I laid the flowers to rest and traced my mother's name with my fingers.

Perhaps I was being paranoid, but my gambling life had taught me one thing: someone's always watching and it's usually the person you least suspect.

Leaving the cemetery, I went downtown. Just as I anticipated, I found cousin Jim playing cards in one of the first bars I checked. As I came through the door, he saw me first. "By God, you old bugger. You are alive." He stepped out of the shadows and slapped me on the back.

We hugged and we laughed and we both had tears in our eyes. He bought me a drink and we talked of everything except for the one thing on our minds. Then, when we had exhausted all other sources of conversation, we spoke of what occurrences happened to us during the night of the storm.

I told him of how I was playin' cards at John McLaren's house trying to ignore the danger. He told me of how he and the other soldiers hadn't been afraid either, at first. His experience was much different than mine, being a soldier and all.

He had been out at Fort Crockett near Vedder's Park. And he talked of how the ocean's water turned a phosphorus color. A soldier who had been stationed in the West Indies once told him that meant a hurricane was on its way. They watched from the shore as the nearby bathhouse was destroyed by the high winds. I told him I knew the bathhouse he was referring to—it had a rooftop garden. "Had a rooftop garden is right," Jim said. "It's all gone now."

He then told of how one of the soldiers noticed the most ominous sight of all: fifty-foot wall of water coming straight at Galveston. For as far as they could see there was nothing standing between it and them. He told me he almost pissed himself as they ran to seek refuge at the fort. But they were too far away. As the water rose, they ended up hightailing it inward. In the hurricane-force winds, they only made it as far as one of the beautiful houses in the newly built suburb close by.

Many people were in this particular house, he said, and they all survived the storm. However, most of their neighbors did not. "Why did this particular house survive? It wasn't even as well-built as some of the others," Jim said. "For example, a neighboring house nearest the gulf had been reinforced with a concrete enclosure around it."

Jim told me there were some large timber beams in the area that were to be used in construction on the nearby fort. They broke loose in the flood and started pounding the nearby neighboring homes like battering rams.

In the home in which Jim and the soldiers had sought refuge, one man had single-handedly redirected the timber beams away from the house through an opening in the roof. The effort had left his hands in ribbons. But Jim thought it was this one action that had saved the house full of people. There was no other way to explain it.

I had heard many such stories of bravery in the days following the cyclone. I had also heard some that seemed miraculous. And Jim told me it made him think that if you weren't supposed to go that night, you didn't. We were both quiet as we thought of all the dead. I told him it was hard to think of all those people needing to die that day. He said he supposed so, but it seemed that way to him.

Jim continued on with his story. "When we came out of that house everything was pretty much swept clean," he said, "and we had to walk over

229

the big piles of storm wreckage to get to town. Along the way we saw

people searching for loved ones. Some were screaming and crying as they

went along. Others were silent and stone-faced."

Once in town, he had been conscripted into the militia that would

guard the island. His captain had been injured, and a civilian man had been

appointed by the mayor and chief of police to organize things. "He did an

excellent job—this regular civilian who stepped in and took total charge of

our division and other volunteers," Jim said. "Good thing the man had

been appointed by city leaders, because if our captain had been around, he

couldn't have gone into action without the orders of President McKinley

himself."

"Is that so?" I said. "Then it was a lucky thing it happened as it

did."

He went on to tell me of how most of the cavalry, himself

included, had lost their horses. But new horses were found for the soldiers.

The horse he got had never seen a saddle and he rode him bareback as he

patrolled. "Hadn't ridden a horse like that since I was back on the farm,"

Jim said.

Jumping smaller piles of rubble and crawling up larger ones on

horseback, the cavalry did whatever it took to patrol and maintain order. I

had seen what Jim was talking about myself and thought it incredible the

way the horses made their way around the devastation.

"Come outside and meet my new friend," Jim got up and pulled me out of my seat. "I've been telling him about how you were my favorite cousin."

Once outside, Jim took me over to a beautiful pinto. The horse reared back his head and whinnied loudly. Then he cocked his head and looked at me with one eye. I could see his wild spirit gleaming inside.

"Dean," Jim smiled as he addressed the horse. "This is Dean." He gestured back at me.

Jim's actions brought a smile to my face too, and I heard myself saying, "Since he's named after me, can I ride him?" I rubbed the horse's nose.

"Well, I don't rightly know if he's that tame yet…" Jim saw my disappointment. "Ah, hell you can try and ride him. Head out that way—there's some open field just outside of town."

I jumped on the pinto's back and rode in the direction Jim pointed. In the area that had been cleared, I could almost imagine it was the old Galveston. I rode hard and fast, giving the pinto full lead, and soon we were running down an almost clear section of beach. The sun was setting in a glowing ball of fire on the water, spreading pink and gold streaks in a fan above it. Out on the ocean, I could see sailboats gliding across the colorful reflections mirrored from the overhead sky. It was majestic. I felt good in a way I hadn't felt in a long time as the horse slowed to a trot.

I was slightly chilled by the cold ocean spray hitting my jacket. The taste of salt was on my lips. A stiff wind whistled by my ears lifting my hair from my eyes. Everything was right in the world. Everything was perfect and I tried to make it last as long as possible before I had to turn and take the pinto back.

Jim was still playing cards. When I returned, he came outside the bar as I tied up the horse.

"It looks like you two had fun," he said, smiling.

"If I wasn't a changed man, I would steal him from you."

Jim gave me a knowing wink and said, "Yessir, but you are a changed man so I don't have to worry about nothin'."

I could trust Jim for anything just as he trusted me. And I was grateful he said he would oversee the raising of my mother's grave when the work crews got near the cemetery. Seems they planned to do the whole island in sections. I left money for him and anyone he got to help him.

That night, I stayed in Jim's tent. It made me remember how lucky I was to have a posh hotel room. The next day we parted, both unable to believe the other was alive.

I left feeling assured that the former glory of Galveston would return in these people's capable hands. A seventeen-foot seawall … I am amazed at what is humanly possible these days.

Dean was recovering from the hurricane faster than most. Perhaps it's because he had the least to lose, notwithstanding his monetary fortune. Tragedy had kicked him down so hard he had broken ties with friends and family. In a way, the storm was giving him all that back, swirling away the walls he had put up around himself. Freeing him. Pushing him forward. I could feel him coming back to life as we rode the pinto down the beach.

JOHN

I was still in the same position I had fallen asleep in the night before in the bar. "Don't suppose they'll give me a refund on my room, do you think?" I asked the man sweeping the carpet. He shook his head "no" and gave me a hand getting my coat and hat. I thanked him and walked unsteadily out the door.

In the hallway, on the way to my room, my brain told my body it was still drunk and that's why my legs seemed unable to coordinate. Oh my God, I must be seeing things, too. Standing right there in front of me was Dean Johnson. "Dean," I said, way too loud. "Dean, oh boy!" If he noticed I was drunk, he didn't say anything about it.

He greeted me warmly and put his arm around my shoulders. Then he led me down the hallway to a room door. He fished in his pocket and brought out a key. "Hey," I said. "You're staying in the same room I am." I think he told me it was his room as he put me on the bed. Or maybe I figured it out when I woke much later that afternoon. He was sitting in a chair across from me looking out the window. I don't know how he knew I was awake, but he did. Without looking at me, he asked, "Did January take the baby?"

I looked at him like he was insane. Then I remembered he didn't know January had been hurt in the storm. I remembered he didn't even know January had come back to Galveston for me. And he sure as heck didn't know that Lucky was my child and that Sarah Michelle had left. So why would he ask if January took Lucky?

Since I couldn't figure out what he did and didn't know, I decided to answer his question with the truth. "January is in the hospital with a head wound. The nurses wanted to keep an eye on the baby because they didn't want his cold to turn into pneumonia and ... and ..." I looked down at my grimy hands and then I ran them through my dirty hair. I could smell myself now that I was fully awake. "... and they took him from me, I think, because they thought I might be drunk."

He sat still, looking out the window. No comment. No judgments. He was the same Dean I'd always known, only different. Even though he had barely said a word, the way he held himself was different. His whole demeanor was different. More confident.

After I had washed my face and eaten some of the cold lunch he had ordered from room service for me, Dean finally spoke. "I'm going to the hospital to check on January and Lucky. Why don't you get cleaned up?" He went out the door. A moment later he stuck his head back inside. "There's a clothing store three doors down, you might stop there." With that he was gone.

I put down the sandwich I was eating and called for him, "Dean!" He stuck his head back inside the door. "Lucky's my child," I said flatly. His hat brim shaded his eyes, but I could tell they didn't register surprise—the gambler in him never showed his emotions except the ones he wanted you to see. He was still standing there so I continued, "… and Sarah Michelle left me."

"Is there anything more?" he asked in a calm voice.

"No, there's nothing more."

He looked down at the floor and back at me. "I'll be back soon," he said. Not too long after that I heard a knock and thought he must have forgotten something. "Come on in, I'm decent," I yelled.

The door slowly opened and this time it was Sarah Michelle's head that peeped around. My heart leapt in my throat before settling back in my chest where it pounded so hard I couldn't hear what she said. She said it again and I still couldn't hear. I looked down and my right hand was shaking hard and I didn't even notice my hangover anymore. She came and stood beside me. All I could do was shake. Now I could hear her, she was saying, "Are you alright?"

"No," I answered. My mouth was dry. My head ached. I was definitely not all right. What was she doing coming into Dean's room?

SARAH MICHELLE

I had been reluctant to go to Dean's room at the hotel, but I wanted to tell him I had heard of a benefit show to aid the flood sufferers tonight. Wouldn't it be grand to go to a show like I used to do? While things certainly weren't normal in any way, I could pretend for a few hours.

Imagine my surprise when I opened the door and saw John. Pardon my language, but he looked like hell. At first I thought he might have come to Houston searching for me, but immediately he told me of bringing January to the hospital and how Dean had found him in the hallway. He also demanded to know what I was doing knocking on Dean's door. He thought I had run off, he said, but he never dreamed it would be with Dean. His voice was angry. Accusing. His eyes flashed with each word.

"John, I believe you are still drunk," I said.

This seemed to incite him even more. So in as few words as possible, I told him of my plan to start over in Abilene. I reminded him the few people I knew in America had been killed in the storm. "Dean and Sean were all I had left ... I decided to go live in West Texas with them. It was either that or go back to Europe," I explained.

"You could've stayed in Galveston," he said with anger in his voice. "With me and Lucky. What, am I not fancy enough for your taste?"

"No," I answered quietly. I didn't want to say anything bad about January.

"Were you afraid to be seen with a dockworker?"

I ignored his last comment and asked him if we should join Dean at the hospital. Frankly, I was surprised Dean hadn't come to my room right away and asked me to go to the hospital with him when John told him January and Lucky were there.

"I need to bathe and shave," John started toward the door. "And I'll need to do that in my own room." He picked up January's travel bag and started to leave. My impatient look was not lost on him. "Go to the hospital. I'll meet you there when I'm clean."

Trying to look proper, I didn't run. But I did walk very quickly. A man in a carriage must have felt sorry for me as he asked where I was headed. When I said the hospital, he said hop in and I'll take you there. It was an automobile. I had never been in one before and was frightened by it. Still it could move fast. Like the wind, we were off and in moments he delivered me safe at the front steps of my destination. I couldn't thank him enough and he said, "No problem, just love to drive the thing." I pushed my hair off my forehead, "Well, it certainly is nice. Never imagined I would ride in such a wondrous machine."

My nerves are like steel now. Before the storm, everything used to jolt me into a fit of excitement. Now nothing does. Well, maybe finding John in Dean's room. But not like it would have before. While I was surprised to see John in Houston, I had recently learned to flow with the twists and turns life takes. For instance, I would never dream that someone like John would turn angry and bitter while someone like Dean would become kinder and more sympathetic. Strange how adversity brings out people's best and worst.

At the hospital's front desk, I told the receptionist I was there to see January. I did not use a last name because I suddenly realized I did not know January's last name. The receptionist told me a room number, but reminded me only close relatives would be allowed in as she was in dire straits.

Once near the room, I didn't ask for permission. My husband used to tell me sometimes it is better to beg forgiveness than to ask permission. I believed this was one of those times. Wait, someone was inside her room. I peered in through the slightly open door. I could see Dean on one knee with his head bowed. He was slipping a ring on her finger. I could hear him say, "This is the ring I promised you on our wedding day." He turned her limp hand toward his closed eyes. "Look, the gem in it is a garnet," he said. "For the month of January. Yes, I know you were born in October, but I thought it was pretty. A fashionable young woman selected it, so I know you'll find it to your liking…" I backed away from the door and went to sit down.

Just when I thought I was beyond caring, I found a new hole in my heart. I looked up and saw John and a nurse coming toward me. The nurse was carrying baby Lucky in her arms. John had decided not to clean up after all. The nurse handed the baby to me and John took a seat nearby. "I'm a little too dirty to get close to Lucky."

I thought of the first calls for relief aid to go out of Galveston— "send quick-lime and disinfectant as soon as possible or the survivors will surely perish."

"Baby Lucky, Baby Lucky," I sang softly as I rocked him gently with a back and forth motion. It seemed to calm us both. He reached to touch me with his tiny hands. In my mind, I tried not to let the bad thought slip through that if January didn't recover, John might give Lucky back to me … no bad thoughts … I wouldn't let them through. I did care about January. What is wrong with me? I may not have liked her as a person, but I didn't want her to die.

Dean walked out of January's hospital room. His face was grim. "Is she better?" I could hear John anxiously ask him." He shook his head and said, "I don't think so, she didn't respond." As he said it, I thought of a teenage boy that had been hit on the head in the storm, he had returned to his wits when no one expected him too.

Talk of miracles like his were becoming as commonplace to us survivors as stepping over storm debris. But death was just as common, if not more so. I remembered a day after the cyclone, a man burying his wife and children where he had found them in shallow graves and marking them with a board he stuck in the ground. He had crudely written all their names on it. After he had finished, he went off to help where he could. There was a certain hardening of the heart to horror and a dazed acceptance of life after the storm and I often still felt a sense of bewilderment. It was hard for me to concentrate at times like this, but I willed myself to listen in on Dean and John's conversation.

Dean had taken John to the corner of the room and was saying something about a colleague he had gone to school with up North. Dean was from Texas. He had never mentioned going to college, especially one up North. Later, I discovered his friend was a medical specialist.

For the first time since January's accident, I saw hope in John's eyes.

Many of us were holding hands and forming a line of defense around January's prone form. We didn't dare break the bond to each other lest any evil slip between us. We sang songs of praise and raised our voices to the edges of eternity. January was the only human who heard and she thought herself to be in heaven. But she wasn't. Not yet.

THE BOY "ROBERT/SEAN"

Big adventures often start off mundane, I told myself as I settled in on the train. Kitty and G.K. had helped me with a disguise. Kitty had cut my hair short and used peroxide to lighten it. G.K. had given me some spectacles to wear that actually seemed to help my vision. I might keep these on all the time, even when I'm not in hiding.

I must say I was thin compared to my usual slightly pudgy self. I didn't think most people would have recognized me even if I had done nothing. But it was better to be certain. My satchel was filled with gifts and a few articles of clothing. I had some spending money and food. G.K. and Kitty were overprotective. They wanted me to send a telegram to assure them I had met safely with Dean and Sarah Michelle.

"Ha," I thought. If they could even fathom the danger I had lived through a few months earlier, they wouldn't have worried about a simple train ride. Or, maybe living through what I did would make people more anxious about seemingly ordinary days. The day of the hurricane, September eighth, had started off ordinary enough.

Once safely seated in a passenger car, I noticed the man I had seen in town. Virgil was his name. Apparently, he was on his way to find work in Galveston like he had said.

I guess I could talk to him a bit. He knew me as Sean, not Robert, and it would only be to my advantage if anyone asked questions that he could vouch for me. What's more, he would believe he was doing it honestly.

The train ride went without a hitch. It was exciting in that I hadn't ridden a train often, but overall it was a long, somewhat boring ride. I was glad I had someone to talk to occasionally. I found out a lot about Virgil on that trip. He didn't seem to notice he found out very little about me.

DEAN

The hospital office had a telephone. It would be easier to call than send a cable. I sat down to collect my thoughts in a small room outside the office. Suddenly, tears sprang from my eyes. I leaned forward in the chair and began to cry. Seeing January like this had been the last straw. Apparently it had been for John, too. He looked like a madman when I found him drunk in the hall ranting and raving at God and the world in general.

John had been my source of sanity when I met up with him right after the storm. People everywhere were still walking about bewildered, many of them screaming and crying. John had been so purposeful, so sane, when I found him in what we would refer to later as "Tent City."

He reminded me of the carefree life I had just lost. Now, we both had seen things on the work crew detail that will stick with us for the rest of our lives. It had been a particularly harrowing day for me right before I came upon John.

We were both strong men. But life was too much at times. I felt my humanity. My fragility. Shaking my head, I wiped my tear-stained eyes. I blew my nose, checked my emotions, and started doing what I could to save January. Tomorrow I would fall apart.

The telephone crackled, but I could hear him well enough. Yes, he would come. Yes, there was hope. It was an experimental surgery. Then he

244

surprised me. He said he wanted me to go as soon as I got off the phone and drill a small hole in January's skull. He explained the procedure to me in detail and stressed for me to do it *now*.

I didn't know if I could, I hadn't practiced medicine in five years. These days, people thought of me as a two-bit gambler. What's more, I was no longer welcomed in this hospital thanks to another experimental surgery I had performed years earlier—a procedure that had gone badly. It had dashed my confidence, but I knew in my heart I still had what it takes. Many of my experimental endeavors had positive results and I would try my best now to persuade the chief of surgeons to let me try. He had been on my side when the family of the patient had turned against me after the surgery.

John and Sarah Michelle met me in the hall. Baby Lucky was in the nursery taking a nap. I told them my specialist friend was coming, but he wanted me to do a medical procedure on January now.

Both of their mouths popped open in surprise.

I had been so distraught, I forgot they didn't know I was a surgeon.

John started to protest. He couldn't—or wouldn't—believe I had been a surgeon. He became hostile, pushing me up against the wall, saying I wasn't qualified. "Yes, I am. I am," I told him. And what I said was true. I had kept my medical licenses valid. I had worked too hard to earn them to ever let them go so easily. Finally, John released me. I rubbed my arm where he had been holding it.

"I'll explain later," I said to both John and Sarah Michelle. "I promise. I'm good at what I do."

"Then why haven't you been doing it?" John's voice spewed venom.

I shook my head and turned to go. With a few quick strides, I found the chief of surgeons and the head of the hospital standing nearby. They listened attentively to my plans. Then they started to ask questions. They didn't like the fact that it was an experimental surgery. January's family would have to release the hospital from liability.

"Is this man her husband?" asked the hospital head. He was looking directly at John, who was coming up behind me.

John was opening his mouth to answer when I pulled a document out of my right coat pocket. Before leaving for the hospital this morning, I had the good sense to retrieve it from the hotel safe where I had put it the night January and I were married. The two men opened the folded document and looked up in surprise. The chief of surgeons said, "Dr. Roland, you are the patient's husband."

John clamped his hand to his forehead and cried out, "Mercy be to God man, ain't you full of surprises."

I said nothing. Silence ensued. I didn't look at John and Sarah Michelle because I couldn't. It felt odd to be called by my real name.

The hospital head said, "Come this way, Dr. Roland, and we'll get the papers drawn up releasing the hospital from liability. This procedure needs to be done STAT."

"I'll need a surgical gown and an operating room," I yelled to the chief of surgeons as I followed the other man to sign the papers.

Without looking back, I knew John and Sarah Michelle were watching me go. I felt a stabbing pain inside my chest as I overheard Sarah Michelle say, "I didn't even know Dean knew January until today."

JOHN

When I asked Sarah Michelle for word about the boy Robert, she said we must always refer to him as Sean. She threw up her hands and said, "I've got to get to the train station. He's coming in today from West Texas."

For several minutes, we struggled with if I should stay here during January's surgery or go with her to get Sean. She insisted I stay. As soon as she was gone I went into January's room. The nurses were making preparations for the procedure.

One of the nurses told me she had seen this procedure done before and it had been a success. Please let January survive. I didn't care if she was a little off. I had heard one of the nurses say that people who survived a head wound often were. I could take her with scars. I could take her being a little different than her former self. I could take her being slow. All I knew is, I couldn't take it anymore without her. And, at the same time, I hated myself for needing her—especially considering the way she had treated me. Dean had a lot of explaining to do about that marriage license. I would deal with him later.

And, oh my God, I hope I haven't hurt Sarah Michelle.

"There's a garden sanctuary on our lawn if you want to wait there. This may take a while," the nurse offered as she wheeled January off. I wasn't a praying sort of man, but I decided it was as good of a place as any to go and think things out.

THE BOY "ROBERT/SEAN"

When Sarah Michelle arrived at the rail station, I was seated reading a newspaper. She wouldn't have recognized me if I hadn't given her a small wave. I tried not to seem concerned that no one had been there to meet me.

I looked up as she approached and smiled. We greeted each other with as little fanfare as possible so as not to draw stares. "So sorry I'm late," she apologized. Just then a man with an electric automobile drove up. He was inquiring about the arrival of a package. He hadn't seemed to take note of us at all even though there were few people left in the rail station that morning. I took Sarah Michelle's arm and spun her in the other direction. "Let's go this way," I said under my breath. "That man is my father."

We walked at a normal pace in the opposite direction without once looking back. Soon we heard the automobile's engine behind us, but it passed us without slowing down. A large brown package was in the passenger seat. "It looks like my father got one of the new automobiles," I said out loud to myself as well as Sarah Michelle. "He had been talking about it a few days before I left." I looked at Sarah Michelle's face. Her mouth was closed in a grim line and I could tell she was thinking hard.

"Sean, we need to go to the hospital first," Sarah Michelle said. With that, we slowly turned and started walking back in the direction in which we had started. Sarah Michelle continued, "There's a lot I have to tell you."

A pit formed in my stomach, "Who's in the hospital, Sarah Michelle?"

"A woman named January."

"Not Dean's January?"

"Do you know January? Did Dean introduce January to you?" Sarah Michelle tried to sound nonchalant, but her high-pitched, nervous tone betrayed her.

I acted like I didn't notice.

"No, but I heard him say the name January. Dean told the policeman she was his wife to give him an excuse to cross to the mainland." I continued, "Remember in those first few months, they were still watching everyone's coming and going very closely." Sarah Michelle remained quiet so I started talking again, "Later Dean told me he had made it up that January was his wife." I noticed Sarah Michelle relaxed a little as I said these words. But then she appeared anxious again.

"Apparently she is his wife and she's in the hospital now," Sarah Michelle said. "Dean is operating on her injury even as we speak, and John is in the waiting room with Lucky." Sarah Michelle looked like she was going to burst into tears.

"Dean is operating on a person? Surely, there's someone better qualified." I said, confused. "Maybe you should start at the beginning and tell me what's happened."

We had a long walk to the hospital and Sarah Michelle told me everything in an unemotional monotone voice. Well, at the time I thought it was everything, but she left out the part about Lucky being John's real son. This I would have to find out later on my own. Soon we arrived at the hospital waiting room. John's eyes lit up when he saw me. He looked awful, but I didn't say anything. I knew it was hard to keep clean while living in a tent in Galveston. But he looked very haggard and unusually run down. I noticed he had lost a significant amount of weight.

"I swear you've grown in the short time since you've been gone," John said as he led me to a chair. He took Lucky from his basket and put him in my lap. Lucky was getting big. He stared into my face and followed my eyes. He was an exceptionally happy baby. I guess you have to be somewhat carefree to swing from a rafter in a cyclone, I thought to myself and smiled.

I felt a presence nearby. It was the doctor that had put the cast on my arm originally. He was standing right beside me looking down at the baby. I started to bolt, but his kind tone stopped me. "It's about time for the cast to come off, boy," he said as he examined it. "Why don't you come with me down the hall and I'll take it off now?" John took Lucky back and Sarah Michelle nodded "yes".

Once in his office, the doctor said, "That's a pretty good disguise you've made for yourself."

"It didn't seem to fool you. You spotted me right away."

"No, I spotted the sling. My wife sews them for me. That's when I realized it might be you." He felt around on my arm and then started to get out a medical saw and some other instruments. "Now, don't worry. I know what was happening. I actually helped Hansen with the plan."

"You did? Then thank you sir, you saved my life."

"Did you know Hansen's had hell to pay for helping you?" He began to use the saw to remove the cast. "Your father fired him for letting you run away again." He must have sensed how upset this news made me. "Now don't worry. Hansen found another job working at the stables. He's good with horses. Most Texas-born men are."

He called, "Nurse, would you come in here a moment, please? I need a little help." Together the two of them finished the job and once they took the cast off, I looked down at my arm. It was thinner than the good arm and looked yellowish-green under the white plaster dust from the cast. The nurse began to wash the arm and then the doctor took another look. "Yes, I think it healed nicely. Soon it will fill out to match the other arm. Now let's give you a thorough once-over." He poked around on my knee.

"How's the stiffness in your leg?" I told him it was still there, but not as bad. "It's likely to bother you, on-and-off, for the rest of your life. But I think overall you're in fine shape."

"What do I owe you?

"You owe me nothing, Robert," the doctor said. "Your father has already given a lot of money to this hospital, I probably owe you money."

"Please call me Sean." I extended my hand.

He shook it and said, "Good-bye Sean." I didn't know it at the time, but he would be the last person to ever call me Robert. I should've taken more notice of the occasion.

SARAH MICHELLE

Sean walked back to us in the waiting room. He was smiling and touching his arm where the cast used to be. "It itches a little," he said. John and I were happy to have a break from our present conversation. We had been discussing what Sean had told me on the way to the hospital, the part about Dean telling him he was not really married to January, that he had only used the story as an excuse. I also speculated to John that perhaps Dean had married January because she was pregnant. I reminded him that it would have been very difficult for her to be unwed in her condition.

John said, "January hadn't wanted to marry, she had wanted ..." his voice trailed off before continuing. "That was a real marriage license Dean had." I could see John was still troubled, but he was much less angry. I had been afraid he might physically hurt Dean before anything could be talked out in a rational manner. Sean had arrived back at just the right time to end our conversation, and since I didn't really know what to say, I said nothing.

Sean opened his satchel and pulled out a toy for Lucky, one of many gifts he had brought with him. He and John began to play with the baby. I closed my eyes and must have fallen asleep because when Sean shook my arm, I found myself waking. "Here comes a nurse with news," he said.

The nurse walked up to us. Her expression gave no clue as to the outcome of the surgery.

"How did it go?" I heard John say to her.

"It went as expected," she replied. "We really won't know more until the experimental surgery tomorrow. The specialist is expected to arrive in the morning. But the patient is stable."

"We'll take this as good news," I said.

"Dr. Roland said he expects the best," the nurse offered.

"Who is Dr. Roland?" John asked the nurse.

"Why, Dr. Roland," she said it as if we were supposed to know this man. "January's husband, who performed the surgery today."

"Yes, of course." I tried to cover everyone's surprise. "We're used to calling him by his first name, Dean."

"Ma'am, his first name is Jackson…Dr. Jackson Roland," the nurse blurted.

"But we call him Dean," John said quickly. "It's a family nickname."

"I thought his nickname was Stone …" the nurse stopped mid-sentence. "Really, it doesn't surprise me the doctor wouldn't go by his given name after what happened," the nurse looked at us conspiratorially. "I don't often state my opinion, but I believe it was that woman's last chance." The nurse paused a moment then continued, "She would have died anyway if

Dr. Roland had not tried something. It's just that her husband was a wealthy benefactor of the hospital..." Our faces must have looked stricken at her words. "Oh dear, I've said too much, it's not my place. I just wanted Dr. Roland's friends and family to know that I believed he was an extraordinary surgeon..." She stopped talking abruptly and left.

None of us knew what to say. After a few moments of sitting and staring at each other, John said, "I believe I'll go back to the hotel and clean up."

I left the baby with one of the nurses. Sean wanted to know why I didn't take him with me. I told him Lucky had a fever a few days ago and it seemed like the right thing to do to leave him at the hospital. Sean seemed to accept my answer.

As John, Sean and I went back to the hotel, we walked slowly, taking in all the sights of the city during the height of the holiday season. Everywhere we looked there were signs of celebration.

"It's a lot different in Abilene," Sean spoke.

"I'm sure it is. Houston is a much larger city," I said.

"Folks say Houston is poised to get much bigger as it takes away the port trade of Galveston," Sean continued, perhaps thinking of his father. "Houston's got the railway, and it has a lot of other positives."

Changing the subject, I said. "Let's go in here." It wasn't hard to pull him and John into the front door of Mario's Ice Cream Parlor &

Restaurant. Once we were seated, Sean reached into his satchel and brought out a gift for me.

"Would you mind if I save this gift and open it on Christmas Eve?" I asked him. "Because I want to buy a gift for you, too. And we could open them on Christmas Eve … maybe have dinner if we can find a restaurant open."

"I think the only thing we'll find open is a saloon," Sean laughed.

"But saloons serve food as well as liquor," John added.

"Yes, it won't be like any holiday either of us has ever celebrated. Nor should it be, as … " I stopped mid-sentence before adding " … as we have to start anew."

"Yes, when everything is swept clean away, you have to start everything anew," John said. I acknowledged this fact, but I would never forget Thomas and Tommy, or my life with them. Sean held his soda glass to mine and we clinked them in a toast. "Here's to our new life together in West Texas," he said.

"To life in West Texas," I repeated and we clinked our soda glasses again. John raised his glass and touched it to ours.

We had a wonderful time and I pondered the fact that I could feel so good this evening considering how bleak I had felt this morning. My mood was at the opposite end of the spectrum and it hadn't even been twenty-four hours. Maybe that's why my father said to wait twenty-four hours before making any life-altering decisions. It made sense to me this evening. I would never take feeling carefree and being at some degree of peace for granted again. I was thankful to be alive, thankful to have such good people in my life—if I couldn't have the ones I had made my other life with.

"Tell me about school, Sean," I asked, trying not to sound like a mother. "How are you getting along?"

DEAN

After the surgery, I went into the surgeon's quarters and slept one of the deepest sleeps of my life. No dreams. No waking up. Just plain simple sleep and I desperately needed it.

I had done exactly as my friend told me. Now, we would wait until he arrived. Hopefully, we hadn't waited too long before taking the pressure off the brain for the experimental procedure to be successful.

It felt strange to be here in these quarters. To be addressed as doctor, or Dr. Roland more specifically. Or signing medical papers with my full name—Andrew Jackson Roland—but, honestly it had always been strange to sign my full name having been named after the famous general and seventh president of the United States.

My father had been killed in the Civil War in 1865, only months after I was born. He had served under General "Stonewall" Jackson in 1862 and had admired him like no other officer. My mother told me he wanted to call me Stonewall Jackson Roland. They had compromised on Andrew Jackson Roland. She thought it seemed more proper to be named after a United States President. But it seems everyone ended up calling me Jackson instead of Andrew. When I was younger some even called me by the nickname "Stonewall." As an adult, January was the only one who had ever called me "Stonewall." She did it whenever I didn't do what she wanted, which was often.

I shook off the heavy sleep and got up and walked around. Stretching felt good. The procedure had left me stiff. Every muscle had been tense as I tried to achieve perfection. Performing surgery came back to me easily, even after five years.

In the hallway outside I heard a familiar voice. I looked out and saw my specialist friend from the north coming toward me with the chief of surgery. They were talking animatedly. The men saw me watching them from the doorway.

"January opened her eyes and is responsive," they both said at the same time.

I hoped the good news would distract John from killing me. I had no idea how I would explain my way out of this one.

What would I say to Sarah Michelle to make her love me now that she thought I was a married man? Oh January, it seems you always blow in from out of nowhere and leave everything in your path in shambles.

8 TIME TO REJOICE

I was fighting the fight against the fallen angels as January struggled to wake. Prayers were being said. We could hear them in the halls where nurses crossed themselves. In the waiting room, Dean, Sarah Michelle and Sean prayed inside their heads. John also prayed out loud in the sanctuary. I could hear prayers by the surgeon and the assistant in the operating room. And I heard a good many more prayers for January by people that didn't even know her personally. They made us stronger. They made us fight harder. Of course, prayers are not always answered, but God willing, they are when it is in the plan. In this case, the prayers made the difference and the victory was ours.

DEAN

"January's opened her eyes and is responsive," I repeated after the two physicians. My friend grabbed me and started to talk very animatedly. It seems January was in better shape than we had assumed. He had already checked her thoroughly. By taking the pressure off the swelling of her brain, she had recovered enough to open her eyes. But, of course, he reminded me it was too early to know if there was brain damage. "Please," he said. "Come with us so we can determine if she recognizes you."

John met us in the hallway. He was clean and looked much better, although he still had dark circles under his eyes indicating he had not gotten much sleep. We told him our good news and I introduced him to my friend, Dr. Darcy Simmons. Then we all went to January's room.

Her eyes opened wider as we entered the room. She didn't seem to recognize us as people she knew. "Perhaps we're overwhelming her by surrounding her all at once," the chief of surgery said. "Jackson, you visit with her first since you're her husband."

It was an uncomfortable moment for John and myself. I could tell he and I needed a moment alone, too. But it would have been more uncomfortable to say that I wanted John to go first. So I didn't stop him when he left the room with everyone else.

I pulled up a chair at January's bedside, not wanting to rush her. She looked at me. I wanted her to recognize me, but I knew she did not. I asked her if she liked her new ring. She looked at it and repeated back "ring". Her voice was soft and childlike with none of the coyness that made her January.

Next I tried asking her if she remembered my name. I asked about John and Lucky.

"John," she said. "I remember John."

"What do you remember about John?"

"I remember John," she said it slowly with a confused look on her face.

I stepped in the hallway and motioned for John. "She wants to speak with you, John." The relief in his face was obvious. Outside the door, I reminded him it would take time for her to recover. "She seems to have lost some of her memory," I said, but he moved past me into the room without acknowledging what I was saying.

January's face broke into a smile. "John."

JOHN

Things had been so bad for so long, I wasn't used to a good thing happening and I cried at January's bedside. She reached up and touched my tears. I looked into her face. Tears were in her eyes. "John," she said again.

"What, January?"

"Ring," she said and touched her finger. "Ring."

I had not noticed the ring before. "It's beautiful," I answered her, not knowing what she was trying to tell me. "John," she said again, smiling. Then she touched her head and mouthed "Ouch!" I knew the scar would devastate her. Her obvious vanity was one of the things that drew me to her. Unlike most women who were humble about their beauty, I loved the way January used it to her advantage in a most powerful way.

The specialist, Dr. Simmons, stuck his head inside. "How are things going?"

"She remembers my name and that's enough for me."

She said "Ouch" again and pointed to her wound. "I think she might need some headache medication."

He stepped closer to the bedside. "Let's give you something for your pain and let you rest." He turned to me, "Soon she'll regain strength, but these first few hours she'll be in and out." He wrote something down and handed it to a nurse that had followed him into the room. I hadn't even noticed the nurse.

Dean stepped into the room holding Lucky. He took him to January and the baby stretched his arms to her. She didn't respond back and said in a strange voice, "I lost my baby ..."

"No, January, I believe this is our baby. Our baby lived through the storm," I said as I took Lucky from Dean's arms.

Dr. Simmons and the nurse disappeared as if on cue. They understood that what I needed to say was private. Of course, they must have thought I was referring to the thunderstorm in which January was hurt. They couldn't have imagined this tiny newborn living through a hurricane all by itself. It still amazed me.

Dean whispered to me, "John, I don't think it's wise. January told me in Houston that she lost the baby she was carrying."

I told Dean to sit down beside January. Then I tried to make sense of it for everyone, myself included. "January, the night you were hurt you had just confessed to me in our tent—where Sarah Michelle could overhear—that you had not lost a baby, but had given it to Sister Elizabeth at the orphanage only days before the storm." I looked over at January and she was asleep. I was still holding the baby. Lucky began to cry and a nurse came in and ushered us all out.

We went down to the outside garden sanctuary to talk in private. Once there, I confided. "Dean, I had helped Sister Elizabeth hang a swinging crib for a newborn from the rafters. It was only days old." He looked at me and he looked at Lucky. He leaned forward and waited for the rest of the story.

"Right after the storm, Sean and Sarah Michelle went with me to help the orphans. The three orphan boys in the tree had already been found by that time. No one had noticed the tiny sleeping baby high in what was left of the roof of the building."

Dean ran his fingers through his thick dark hair and grimaced.

I continued, "Seeing as you're married to January, I now realize it could be your child. I would have told you sooner if you had clued me in on your marital status." My tone was defensive, somewhat hostile.

"Lucky's your child," he said plainly. I could see pain in his eyes.

"How can you be sure?" His calm demeanor took me aback.

"I had the mumps in my early twenties," he grimaced with the words. "Doubt if I'll ever have children of my own."

We were both silent for a time. Then Dean asked me why we hadn't reported finding Lucky at the orphanage. I answered, "Sarah Michelle believed, and rightly so, that the authorities would never let a single woman adopt a child alone. Especially in the condition her life was in after the storm—penniless and alone without a proper home. I believe God gives you at least one thing to hold onto to get you through in life during a crisis. For Sarah Michelle, that one thing was Lucky."

Dean sat very still. Then he looked at me directly and said, "The wedding license I have with January ..." He ran his fingers through his hair again before continuing, "I owed January a favor. She knew things about me ... She said she needed a father because the real father didn't want to be one."

"She didn't want to marry me," I said.

Dean responded back. "She knew you didn't want to marry anyone."

"No, but I would have..."

"Two wrongs don't make a right, John." I knew what Dean said was true. Still it bothered me that he had the nerve to ask me in the first few days after the storm if I had heard from January, and I told him as much. I also knew I had not wanted the responsibility of a family. I looked down at Lucky and knew I would gladly take on that responsibility now even though I was the weakest I had ever been in my life.

One side of me wanted to kill Dean—to hurt him for his betrayal of our friendship. Although it was not really a friendship at the time, but definitely an acquaintanceship. I thought about punching him, but instead I calmed my nerves, and said, "Sarah Michelle and Sean are waiting for us back at the hotel. They want to see a play."

"I'm a little low on cash," Dean said. "Expect I'll need to find some work here shortly if I want to keep a roof over my head."

"You can have some of the reward money I got from the Stockton's. Sarah Michelle gave me half of it even though I don't deserve it."

"Maybe I'll take a small loan to pay January's hospital bills, seeing as they listed me as the responsible party," Dean said. Then as if he had just thought of it, he added, "I'll stop by the stables tomorrow and see if they need any help with the horses. I'm good with horses." Dean sat perfectly still and stared off into space. After a while he said something. I bent my head closer to hear Dean's words. I noticed tears were streaming down his face. As I moved even closer, I heard him say, "I was trying to do the right thing, John. I was just trying to do the right thing."

SARAH MICHELLE

Dean knocked on my hotel room door moments after Sean and I arrived back. We had unloaded our arms of all the packages we had bought: Christmas presents for everyone. "Just a minute," I called out as we tried to hide everything in the closet."

Sean and I were both flushed when we finally opened the door and allowed Dean to enter. As Sean moved away from the closet door, it opened and everything fell out. We both rushed to push it back in. "You didn't see anything, did you?" Sean yelled from inside the closet where he was pushing things up on a shelf.

"Christmas presents," I said as I bent to pick up a package.

"Christmas presents … I've got my eye on a few things to buy for the both of you," Dean grinned broadly showing his fine straight teeth and deep dimples. It was the same smile he had used the first time I met him in the tent.

I remember thinking how handsome he was, even covered in mud. Back then I had taken him for an uneducated man that had smart wits. Now I understood that was the way he wanted people to perceive him.

He reached into his pocket and took out a bag. "Sean, you may need this someday. I retrieved it after you left abruptly that day with Hansen."

Both Sean and I gasped, we knew what it would mean if Dean were caught with a bag of jewelry. Dean held it out to me. "Perhaps you could put it in your trunk, Sarah Michelle. Keep it safe for Sean."

Sean looked at me in a most pitiful way and said, "Most of it belonged to my Aunt." Then he started to tremble, "The rest of it I stole, and I'm sorry. I didn't know how wrong it was until I did it."

I put my arms around Sean and comforted him, "We all do things that are wrong sometimes. It's part of being human." Dean was still holding the small bag toward me. I took it from him and dumped the contents on the dresser. It contained some beautiful gems. Very expensive rings, earrings and necklaces glistened alongside a broach and tiara. I had not seen jewels like this since I had left my family in London.

The latch on my trunk was stiff and hard to open. Even as I put them in a small tray inside, I knew I would never sell them or wear them. To do so would remind Sean of his wrongdoing. Many people had stolen after the storm. But in the light of day, I knew Sean was mortified that he had participated in defiling the dead. One day we would find a way to make this right.

The mood became lighter when Dean told us the good news about January. He also told us John had come clean about the way we found baby Lucky. "Excuse us a minute, Sean," I guided Dean into the hallway. "Did John also tell you that we believe Lucky is January's child?"

271

"Yes," he said.

I was relieved to hear him say it out loud. "So you think Lucky is John's child?"

"January never told me that, but I always suspected." Dean looked down at the ground. "I owed January a favor, I didn't ask a lot of questions."

We went back inside and immediately stumbled upon Sean, who had his ear to the door. "Sorry," he said. "I'm not only a thief, I'm also a snoop."

"Well you wouldn't have to be a snoop, if I wasn't a liar," I tried to laugh. Then we all laughed for real.

"Oh, what a tangled web we weave when first we practice to deceive." Dean added.

"Quoting Sir Walter Scott. Sean I believe there's a lot more to Dean than he lets on." I giggled. Sean's face lit up like a small boy, as he said, "Like a whole other person—Dr. Jackson Roland."

Dean laughed uncomfortably and to change the subject he suggested we get John and all play a game of cards. It seemed a perfect way to spend the evening as it was beginning to rain outside. I was surprised to see John arrive at my room with Lucky in his basket. I had assumed he would leave Lucky with the nurses.

As we played cards, we made our plans for Christmas Eve. Outside we could hear music and laughter as people shopped in the rain. It was a light rain. More like a heavy mist, but I didn't want to get out in it. None of us did, really, when we could stay warm and dry inside. It was still strange to be with this new family of mine, but I was thankful to have each one in my life.

The feeling was bittersweet and it brought tears to my eyes. Each person acknowledged my tears in their own way, but didn't push. We understood we might never fully recover, but we would get by.

DEAN

On my way to the stables, I thought of Hansen losing his longtime job as Robert Stockton's right-hand man. Damn that Stockton. Did he value anyone beside himself?

The sound of a crowd gathering caught my attention. I whirled and saw some kind of commotion behind me. I could hear Sarah Michelle's voice saying, "Let him go, it's not him."

Then I watched as John tried to cut through the knot of people. He had a determined look on his face. Next, the crowd backed off to reveal a young redhead man pulling Sean one way and John pulling him the other.

"It is Robert Stockton, Jr.—I compared him to the reward poster," the redhead cried. "See, there's one pinned there on the post." He pointed to a nearby sign. Someone ripped it down and brought the poster over to Sean, putting it up against his face. I could see the large print offering a sizeable reward for his safe return.

Hansen came out of the stables and walked right past me. He went straight up to the group and took the poster, "Let me see. I've known Robert Stockton, Jr. since he was born." He took Sean's face in his hands and looked him over carefully. The crowd waited. "This isn't him. Looks like him though."

"Sir, I know Robert too." The redheaded kid would not be deterred. "I went to school with him and I recognize his voice." He continued, "He's changed the color of his hair, but it is him."

"No, it's not him," a man in work clothes came forward. "This boy's name is Sean Kalo. He lives in Abilene. Rode the train up with me to look for work rebuilding Galveston." Then he added, "I assure you he ain't no wealthy man's son."

I stayed back and watched the show from a distance. If things got out of hand, I would step in but for now I didn't want anyone to believe Sean was with me. Some people might remember seeing me with him and Hansen when we were in Houston before.

The man took Sean by the arm and said in the direction of the crowd, "Let's go. We're not going to find any work standing here." Sean walked off with him and Sarah Michelle, and John followed close behind. I watched them turn the corner. Then I went into the stables and asked Hansen for a job.

He asked me in his office to discuss it. When we were alone from prying ears, he demanded to know why Sean was not with his cousins, George and Kitty Kalo. I explained how my original mission had been to come to Galveston to get Sarah Michelle. Once here, I had sent for Sean so we could spend the holidays with John and Sarah Michelle in Houston and possibly see his sister. He needs to have some fun. We all do. The holidays are going to be hard this year."

As Hansen listened, he leaned back in his chair and his face lost some of its anger. "I wanted to see him myself. I can only imagine how his sister must miss him," Hansen said quietly.

"We also wanted to attend the New Year's memorial for the victims of the storm in Galveston…"

Hansen cut me off. "That sounds like fun," he said sarcastically.

"Not fun, sir, but important in a way none of us can verbalize except to say all those people need a proper sendoff, if nothing else to ease our own guilt for having to dispose of their remains quickly." I closed my eyes and could see the red flames burning in tall columns from the funeral pyres. As with all things one wants to forget, the horrific sight would always be one I could conjure up easily.

"I could use some extra help for the few weeks you are in town," Hansen surprised me by changing the subject. "Some of my men want to take the holiday off leaving me short at a very busy time. Come back tomorrow and bring Sean. Perhaps I could arrange for his sister to be here too." He stood and motioned me toward the door.

"What time would you like us to arrive?" I shook his hand good-bye.

"Ten o'clock in the morning," he replied. Then added with a smile, "I know Sean likes to sleep in when he isn't in school."

JOHN

Once we were away from the redhead kid and the crowd, Sean introduced us to Virgil.

Indeed they had ridden on the train together and it was very obvious Virgil did not believe for a minute Sean was any wealthy railroad magnet's son. When Virgil discovered I had been working on some of the cleanup crews in Galveston, he immediately started picking my brain for information. I gladly told him everything I knew. I told him names to ask for to in order to get on the list for the reconstruction work that would be starting in the next few months. Sean and I both noticed he wrote them down in a beautiful handwriting with even, looping letters. When I commented on his skill, he said I can read well too. My dear mama taught me. She was a schoolteacher.

Clearly, Virgil was a man made of the same cloth as myself. I remember at his age how eager I was to take on the world and make my fortune. Now, I was reduced to half the man I used to be. I wished good things for Virgil, but I was a little envious of his obvious zest for life. He had what I once had. Now, my innocence was lost as surely as the city of Galveston. Uneasy feelings weighed upon me, and my heart ached for the situation with January.

I left Sean and Virgil playing checkers outside of a pharmacy. They were laughing in a way that I hoped to hear more often from Sean. He was too young to have seen the sights he did. But, unlike my own, his spirits were starting to lift. I had seen Sarah Michelle's spirits soar in the past few days. I remembered when she was so despondent she couldn't utter a word. The human psyche was amazing in its ability to heal.

Sarah Michelle was some woman and quite a beauty now that her bruises were fading and her cuts were healing. When I had thought January had left me for good, I had feelings for Sarah Michelle. But I didn't feel it would be appropriate to mention such things when she was grieving her lost family. She had told me she had guilty feelings about being the only one of them to survive. Over and over, she tried to imagine how events might have turned out if she had done this thing or that thing differently.

I had told her sometimes a person just has to decide to be happy. My mind wandered on aimlessly like this for some time. In my head I told myself I would be happy again. I would take my own advice, but first I had to expect some sadness and some anger. You can't go through something like we did and not be touched to the core of your soul.

My steps quickened as I neared the hospital. I was anxious to check on January. I was fearful to love her. I might not be able to take it if she left me again. Either by walking out or … I wouldn't even think it. January was going to live. She had opened her eyes and spoken a few words.

That was something to rejoice about. Something was going right and I was going to hold on to it. This was a good thing. I still had hope in me. I didn't view the storm as some kind of punishment anymore, but rather a correction in the direction of my life. It may be the devil's world, but there was evidence God lived in it, too. I looked down at the sleeping baby in the basket I was carrying.

"I have a son." I said it out loud to the world as if doing so would confirm it were true.

DEAN

Hansen was right. Sean did love to sleep in late. I went by John's room where Sean was sleeping and woke him at seven thirty in the morning. John wasn't in their room. Sean said he never came home from the hospital last night. I thought Sean was awake, but when I came back at eight o'clock to take him to breakfast he was asleep again.

I woke him every fifteen minutes until nine o'clock when he finally rolled over and sat upright on the side of the bed. "Boy, how do you ever get to school on time?" I said, half-joking and half-serious.

"If it had been a school day, I would have gotten up easily," he rubbed his mess of hair and yawned. "But because I knew it wasn't a school day, my brain wouldn't let me get up."

"I guess that makes sense in some world," I handed him his shirt. "Get dressed. I need to eat before I work."

When I was satisfied he would stay awake, I left and went down to the dining room to wait for him. As I rounded the corner near the bar, I saw a sleeping figure on a bench. It was John. I woke him and he was completely sober. He looked at me and said, "I ain't been drinking." I knew it was true.

"I wouldn't blame you if you had," I said which was also true. "Just didn't want Sean to come down and see you passed out if you had been. It might make him feel uneasy seeing the way his father gets ..." I stopped myself from rambling. "What the hell are you doing sleeping down here on a bench?"

"When I got here from the hospital it was late at night and I sat down on this bench a minute to rearrange the baby in the basket, when who but Virgil comes out of the bar and starts talking to me."

John must have seen a look of panic cross my face as I looked around for the baby. "Nah, nah, nah. I didn't lose Lucky. Sarah Michelle couldn't sleep and she had come down to the front lobby to sit awhile. She took Lucky back up with her."

"And you decided the bench looked comfortable?" I patted the hard wooden surface as I said it.

"Virgil and I talked until five in the morning and I was so tired I went to sleep here."

"That must have been some conversation."

"Yes sir, it was. Virgil got a great idea when he went to find work in Galveston yesterday," he smiled up at me from the hard bench. "We're going into business together."

As John got to his feet, Sean came around the corner. "You two hurry and go eat," John said to Sean. Then he turned to me and said; "We'll discuss it more later. Right now, I need to sleep in a bed and you need to—"

"Go shovel horse manure for money," I finished his sentence.

"I've done worse," he said as he walked off, "Whatever it takes to make a buck." Then he turned, and I knew he was sincere, "Dean, I hate that your hard-earned money is at the bottom of that ocean out there. It seems hateful cruel to lose it all at a time when you need it most."

"There is one upside to not having money," I called out to John as he walked away. "I've discovered who my true friends are."

John stopped walking, turned and pointed at me saying, "That's real pretty Dean. Someone ought to write that down and put it in a fortune cookie or something."

Sean smiled and I could see his face was still puffy from his long sleep. Hansen was going to be happy to have him around for a few days. I had not told Sean his sister might come to the stables, too. I didn't want to disappoint him if Hansen couldn't get word to her.

We ate our breakfast silently as Sean struggled to gain full consciousness. I noticed he wasn't a breakfast eater, but he made up for it at lunch and dinner. Sean's voice was beginning to change and become deeper like his father's. And he was starting to look more like him as his face thinned out of its boyishness. We were going to have to be careful if we ever came to Galveston again. His identity would be hard to disguise.

"What are you thinking about?" Sean's words shocked me out of my thoughts.

"About how much you've grown. You're starting to look like a man." I dabbed my napkin at my mouth. "We're going to have to teach you how to shave soon."

"I'd rather grow a great big wooly beard." He stroked an imaginary beard on his pale chin.

"You better ask Penny Welbourne about that first." I prodded him about his schoolboy crush back in Abilene.

"What do you know about Penny? Has Kitty been talking?"

"What did G.K. Kalo tell you? No one keeps a secret—everyone talks to someone else about it."

THE BOY "SEAN"

Dean didn't tell me my sister Jane would be at the stables. It was
overwhelming to be with Hansen and Jane. All I could do was grab them
and hold on to them. I was choked up. Hot tears ran down my eyes and
made a dark place on Hansen's light blue vest, and I tried not to mess Jane's
pretty dress. I knew it probably cost a fortune. Jane was such a
clotheshorse— only the latest fashions and hairstyles for her. Otherwise she
was quite sensible. She even rationalized her affinity for fine apparel by
telling me that people thought you were a smarter, better person if you
looked your best.

Hansen ushered Jane and myself into his private office so we could
catch up on each other's lives. I looked back for Dean as I went through
the door. He had already made himself busy shoveling out a stall. It was the
first time I had noticed what a tall athletic build he had. Obviously he must
have done some heavy lifting at some point in time to build his muscular
physique. Jane was looking at him too. I could tell she liked him and he
liked her back. But the thing I noticed about Dean was he liked every
woman. Tall or short, plump or thin, he found something to like in them
all. But no need to warn Jane, she wouldn't be seeing much of him in West
Texas.

After Jane left, Hansen came in with a warm lunch for the two of
us. He had cooked it himself in the small kitchen next door to his office.

285

We talked, and then we just sat for a while in the way that people do who are real comfortable with each other.

Hansen told me the story of how he came to be looking for me in Galveston the day he saved me from getting shot. Turns out after the storm no one was allowed into Galveston without passes and proper identification for relief work. They were very strict because of all the stealing and such. I visibly winced at his words, but he didn't notice. He continued on about how upset the people who were trying to get into Galveston to help relatives and friends were about being kept out. He was right, martial law was being strictly enforced and, as I remember, I was really glad there was a soldier posted on almost every corner.

But even though people couldn't get in, people could leave—and hundreds started streaming off the island and into Houston the next morning after the storm. Hansen said my entire family set out to watch everyone coming into the city of Houston to see if I was one of the survivors. He told me he felt like I might have survived. But he was uncertain because from the stories he was hearing, the storm took many a strong man while leaving a weak child alive right beside him. He knew I was resourceful, but it sounded like it had been a game of chance as to whether I made it out alive.

Next, he told me of how some tattered storm survivors came walking into Houston barefoot after having managed to sail across the bay in beat-up boats. In the days following, when the waters had calmed down, they brought in a heavy-duty tugboat from New Orleans to help with the large vessels. Some of them had run aground and quite possibly would never be seaworthy again. He asked me if I had seen where the one ship had taken out the railroad trestles and the bridge when it had been tossed about in the high winds.

I told him that happened in the early part of the storm. "I know," Hansen said. "Your father and I tried to cross right after it happened. We had to turn back. Your father had wanted to bring you and his sister's family here to his house. We were on one of the last trains coming back into Houston. I heard the train behind us did not make it back."

"I heard about that," I almost whispered. "Everyone in that train except ten people who walked to the Bolivar lighthouse were killed that night."

"It's a shame, who would have thought the storm would get so bad so quickly?" Hansen continued, "Much was certainly lost—not only in the cost of lives and property, but when the rail lines went down it cost your father and his associates a lot of money.

"I remember thinking of father when I saw the chaos after the storm. I know how important his business is to him," I replied without emotion.

"Actually, your father was very upset about your welfare. The storm had been bad in Houston and done a lot of damage—so we knew Galveston had taken a beating. From the looks of the ragtag bunch of survivors that flooded into the streets here, it had been worse than anyone could've imagined. You should have seen them. Shoeless, hatless, dressed in rags and tatters of clothing. Many were bruised all over their bodies." Hansen paused for a moment. "Anyway, your father was standing in the streets with your photograph asking every person who came into the city if they had seen you."

"As the days went by, we didn't give up hope," Hansen remarked. "Jane went to the emergency tents set up in Emancipation Park for the overflow of survivors coming in to Houston. We had heard they were taking most of the women and children off the island and putting them there until the cleanup was complete. So, one day a young girl said you were living in a tent near her family on the island. She drew Jane a picture of where to find you amongst the sea of tents she referred to as Tent City."

"That's how you ended up outside of my tent at just the right moment," I said.

"It wasn't that easy. Your father got me a pass to do relief work for the railroad. It was the only way I could get onto the island. The repair crews had already gotten an emergency bridge back up in the first few weeks. Some of the rail lines were starting to be restored."

"It was amazing how fast the crews of people were able to restore things. It certainly gave us all hope where there had been none." I thought of all the people that lived on the island as well as relief workers that had flooded in. No pun intended. It was truly amazing the amount of money and time people donated to the cause of helping out.

"Like I said, we had hoped you would be in one of the groups of people starting to come off of the island, but you weren't. Jane and I didn't tell your father about the girl's map to your tent. We thought you might be letting everyone believe you had perished." His voice had been deepening and becoming even more gravelly with each word he spoke. I could see tears building in his bloodshot eyes.

"I did want to at first," my voice was too high and defensive. "But I always intended to let you and my sisters know I was alive." I looked down at the floor in shame for the pain I had caused everyone.

"I understand your plight, boy." Hansen regained his composure. "I was watching you for a few days to make certain things were okay with you. I heard the woman call you Sean. I knew it was you. I had decided you were in a good place as far as the situation on Galveston could be at that time and I was going to leave you be until …"

"Thank God you were there. I would be dead now for my stupidity." I thought of the jewels in Sarah Michelle's trunk. "I never should have done it."

"It was wrong, but I can tell you're truly remorseful." Hansen got a pipe and loaded it with tobacco. He didn't light it right away. He just tapped the tobacco around inside. Before long he started talking again. "People do bad things they regret. That's why there's forgiveness." He lit a match, but did not light the pipe. He put it out again. "And, I should be honest with you, your father grieved for you after the storm. I thought he would never do anything violent around you again. Then, not two days after your safe return, he almost killed you. I'm sorry boy. I'm sorry I brought you home."

"I thought things would be better too. I was so glad to be home safe in my own bed that first night."

"How is your new life going out West?" It was the first time Hansen inquired about it.

"It's great." I took out the harmonica Dean had given to my sister to give to me. "Listen, I'm learning how to play the harmonica." I couldn't play it very well, but Hansen sat and listened to it as if it were the best music in the world. When I finished he had a smile on his face.

We sat again in silence. We were happy to be in each other's company again.

SARAH MICHELLE

Lucky was fussy all day. I tried to get things done around his outbursts of crying—wrapping presents for everyone, washing the few clothes we had in the sink and then hanging them to dry in the bath. I would be glad when I had a home of my own again. And I wondered if we should leave for Abilene right away as opposed to celebrating the holidays here in Houston.

But I wanted to attend the memorial service in Galveston on New Year's Eve. Everyone needed the memorial service. Especially me, as I didn't have a proper funeral for Thomas and Tommy. Perhaps that's why I couldn't leave the island right away. I needed to stay there as long as possible while they searched for bodies to make certain they were found. It broke my heart that they had to be burned. I decided at once not to dwell on it. Not to start the day off with bad thoughts. If I was going to survive, I would have to be tougher than this and I knew they would want me to survive—to get up and get on with it. At times I could almost feel both of them beside me picking me up and prodding me on—especially in the beginning when I could hardly breathe without pain, let alone move.

Christmas was going to be bad. But it would be worse to ignore it all together. I thought of the new people in my life and how important they were to me. But I still felt strange at times, as if I were floating in a stranger's body. All things seemed unreal, and sometimes I felt totally unconnected from things that were happening around me. Lucky was just a baby and would never remember this time in his life. Once again, I thought what an appropriate name Lucky was. Still, he did need a formal name. But that would be John's job if he ever decided to get around to it. Or January's, when she recovered.

John hardly left January's side, which I felt was a good thing. I'm the type of person who believed that love could help one recover. A person could give another person their strength just by being there with them. The mind was a powerful thing when it came to healing. I had seen this when my own mother recovered from a mysterious illness that almost took her life. She wasted away to nothing in a very short time only to will herself back. But I also knew that the mind could only do so much. Sometimes there were no happy endings, but John seemed satisfied to settle for just having January alive.

The specialist friend of Dean's wanted to take January back to New York for special head trauma treatments, he had said. I know John was considering it. January couldn't take care of herself on Galveston while he and Virgil worked there. She needed to be in a clean hospital-type environment. The specialist had said she needed the therapy now, right at the beginning of her healing.

Dean actually got to make the decision about January because he had registered her in the hospital as his wife. But I knew he would do as

John wanted. Dean said January did not have a family to care for her. They had written her off because of her rebellious nature and scandalous behavior. It seemed to me there had been a lot of scandalous behavior these days. Maybe it's all the new inventions and the turn of the century. Or maybe people have always been scandalous, and it takes people who are not scandalous by surprise, as if it could only happen in our day and age, as if it's something new for the world to be going to hell in a handbag.

When Dean came home that evening, he stopped in to check on us. Sean was out and about and it gave Dean and myself a few moments alone. I asked Dean his thoughts on the subject. He said he thought the world had always had both good and bad influences in it, and he didn't feel that a person was all good or all bad, but rather was struggling at any given time to go one way or the other. So, society in general was not worse today than it had been in the past. It was just about the same as always. Our generation just thought it was special.

I went to my trunk and brought out a piece of paper and handed it to him. "What is this?" he asked.

"It's a typed poem someone was passing out on the street corner where they were collecting money for the storm victims." I pointed at a particular passage, "Read this part."

"We ask forgiveness for the people of Galveston," he read aloud.

293

We both agreed it appeared that the author of the poem felt God

had sent the hurricane to punish people for being bad. But we both knew

there were good and bad people on the island. Little babies, nuns, every age

group, every race, every income level. But indeed it did seem like the wrath

of something was raining down at the height of the storm. Dean said he

would have to think on it some. I told him I had thought on it. It felt funny

to be judged by people who knew nothing about me. Did not a certain

amount of bad times befall everyone?

"Enough dark thoughts," he said. "Let's plan our Christmas Eve

dinner. I hope you don't mind, but I've invited Hansen and Sean's sister

Jane, if she can get away."

"And John's invited Virgil, so remind everyone not to say Jane's

last name." I paused before continuing, "I hope January can sit and eat with

us."

"Did John not tell you?" Dean became excited as he spoke, "he's

decided to send January for the treatments in New York. She will be leaving

on the first train out tomorrow."

"Oh, Dean that's wonderful news," but I was always practical.

"How will he pay for it?"

"He's using his half of the reward money for now. The rest we'll

worry about as it comes due." Dean reminded me that even some treatment would be better than none. Then out of nowhere Dean said, "The book of Job." I looked at him as if to make sense of his last statement.

"In the Bible," Dean held me by my arms as he spoke and slightly shook me. "Job didn't do anything wrong and he had terrible things happen to him." Now I understood he was answering my question about the poem and whether we had done something to bring this great tragedy on ourselves. "The book of Job," he continued. "You shouldn't judge a person because you never know what's going on with them."

I stood and thought about what Dean had said and told myself life is a mystery and wondered out loud why God had seen fit to change the course of my life in such a radical way. "Dean," I said. "You surprise me with the things you know about." In my mind, I tried to imagine Dean sitting under a tree reading the "Book of Job." Then I tried to put him in church. Then I went back to him under a tree. And once again I was reminded of how little we knew of each other and the way the world works. For the first time, I saw the cyclone as an event that would have a positive outcome for me even though I had lost much. I was gaining deeper insight. I was growing, and it hurt.

Perhaps this is why we live at all—to grow and learn. I had noticed some people came by this naturally at a young age and others seemed never to achieve it. Thoughts like this would never have crossed my mind six months ago.

I looked at Dean, who was playing with little Lucky. "Sarah Michelle," he said as he barely tickled the child's feet. "John wants you to take Lucky to Abilene." It was the answer to a question I had dared not ask out loud, "Who was going to take care of Lucky?" Once again fate had declared it would be me.

Sarah Michelle was learning to let go and love. Sean was growing up and remembering how to have a good time. Dean was recovering from his past and moving forward. But John was hanging in the nether world of what was now and what could have been.

9 CELEBRATIONS OF LIFE & DEATH

JOHN

Putting January on the train to New York was difficult. She didn't understand why she was leaving, and she was so pale. Dean's friend promised to send progress reports and assured me I was doing the right thing. I held January's hand until the last moment and I couldn't help but notice the beautiful ring. It hadn't been on her hand until recently and I wondered where it came from. I felt I should tell her family, but I didn't know how to contact them. What had January done so wrong that they couldn't forgive it?

I watched the train pull out of the station. Dark smoke filled the air and made me cough. Rubbing my shoulder, I wondered if the damage done to it in the hurricane would haunt me with pain from now on. It hurt especially bad on cold days like this.

January and the doctor waved to me through the train window, and January blew me a little kiss with her hand. It was a small thing, but January-like enough that I knew her personality would soon shine back through her current confused state.

Sarah Michelle and Sean had planned a Christmas Eve dinner and I guess I needed to attend. I understood their attempts to celebrate, but why did it have to be tonight of all nights? The day January left me. I had never enjoyed holidays even in the happiest times of my life. Damn them, I didn't feel like being anything other than sad.

Our dinner was planned for seven o'clock in the hotel bar. The dining room was closed, but the bar was staying open on the holiday. We were going to meet at Sarah Michelle's room around six-thirty to give each other gifts. My gifts consisted of different kinds of candy and cakes for Sean and Sarah Michelle, and whiskey for Dean. I had bought them yesterday on my way to the hospital. I wasn't good at gift-giving, and I hoped they liked them.

As I bathed and dressed, my mood was bleak. I really didn't feel like going to a gathering. I had written to my family back in Ireland a few weeks ago to tell them I had lived through a great hurricane. I had finally received a letter back from them this morning. The postmaster in Galveston had been kind enough to forward it to the hotel. My parent's letter said they had read of this great hurricane in the newspapers and had feared for my safety. My mother had written. She and my father were relieved to know I had lived.

I needed to write them and tell them the miracle of how their grandson had survived too. But first I would need to tell them they had a grandson. I could send the photo from the newspaper of Sarah Michelle, Lucky and myself. However, I would need to tell them about January.

Maybe I wouldn't tell them everything. Maybe I would just write to them that they have a grandson. My mother would cry because I was not married. Or, if I were married, she would cry because she had missed the wedding. Maybe I wouldn't tell them about Lucky until January and I had officially married.

I looked in the mirror. I guess I looked presentable. My thoughts were heavy and it showed on my face. Tonight I would need to tell Virgil I didn't have the money to start the business because I had to pay for January's treatments. The railroad had given her free passage as they had for many of the storm victims. They didn't even ask which storm she had been injured in. They just assumed it was the big one. Many people had given so much without even being asked. It inspired me and gave me hope. And hope was what we needed. It broke my spirit when I heard someone write off Galveston. Just the other day, I had heard some men at the hospital saying everyone should leave the island and start over somewhere else. They hadn't even seen all the progress being made. Just wrote us off. They talked of oil replacing cotton and of bright prospects for Houston.

As I walked to Sarah Michelle's room, I remembered I had forgotten the gifts. I turned and went back for them. Then as I came back out of my room, Sean's sister Jane came around the corner carrying a suitcase. "Are you checking in?" I asked.

"No, I'm on my way to Sarah Michelle's room," she replied happily. "I've brought gifts for Sean."

Once inside Sarah Michelle's tiny hotel room I began to feel nervous and antsy. My heart pounded and my ears roared. Everyone had been exchanging gifts and all seemed to be enjoying it except for me. Don't get me wrong. I loved the small gifts I had received: a new shirt, a new hat, and one that I really needed—some new work boots. The baby had received several gifts, including a handmade ornament from Sean's sister, Jane, inscribed "Baby's First Christmas, December 25, 1900". It reminded me I had not bought a gift for my son. I wasn't used to the ideal of having a son. What would a baby want? I would need to think of it before tomorrow morning.

Jane was searching in her small suitcase for one more gift. She brought out a small flat package wrapped with ribbon. "And the last gift is one from Sean to John," Jane said as she handed it to me.

I took the small package and shook it near my ear. She laughed, and Sean's eyes gleamed. "Open it," Sean said excitedly. "Open it."

I carefully took off the paper and opened the box. Inside was a check for a large sum of money. Jane said, "Sean had me sell a few things for him to get your gift. Please accept it as our faith in your dream and, of course, as an investment in the rebuilding of Galveston."

Tears flowed from my eyes. I knew what items Jane must have sold for Sean. "Sean, you may need this money in your future."

"No," he said. "I kept what was my Aunt's and gave it to Jane for safe-keeping. The pieces that weren't our family's are the ones I sold."

"Please take it," Sarah Michelle stood and walked toward me with Lucky in her arms. "It's Sean's way of making right with the world."

I put Sean's gift into my front jacket pocket and patted it. "Of course, I'll take it." Then I turned to Sean and said, "I wished I had given you more than candy and cakes."

"I like candy and cakes," Sean said as he wiped the sugar from around his mouth with the back of his sleeve.

"It's time to go downstairs and eat." Sarah Michelle busied herself getting the baby in its basket. "The bartender told me he would have the kitchen have our meal ready right at seven o'clock."

"For people who've lost everything, we certainly are having a fancy Christmas," said Dean as he escorted Sean's sister Jane down to dinner. "I hope everyone doesn't mind, but I told my cousin Jim to meet us tonight too."

It was a strange gathering of people, but it proved to be a happy event, perhaps because it was important for us to have a cause for celebration in our lives at this time. I looked around the table at Sarah Michelle, Dean, Hansen, Jim, Jane, Sean, Virgil, Lucky and myself. We took nothing for granted and we all enjoyed ourselves right past the hurt into some kind of happiness … if only for a short while.

Jane said her stepmother and father had taken the younger sister and gone north for Christmas. She had to beg them to leave her here so she could prepare for her new school in the next few weeks. She told the servants she was at a friend's house tonight, which meant she could spend as much time with Sean as she wanted. I watched them together and knew it couldn't be easy for a kid as young as he was to leave his family and all the comforts of being wealthy. His life must have really been bad to not go home after the hurricane. I remembered back to how Sean had let Sarah Michelle and me believe he was an orphan. But every once in a while he slipped into his true identity. He once mentioned the taste of caviar and he had played the piano for Sarah Michelle when they discovered it in the debris. His ability to read and write at an accelerated level all gave him away, as did his extensive vocabulary. I heard him say the word "pertinacious" the other day in reference to myself. I didn't know what it meant, but I acted like I did. I know Dean knew what it meant because I saw laughter in his eyes. Damn him.

That Dean, he was another matter altogether. He had us all completely fooled. But it's hard to hide things when everything's been stripped away from you in hurricane-force winds. All life's secrets tend to come to the surface as if they are not worth hiding in the first place. I would write my mother and father about Lucky. I would tell them the truth. The whole truth. They deserved to know the truth and they would accept it or they wouldn't. If any baby was meant to be in this world it was Lucky.

After we ate, a few regulars and a few holiday travelers began to fill the crowded little bar, which gave it an even more festive atmosphere. A young man played the piano and I thought how nice it would have been if January were there to sing. Dean asked him if he knew the "Maple Leaf Rag" and he did.

Later, I saw Dean and Sean talking to the piano player. They said they had crossed over the bay in the same boat as him. He had been injured in the storm and his parents were taking him to the hospital. A head injury, they said. Obviously, he was much better now and I hoped the same would happen for January.

When the boy finished the song, he sat and talked to Dean and Sean. Apparently he now made a living as a musician. He thanked Dean for the sheet music he had brought him in the hospital; knowing the new popular music had helped him land the job here at the hotel bar.

Sean showed him the harmonica Dean had given him, and the boy showed Sean how to play it even better. That was the thing about the young; they were so willing to get to know new friends. I wasn't much older than Sean, but I had lost my openness around strangers. I had become guarded and jaded in a few years' time.

I noticed Virgil was somewhere in between Sean's age and mine. He was an eternal optimist, and I needed him. I also needed the money Sean had given me. It's strange how sometimes you get what you need from the people you least expect it. I looked at Sarah Michelle and Dean. They were dancing together as Virgil and Jane whirled around them. The piano player was taking a break. The music was coming from a phonograph. Sometimes it would scratch and skip, messing up their tempo and steps, causing them to laugh even more. All four looked like they were having the time of their lives. I felt okay too. At least I didn't feel bad. I bent over and checked Lucky's heartbeat with my two fingers. He was completely still as he slept in his basket, but the strong, even beat of his heart assured me he was fine. I rubbed my aching shoulder again. And thought about the fact Sarah Michelle was going to be leaving soon with Dean and Sean. I'd miss her, all right. Guess she decided it was too much to rebuild her house. Women. Who knew what went through their heads? I watched as Dean leaned Sarah Michelle back at the end of the dance. I thought he was going to kiss her for a moment. It made me mad. Real mad. But I had no right to be mad. So I smiled and gave a little wave when they looked my way.

I was going to rebuild. Still had the front door I rode out the storm on in back of what was left of Sarah Michelle's old house. The door wasn't much, but it was a start to a new place … and every time I entered through it, I'd remember I didn't die that night. There must be some purpose to my being here. And this thought comforted me.

Damn, Dean. Now he had his hand on Sarah Michelle's back as he guided her over to the table. It looked like they were going to have coffee and dessert.

DEAN

The knock on the door came at about two in the morning. I knew it wouldn't be good news at that hour. It was Jane. She and Sean had stayed in John's room. John had gone to sleep on a cot in my room. Now we both were up and putting on our pants. "Just a moment," I said as I fumbled with my belt.

Once we were in the hallway, Jane led us inside John's room where we could hear agonized sobbing. "It's Sean, he can't stop crying. He was crying in his sleep and I woke him. He can't stop." Jane was terrified.

"It's normal," John said matter-of-factly.

"We all cry in our sleep sometimes now," Sarah Michelle's voice made us all turn and look toward the doorway. She moved past us and put her arms around Sean. "He's not really awake. Shhh... shhh..." she said as she comforted the tortured boy. Slowly he woke for real and tears still flooded forth. "It was just a dream," Sarah Michelle said. "Just a dream." She wrapped her arms around him and held him close.

He hiccupped and gulped for air. Jane held out a handkerchief. We had become accustomed to our ways of dealing with the storm's aftermath. Only Jane's panicked face reminded us this was unusual. But we knew it was all part of it and we knew Sean was healing. We didn't have to ask him what he was dreaming about, we still dreamed those dreams ourselves. However, I had not had one in weeks. This I took as a good sign.

Sarah Michelle told John to take her room and stay with the baby. I started back to my room. Jane sat on a chair staring in horror at us all. Sarah Michelle held Sean in her arms and gently brushed his hair with a delicate touch.

The next morning was Christmas Day and Sean came downstairs with a smile. Apparently his storm had passed in the night and his face shown with happiness. Jane was smiling too, but when Sean wasn't looking she watched him with a worried look. There were no answers. This was the storm after the storm, and we would weather it the best we could in our own individual ways.

John showed up with the rocking horse I had bought for Lucky. I had given it to him this morning as he had forgotten to buy a gift for Lucky. Small wonder, with his mind concentrated on January for so many weeks.

Sean held the four month old on the back of the horse as John gently rocked it back and forth. A smile appeared on Lucky's face and his blue eyes danced with delight. It didn't matter that I wasn't the gift-giver. What mattered was seeing the happiness light up and take hold. Lucky wouldn't carry the emotional scars we did; he could remind us of our own childlike innocence, and that made us happy in and of itself.

Virgil invited us to come and stay at his place in Galveston the night of New Year's Eve, as there would be a lot of people gathered on the beach for the memorial service. With that he left us and went back to the job he had found helping manually jack up houses. John would need to go back to his reconstruction job, too, as they weren't quite ready to start the new business. They had been very secretive about this new business.

The two of them talked about how they had witnessed the raising of a cathedral on the island. It was absolutely incredible, Virgil had said, describing the event in detail. John said it inspired him to know that man could do such things when they worked together. Neither spoke much of clearing the debris except that most of it had been cleared slowly, one cubic yard at a time, with the workers saving what they could in the way of lumber, lamps, sinks and toilets. The salvaged items were used in the many new houses being built for the families who planned to stay. "Dean, you're not going to believe how much has been recovered and built in the last three months," Virgil said.

"No, you're not going to believe what a little disinfectant and lime can do," John echoed the words of the first newspaper article about the storm to reach the outside world—and its frantic pleas for cleaning supplies.

It was a miracle there were no major epidemics after the hurricane. Many were sick, but most had recovered. I attributed it to the quick action of the funeral pyres. It was hateful to burn the bodies in piles, but necessary to keep the survivors alive.

I thought of a man pacing back and forth as he told me of his wife and two children burning in one of the pyres. A long, red column of smoke rose from it as he pointed it out. Telling me how timid and fragile his wife had been and how the little one had just learned to say his name. Some people were not certain if their loved ones' bodies had been burned because there had been no time to identify the many corpses. Perhaps they were burned or lost at sea. Either way it would always plague them. At least the man with the timid wife and two small children would know what became of them. That was comforting in some way.

Sean and Sarah Michelle walked with me to my job at the stables. Sean went in and said hello to Hansen. He dared not stay around Hansen too much as people might figure out his true identity. When Sarah Michelle and I were alone, we discussed how this might be a good day for her to lighten his hair again with peroxide. The dark roots were beginning to show and we would still be in Houston for a few more days.

Once they left, I went in to check on each horse. I loved horses. When I get settled into my new life, the first thing I'm going to buy is a horse. I would ask George Kalo if I could pay him to keep it in his barn. He was a good man that loved horses, too. I bet he would know where I could find a good one. Not just any horse, but a special horse.

After I had satisfied myself everything was fine with the horses, I began to clean their stalls. It was hard work, but I enjoyed being worn out at the end of the day and Hansen paid me well. It didn't pay what a doctor or a gambler makes, but it had its rewards.

As I finished each stall, I put the horse back in and gave it fresh food and water. At one point, I realized the food supply was getting low and went to ask Hansen if our order would be here soon. I could hear voices coming from his office. I recognized Hansen's voice and the other one. It surprised me he would be talking to Robert Stockton. Surely, the man had not come to bother him further. To assure myself trouble wasn't brewing, I positioned myself where I could hear better and pretended to be reading the back of a can. I don't know what kind of can because I wasn't really reading it. Just wanted to look busy in case anyone was watching me.

I heard Robert say words like "Beaumont" and "golden opportunity". Apparently he needed a man he could trust. I could hear Hansen say, "Houston is my home" and "I'm too old." Before their conversation ended, I went back to the feed pantry. There would be plenty of time later for Hansen to fill me in on the specifics of their conversation if he cared to do as much. It didn't sound like a hostile confrontation.

Soon, Robert Stockton left Hansen's office. He looked right at me as he flew past without a hint of recognition. He was a man that met many men a day. I would not expect him to remember me, and if he did he didn't show it.

Hansen came out next and I asked him about the feed. He told me to get the wagon and go to the train station to get it. "I don't usually mind a man's private business, but why would you even talk civilly to a man like that?" I hitched up a horse to the small wagon as I talked. Hansen patted the horse and helped me ready the wagon.

"That's just Robert's way. He reacts in anger then tries to make it up with monetary rewards." Hansen checked the hitch one more time. "He wants me to oversee his new financial investment in Beaumont."

"Oh really, what's he got going?" I looked down at Hansen as I adjusted the reins from the front running board of the wagon.

"Secret stuff. Expect I can tell you in a few weeks if I decide to go out there."

"You seriously thinking about it?"

"It's a lot of money, and everything he touches turns to gold." Hansen looked at the veins on his hands. "I'm getting to be an old man. This may be my last chance to retire with money."

"When will you leave?" I asked.

"As soon as I can find a replacement for myself here. Would you be interested? Or would you be interested in going with me to Beaumont? Stockton needs investors and hard-working men."

"No, thank you to both. I appreciate the offers, but I've made my mind up to start over in West Texas."

"Going back into medicine, Jackson?" he smiled as he said my real name.

"Maybe," I smiled back. "Did Sean tell you my name?"

"He tells me everything. But that wasn't how I knew. I recognized you from years ago—you tried to save the life of someone I loved."

"I take it I didn't save them." I could only think of a few people who had died in my care.

"No, but you tried … tried real hard" he took off his hat and pushed his hair back before putting it back on. "That's a lot more than any other doctor did and I thank you for it."

"Why didn't you tell me you recognized me?"

"I figured you didn't want to be recognized, Dean Johnson."

"Noooo sir, I didn't."

"Well that's too bad, you were a damn fine doctor. You almost saved Amilee Stockton's life." After Hansen delivered this bombshell, he turned and walked back into his office.

As I rode to the train station, I thought of what a small world it was. I had been brought in at the last moment to try an experimental surgery on Amilee. Things had moved so swiftly and it looked like she was going to make it. Her husband had been out of town and I do remember her mother talking with me and signing the consent forms. I had never paid much attention to her last name.

But I did know her husband was influential at the hospital because once he returned and found she had expired despite our best efforts, he sued me and threatened to sue the hospital. By agreeing to leave and never practice medicine in Houston again, I had saved the hospital from total financial ruin. I had never met Amilee's husband, but I knew he was a very angry man.

He had called one of the nurses on the phone the night before we lost her, and she cried because he had cursed at her. I remember her saying, "Why would he curse at the person who is trying to take care of his poor sick wife? I would never take it out on the patient, but it makes it hard to go the extra mile." I would think of this often in the months ahead when he drove me from my practice. He didn't even know me and he was reaching out to punish anyone he could for her death without even knowing the specific details. I had tried last ditch efforts to save his wife and I was punished. For what? Him feeling guilty for being absent at her death?

That night I told Sean what I had discovered that day. I knew Amilee was his mother now. He put his arms around me and told me he had only been a little boy, just in the first grade, but he knew she was dying. Hansen and Jane had explained things to him about how the doctor had tried everything, including a new surgery that had a slim chance of working.

He also remembered sitting in his grandmother's lap in a rocking chair while she told his grandfather nothing good would come of my father trying to sue the doctor. He told me his grandparents and Hansen were satisfied that everything that could be done was done.

He also told me Hansen's hair went gray shortly after his mother died—and one time he heard his grandmother whispering to his grandfather it was because of Amilee's death. He hugged me again and thanked me for trying. Then he said, "I'm sorry my father ruined your career. Perhaps I can help make it up to you in some way in the future."

"I've decided to start practicing medicine again when we get to Abilene," I replied.

"When did you decide that?" he asked, beaming a toothy smile.

"Today when I was shoveling manure," we both laughed. But I really had just decided at the moment when Hansen thanked me for trying to save Amilee's life.

SARAH MICHELLE

When we first arrived on the island, I was overwhelmed. More had been restored in the month I had been absent than I ever would have guessed. The streets were clean. New stores and houses were built, or were in the process of being built. Downtown was beginning to look like a glimmer of its former self.

Gone were the funeral pyres and the putrid smell of death. Fresh ocean breezes whipped softly past us as if to say "oh, so sorry" for the wounds nature had left on each one of us just a short time ago. Seagulls cried overhead and the smell of fresh bread came from a nearby window. I could smell an apple pie cooling in a window of one of the new homes. Many homes were undergoing repairs, some of them extensive.

Things felt alive. They felt fresh and it felt good to be here. Sean was carrying Lucky in his basket and I was carrying a small overnight case. Virgil met our small group that also included Dean, John and Hansen. He immediately asked Sean if his sister Jane would be coming as she promised.

"Papa's business brought him back from up north abruptly and he requested Jane spend New Year's with the family." Sean apologized for Jane without saying who their papa was or why he wouldn't want his son with him as well as his daughter. Virgil didn't inquire further. However, Sean could tell he was disappointed. "I will tell her you asked about her. I know she wanted to see you again," Sean said in an attempt to make Virgil feel better. It seemed to work. Only problem was, if Virgil and Jane spent time together, then Virgil would certainly figure out his connection to the Stockton's. Specifically, that he was Robert Stockton, Jr. and not Sean. But I wasn't too worried. He seemed an honest upright person and he was going into business with John.

Virgil led us to a small shotgun style house. It was brand new and painted brightly. "I thought you said we would stay in your tent," I exclaimed as he held the door open for us.

"I did say tent, but John managed to get us this house for rent seeing as he's the lead foreman on our crew," Virgil said with pride as he waved his arm around at the simple but comfortable interior. There were two rooms. One set up with a cot for me and the other made up with pallets and cots for the men. "Very nice," I said as I took a tour.

Once outside, we headed for the beach to see the fireworks over the Gulf. The memorial service would start shortly afterward with readings, songs and a candlelight vigil. I didn't know what to expect. It wouldn't exactly be like a regular funeral, but it would be a proper farewell.

Once at the beach, I spread a blanket and people everywhere started to walk by and say "hello." Like a funeral, there was a certain amount of happiness as people who knew each other, but didn't get to see each other on a regular basis, gathered together and caught up.

"Dean," I whispered. "Do you see that woman over there? Her name is Rosa. I was told she died."

"It appears you were misinformed," he whispered back. "Why don't you go and talk with her, I'll take care of Lucky."

John and Virgil were used to seeing most of the regulars, but were surprised by some of the ones who had left but came back for the memorial. They had heard estimates of about two thousand people relocating after the storm and about six thousand to ten thousand actual dead.

How could it be that we didn't even know an accurate count of the dead? But it was hard to keep my mind on the dead when I was happy to reunite with so many living. Everyone had lost someone. Most had lost multiple family and friends. But tonight we had each other and I could feel excitement everywhere I went.

Soon, a golden-red arc crossed the sky and burst into a thousand stars. The crowd went "awww" in unison as another silver-blue blast followed it. I ran to our blanket to be with Lucky and Dean as a gold one with sparkles burst above the water, creating an incredible display complete with reflections. I apologized to Dean for being gone so long. He said it was fine with him, as he did not have as many people who wanted to see him alive. I laughed because by now John had told me many stories of the crowd he used to run with, and Dean certainly had a colorful past. No wonder January felt comfortable asking him to marry her in her desperate position.

I must admit it gave me a pang of jealousy to think of Dean and January at the altar. Their actual marriage had been a fake, but the marriage license was real, Dean confessed to me. He would need to get it annulled so January could marry John legally. He only hesitated doing it because of her illness. Soon he would file the necessary papers once he was certain January was in good condition. I noticed his surgeon friend asked very little about January and Dean's relationship. He seemed to accept John as her real husband.

Well, here we were at the turn of the century. I guess we were all very modern, even in these Victorian times. I knew there were many who must have gossiped after January came to live with us in Tent City. It was impossible to not overhear every word in the tents around you. If they did dislike me, or John, they didn't show it tonight. Everyone was at peace. I touched the locket at my neck that held my only photos of Thomas and Tommy.

We all watched the fireworks and then sat quietly as candles were passed out. There was a small, lighted stage with a podium for a speaker. In the background were a group of musicians. Sean told us one of them was the piano player from the hotel bar. "Remember, my new friend?" he said with pride as the boy started to play. The crowd became quiet and a speaker stepped to the podium. He asked us to wait to light our candles at the end of the ceremony; we would observe a moment of silence as the church bells rang at midnight.

One after another, speakers and singers came forward to give their special tribute to the dead. Each one echoed the sentiments of the crowd as we remembered our own lost loved ones. Tears welled in our eyes, laughter choked in our throats, and some wept uncontrollably, touched by a simple phrase that struck a chord with their particular pain.

And then we began to feel it. A warmth spread through the crowd and inner peace filled each and every one of us as we said our final farewells to husbands, wives, children, sisters, brothers, mothers, fathers, aunts, uncles, cousins, friends, confidants, acquaintances, familiar strangers. People who had once filled our days, our everyday lives, people we had loved and sometimes taken for granted. They were gone now, and all was changed.

But for a moment they were back and they filled the air. They surrounded us. They filled us with love. And we were overcome. I've never felt such a beautiful feeling inside my being, and I could see the glow on others' faces.

Later, when we would recount that moment, each of us would acknowledge the feeling but be unable to describe it. Just before midnight we lit our candles. It didn't take long as we touched candle to candle and made a sea of light—hundreds, thousands of flickering flames, representing the loved ones lost.

A single voice sang "Amazing Grace" while we lit our candles. When the singer finished, we waited in silence for the church bells. They began to peal. One, two, three, four, five…six, seven, eight…the speaker said on the count of twelve we will remain silent for one full moment in silent prayer…eleven, twelve.

A seagull cried in the night. A reminder of the screams from that terrible night we would never forget. The crowd continued to pray, and a wind whipped up. It threatened to blow out our candles, but we protected them with our hands.

We were one. We were united with our loved ones, dead and living. Love filled our hearts. Tears filled our eyes, and it felt good to cry. It felt good to feel, to be alive and experience this with others like ourselves.

Then, as quickly as it whipped up, the fierce wind died down to a balmy breeze and then the air went still. The speaker came forward and said, "Amen." On instinct we all leaned forward and blew our candles out. We walked home, hardly saying a word.

Together we sang in unison to those still mortal—'Twas grace that taught my heart to fear … and grace my fears relieved. How precious did that grace appear the hour I first believed … the answer to their unanswered questions was obvious yet only a few would see or believe but we did not leave, nor would we … life would go on … and we would sweep in and out to be near them when they needed us most.

***

Later we would discover on that same night that an incredible wind had toppled one of the great pillars of Stonehenge. The people of England stood amazed at this natural occurrence. A wind so great it could easily topple one of the majestic pillars that had stood tall and straight for ten thousand years.

It was New Year's Eve, December thirty-first, 1900. A new century was beginning on the winds of change, the last speaker had said. We knew it was a sign. Each and every one of us knew it to be true in our heart.

I would think of the pillars at Stonehenge often. Who put the great stones there? And why? The answers were as vague as why the storm seemed to randomly kill some and not others. Perhaps this is why the great stone toppled at that precise moment—to remind us the world was full of mysteries and unanswered questions.

The next morning, I overheard Dean and Hansen talking while they ate breakfast. Dean was telling him his cousin Jim might be a good person to take his place at the stables. He certainly was a fine horseman, and his stint with the Calvary was now up as the New Year began. I had seen Dean talking to Jim last night. The two of them with heads bent deep in conversation as they played with Lucky. Two peas in a pod, I had thought at the time. I hoped the job at the stable worked out for Jim.

No one had bothered to wake me, and I had slept in rather late. I noticed Sean was the only person still asleep. John was feeding Lucky milk mixed with rice. I was still rubbing the sleep from my eyes when I heard two sharp raps at the door. Virgil stood and opened it.

"Happy New Year's!" It was Jane and she had brought her little sister too.

"How did you find us?" Virgil asked.

"Why, everyone in Tent City knows you got a new house." Jane's voice must have woken Sean because I could hear him moving around as he hurriedly dressed. When he walked into the room, the younger sister tore past everyone and grabbed him.

"You won't believe this. I was dreaming about you two," Sean's voice was overjoyed. I didn't say so out loud, but I knew he had been dreaming wistful dreams of yesterday because for once he did not cry out in his sleep.

When his little sister did let go, she said simply, "You've got blonde hair."

JOHN

Hansen approached Virgil and myself about the Stockton business in Beaumont as we were eating our breakfast. It seemed appropriate, he said, to start the new year with new opportunity.

We told him we had been planning to start a stonecutting business with some men from Italy. We had met the stonecutters on the crews. Stonecutting was a skill that few men knew, and we wanted to learn it. But Hansen's offer hit us out of left field—and it paid well. Hansen also pointed out that we could go to Beaumont now and in a few months come back to Galveston, even though the rebuilding was moving right along. It would be many weeks before they were ready to do the major stonework on the buildings.

Virgil and I told Hansen we would need to discuss it amongst ourselves. My thoughts were, we might miss out on a once-in-a-lifetime opportunity if we didn't change our plans. I liked the thought of being flexible and hanging out there on a limb so to speak. Virgil was more cautious. He didn't want to offend the Italian stonecutters as we had already given them our word.

However, he was not opposed to going to Beaumont for a month. In the end, we told Hansen he could count on us for a month, maybe longer. In the meantime, we would need to discuss our future in the stonecutting business with our partners. Hansen was very guarded about exactly what was going to happen in Beaumont, but he assured us it was on the up-and-up and we would most likely make a great deal of money. Probably more than we would rebuilding Galveston.

Dean went to find his cousin Jim so Hansen could speak with him about overseeing the stables. Whatever Hansen had under his hat, it must be big for him to just pick up and leave like he was doing. When Jim arrived, the two of them hit it off at once.

Hansen asked me for pen and paper. He and Jim then sat at the little dining room table and discussed specifics of Jim's new stable job. Hansen said he would be leaving tomorrow morning so it might benefit Jim to come check the stables out with him today, meet the owner and all the horses. Hansen told Jim he could also hire someone to replace Dean as he would be leaving for West Texas tomorrow afternoon.

For the first time, it hit me that Dean, Sarah Michelle and Sean were leaving. I needed to have a conversation with Sarah Michelle about Lucky. I couldn't take him to Beaumont and it wasn't the best conditions for him to stay in Galveston with so much happening. Sickness didn't seem to be the threat it once was, but he was a tiny baby. Plus I didn't really know how to take care of him. But it was unfair to ask Sarah Michelle to shoulder the burden of Lucky, then take him back from her when January was better. I asked Dean his thoughts.

Dean said he thought Sarah Michelle would want to take Lucky with her. Then he said something strange, along the lines of he was the person married to January, and by rights, he was the one people would expect to be Lucky's father. Then, he quickly added, he still had no doubts I was the biological father, it was just that people would expect him to be the father. I was going to ask Dean what he was getting at, but I didn't feel like getting into another fight with him.

I felt very pressured. I had to make several life-changing decisions in the next few hours. Would I trust Hansen and give up the opportunity to go into the stonecutting business? And would I send my son off to West Texas, possibly handing him over to Sarah Michelle and Dean for good?

I pondered the situation. If I kept Lucky, how would I take care of him? I knew several men who had lost their wives in the storm, and they were taking care of their children alone. At least one of them hired another woman to watch the child in the day along with her own children.

I needed to talk with Sarah Michelle soon. When I walked into the small room, she knew why I had come. "Please let me take care of Lucky for you, John," there was a certain pleading tone to her voice.

"Sarah Michelle, do you think that it's best for him to grow up far away from me?" I still was reeling from Dean's comments. I knew there was a slight possibility he would fight to keep Lucky with him and Sarah

Michelle in Abilene. I could tell he thought Sarah Michelle and Lucky shouldn't be torn apart.

"January's not going to be well for some time." Sarah Michelle was starting to get nervous. I hated stressing her this way. Still, Lucky was my son, not Dean's.

"Sarah Michelle," I got down on my knee beside her and took her hands. "You and Lucky could stay here in Galveston." I gestured with my arms, "Look, we've got a house now. No more tents."

She shook her head, "No".

"Sarah Michelle, Lucky is my child … Sister Elizabeth and I saved him."

"But I'm the one that cared for him. You would have turned him over to the nurse's station."

She had a point, but I wasn't going to let my son go easily. And that answered another question for me; I wasn't going to Beaumont because I would need to count on the help of the people I knew in Galveston to help me raise Lucky.

It was very uncomfortable for everyone in the small house. Dean didn't argue, but his eyes glared at me from under his hat brim. Sean didn't look at me directly, and Virgil just kept making a coughing sound. Hansen had already gone, thank goodness. I noticed he had left the address of where he would be staying in Beaumont on the dining table.

Shortly after our difficult conversation, Sarah Michelle got up to leave. Dean and Sean went with her. We all pretended everything was fine, and we exchanged pleasantries as we said goodbye.

Virgil and I stood on the front porch waving them off. I had Lucky in my arms. As they left, he reached for Sarah Michelle and began to cry. She kissed him on the head and turned her back to walk away. I could see her shoulders shaking, and Sean took her hand. Dean put his arm around her, and I felt bad inside. But I couldn't give up my son. They needed to understand.

Lucky cried and cried. Virgil finally went next door to get a female to help. A teen-age girl came and she said he was most likely hungry or needed a diaper change. It turned out to be both.

Later that evening, the Italian stonecutter in our crew came by. He had a hangdog look about him. His father had written him a letter. He did not want to take partners—especially two men who would have to learn the trade and would be a liability at first. Lucky started to cry again and Virgil and I told the man we understood. We weren't happy about it, but we understood.

When he left, Virgil picked up Hansen's handwritten note with his new address. "I think fate is telling us to go to Beaumont," he said as he lifted Lucky from my arms and checked his diaper. "And, I think you should trust Sarah Michelle to look after your son."

327

"I can do this," I said as I mixed some rice with milk for the baby.

"But do you want to do it in the way Sarah Michelle does?" Virgil said plainly. He took the bottle of milk and rice and gave it to Lucky. "Look, after we go to Beaumont we'll swing back through Abilene. My folks will want to see me and you can get Lucky from Sarah Michelle then." For the first time all day, Lucky settled down and contentedly sucked on his bottle.

"Let's take Lucky to her now so they both won't cry all night," Virgil started to gather Lucky's few things scattered about the room. "We can probably catch Hansen tonight at the stables and let him know we're onboard."

Damn it, I felt like I was in an impossible situation. I put Lucky in the basket and Virgil packed his tiny suitcase. I remembered Sarah Michelle taking him the day after the storm. She was bruised and battered. It had been an effort to move. She held him and comforted him in her own special way when she was too traumatized to even talk. From the first it was obvious they needed each other.

But what bothered me was Dean's comment about legally being Lucky's father. Why on earth had January married Dean? And why did she tell him she lost the baby after she had blackmailed him to marry her? The answers were obvious, I guess. January knew I didn't want to get married, and January knew she didn't want to have the responsibility of being a mother. We were two of a kind. No wonder we liked each other. And, Dean, well he wasn't turning out to be the bad guy everyone seemed to think he was. And January and I were worse than any one had ever fathomed—myself more so because I was putting on a front of being a forthright honest person that would do anything for anyone, when deep down I always did what I wanted to do. But, enough beating myself up. The decision had been made in my mind. I was going to Beaumont.

Virgil and I caught a ride on the back of a flatbed being pulled by a mule. We then caught a steamer across to the mainland. I couldn't help noticing how happy Lucky was to be out on the water with the wind in his hair. He did look like me quite a bit.

A short train ride later we were on the train platform in Houston carrying our bags and Lucky's basket. It was difficult to maneuver through the crowds, and I wished Lucky were old enough to walk. Soon he would be, and I'd miss him being a baby.

SARAH MICHELLE

Dean and I were dancing in the hotel bar to a phonograph record. The piano player was on break and he and Sean were talking in the corner

"Dean," I said. "How will I go on?"

"Take it one day at a time. And if you can't do that, take it one hour at a time."

"Do you think John is capable of taking care of a baby by himself?"

"I think he'll get help. I think he'll do well in his new business." Dean hesitated before continuing. "Speaking of doing well in business, I think I know what Hansen is doing for Robert Stockton in Beaumont."

The music stopped and we went to our table.

"Don't keep me in suspense," I said as I tugged at his sleeve.

"Can you keep a secret?" he asked quietly.

Nodding, I leaned in to hear his words.

"It has something to do with oil," his voice was barely audible.

10 GREASY WATER & NEW BEGINNINGS

I was pleased to see John was finally coming around. Seeing things for what they really were and acknowledging the good and bad in all of us, including himself. Now he could live to be a better man … a more real person whom we would still admire.

JOHN

Sean and Sarah Michelle were walking behind me, much in the same way they followed me blindly after the storm. Sean would tell me later he thought I was a man of purpose. Today I moved like a man in a fog, pushing past my faults. I would not give in. I would not give up my son. I would make it work out well for everyone concerned. Forward I trod through crowded streets. Virgil and Dean walked beside me, and we could feel the excitement buzzing in our veins like a slow electric current.

Together we made our way across the busy street and hailed a carriage to take us to the address Hansen had given us. Hansen would be pleased to have Sean with him—as pleased as I was to have Lucky with me.

Begging was not my usual way, but beg I did last night for them to accompany me to Beaumont. Dean caved in first because of his love for adventure. Sarah Michelle had no ties to any city or town. She just said she feared the coast, and Beaumont was only about a hundred miles from Galveston.

It was true, I reminded her, Beaumont had taken quite a hit from the great hurricane, but the storm had then traveled clear across the United States and further inland spawning high winds and tornadoes as it went.

Sean said he had read of deaths up north as well as all along the coastline. Sarah Michelle's search for safety was in vain I assured her. We would do well to work with Hansen. We would recover in Beaumont. Dean needed money, too. He could be a part of this new deal. Then, we could all go to Abilene or even further into West Texas at a later date. Whatever they liked. But we would stay together, and Lucky would be near me.

The economy was still reeling from the fallout of the storm. Farmers and cattlemen everywhere had incurred terrible losses; the lumber companies had lost out most of all. Everyone was looking for a new way to make a living. I had even heard some orchards in the area were turning to planting strawberries. It was the nurse Clara Barton's idea, and a good one it was because strawberries would make a quick yield. She was pretty spry for a seventy-eight year old woman, and a godsend to the people of Galveston. She was a tough old gal to come in and help right after the hurricane. Don't know many women that determined, especially at her age. *A true saint, she was.*

The people of Galveston were starting to question how she was allocating the donations and medical attention, but my friend who volunteered and worked alongside her said such talk didn't faze her. Said she told him that's the way it always is after disasters. People always criticize those administering humanitarian aid.

No doubt about it, the after-effects of the storm were still raging all around us in one way or another. They caused a ripple effect, no pun intended, through everyday life and through the economy. People had lost much, and many had lost everything. The donations of food, clothing and money had provided immediate relief, but to survive we were all going to have to change because our world had changed literally overnight. It was hard to verbalize, but the storm had swept life as we knew it away.

Galveston, with its immense wealth, was no more. Six months ago you could walk down the strand and find two-dozen millionaires doing business. Yes, many of Galveston's wealthy were still recovering and rebuilding, but something vital had changed. The ports were already filled with steamers transporting cotton, but the storm had brought boll weevils in its high winds. Others said they had come in the year before the storm. Either way, farmers were going to have a rough time in the coming years. Because of the damage done by the storm's high winds and accompanying floods, this year's crops were all but destroyed. One farmer told us he was only getting about a bale of cotton for every three acres—not enough to profit by any means.

I had not been a wealthy man before the storm, but making money in Galveston was pretty easy and I was starting to amass my fair share. Lord knows how much Dean had acquired. He didn't talk about it. Every once in a while I asked if he still had his lucky one hundred dollar bill in his pocket. He would take it out and hold it in the air, wave it around a bit, then put it back in his wallet.

Dean, Virgil and myself … we knew we were fortunate men to be afforded this opportunity in Beaumont.

Sarah Michelle would profit too even though she was very hesitant to change the plans she had carefully made. She was worried Sean might be noticed, but Dean reminded her that sometimes the best place to hide from someone is right under their nose. And right under Robert Stockton's nose was where we were.

The man had a reputation for making money, a knack for getting in on the next big thing. Why shouldn't his son be a part of it? It would be the world's way of making his behavior right, even if he didn't do it himself. I liked to think that in spite of the hurricane—or maybe because of the hurricane—justice prevailed in the eternal conflict of good versus evil.

Our carriage stopped abruptly at a piece of property just south of town. Hansen and another man were standing out in the middle of a field talking. A warm breeze for the month of January came flowing over us.

"Yes, indeed," I said. "Change was in the air and it smells sweet."

"Or maybe that's one of Clara Barton's new strawberry patches," Dean countered.

DEAN

Soon John, Sean, and I were working right alongside each other drilling in the oil sands. Virgil had landed with another crew on a different shift. Hansen introduced us to the man overseeing the whole operation, whose name was Captain Lucas. He was a leading expert on salt dome formations and he believed the area was worth drilling for oil. Only problem is, he ran out of money and his investors were balking at spending more. Lucas had already drilled some 575 feet. Enough, said some of his investors. It's important to know when to stop, especially when geologists gave negative reports.

Lucas would not give up. He sought new investors. Finally, John Galey and James Guffey of Pittsburgh had given him more funding back in the fall, but they insisted on bringing in Al and Curt Hamill—an experienced drilling team from Corsicana. It turns out to have been just what was needed. Together Lucas and the Hamill had spudded in a well with a new, heavier, and more efficient rotary-type bit. Yet they fought the difficult oil sands every day. It was a constant struggle, and the work was difficult and backbreaking. I worried John's bad shoulder was getting worse by the day.

Lucky for us, Galey and Guffey were friends and business associates of Robert Stockton. Like them, he agreed with Lucas that the sulfur springs and salt domes in the Gulf Coast area indicated a good chance of hitting oil—and it was only a matter of going deep enough. The greasy water in the area had fascinated Stockton from the start. He told Hansen that, even though he had missed out on the funding of the drilling, he wanted to buy land in the surrounding areas. He sent Hansen out to help with the drilling and to secure as much real estate as possible.

Besides giving us all good jobs, Hansen was also eyeing properties for us to buy, as well as Robert Stockton. The only problem is I didn't have much money and Sarah Michelle was worried we wouldn't strike oil. She didn't want to give up her money unless she found a piece of property with a good house for boarders. I didn't want to push her because, being a gambler, I found the proposition somewhat "iffy" myself.

Hansen was working with several different real estate men so as not to call too much attention to the fact of what he was doing. We would each have to cut our own deals. In my case, it would have to be a piece of land that cost around one hundred dollars because that's all I had. However, I felt good. One man, I heard, had a good tract of land for sale for only one hundred and twenty dollars. No doubt, some people wanted to leave the area after the heavy damage done in September. I would go to this man and talk to him myself. Maybe with the money I made at the stable and my lucky bill, I could swing a deal. No middleman to take a cut, more for the man to keep for himself.

In the meantime, I was going to have to take a break from drilling. John and Sean looked like they needed a breather too. We stopped and ate our lunch under a large shady tree. At one point John rubbed his hand over his arm. He stopped and picked something up between his two fingers and held it to the sun. "What is that glistening there?" Sean asked in his newly acquired southern accent.

"More glass splinters in my arm from the hurricane." John laughed and shook his head. "Those demon winds drove'em in deep, didn't they?"

I remembered John's tale of riding his front door right through the height of the storm. Twisting and turning, he managed to negotiate his way through the worst of things with slate tiles, boards and glass flying all around him.

"We'll be old men before they all come to the surface," I added. My rib cage and left hand still hurt every day from a pole that had slapped me hard at the height of the storm. I moved around and got in a more comfortable position but it was only a lesser degree of hurt. Maybe it would heal in time. The gambler in me hoped so. The doctor in me doubted it.

Dean was becoming more thankful for all the blessings of his life. More appreciative of the people he was with on a daily basis. Never again would he take everyday happenings for granted. He was learning to trust. Learning to love. Learning to believe in a higher power. Understanding that like the natural philosopher's explanation of the tiny unseen atom, forces were at work in the universe beyond his comprehension.

SEAN

Jane sold more of the jewels from Sarah Michelle's trunk for me.
At one point she told me she almost fainted when the jewelry appraiser
came from the back and demanded to know how she had come into
possession of a certain piece.

She told him it was a family heirloom given to her by her dear
deceased aunt. "What is your family name?" the stern man had demanded
to know. When he found out she was Robert Stockton's daughter and Tulia
Stockton Lloyd was her aunt, he backed down and treated her kindly.
"Ma'am my apologies. You must understand I'm under orders from the
police to question certain jewelry sales. Many are having economic troubles
these days. Others are trying to profit from…" he put his hand near his
mouth and whispered, "from less than legal means considering the looting."
He held up the opulent broach he had been handling. "See, there's an
inscription to Tulia and Earl Lloyd July 12, 1887. I was a schoolmate of
Earl's. He was my close friend."

Jane told him she would not dare sell the family heirloom if Robert
Stockton hadn't suffered from losses associated with the railroad. It was
somewhat of the truth and somewhat of a lie. Robert Stockton, Sr. still had
plenty of money, but he wasn't spending it as freely as before. However, the
money wasn't for father. It was for me, Robert, Jr.

"I like to think Aunt Tulia would approve if she were looking down from heaven," Jane said with an up and down nod of her head.

"Why didn't we just tell Aunt Tulia and Uncle Earl about father? They might have had you come live with them," she said. I told her, I thought they suspected and that's why I was invited to visit them often. In fact, I was almost living with them the entire summer on and off. "Every school holiday they issued an invita—"

Jane stopped me mid-sentence, "Oh, you are going back to school aren't you?"

"Yes, of course," I lied. Something inside of me felt my course had been altered. Maybe I had learned everything I needed in school. Now I would learn from the real world. Lesson number one: get this money to Sarah Michelle so she can buy as much land as possible for us in her name without having to gamble her nest egg. I had a feeling something big was going to happen. It was my instinct kicking in—the only good thing I had inherited from my father.

As if she heard my last thought, Jane announced, "I'm worried about you being around so many people who know Papa. You look more like him everyday. Even with your hair dyed, I fear it's only a matter of time…"

"I do not look like him," I said as I stared down at my hands. My fingers were long and slender and I often used them to gesture when I talked. I remembered how, as a little boy, I would watch my father's hands as he conducted business meetings. Even my hands were beginning to resemble his. But I doubted anyone would look that closely at my hands. If they did they would also see a jagged scar from September 8, 1900. I reflected on how Dean had insisted on treating the deep cut every night with some medicine he had gotten from the relief volunteers, but I didn't see Dean then for the doctor he was. I believed him every bit a gambler and a rake, I suppose because that's what he wanted me to believe about him. I wondered how many other people out there were like Dean and me. Living in disguise. A good many I supposed.

Jane told me she had been to the stables twice to visit with Dean's cousin Jim. He was teaching her to ride bareback and race barrels like a cowgirl. This was a side of Jane she only revealed to a few people. She was very adventuresome and independent. A secret suffragette, I called her, because I knew she privately believed women should have the right to vote. "Why can we own property and still not vote?" she would say to me when no one else was around. I didn't have the answer. Jane was more intelligent than many men I knew. It must have been hard for her to have to play second fiddle.

We were on the front porch of a beautiful home. Dean was right, it was lovely, but the roof would have to be repaired. I gave some thought again to not buying anything here in Beaumont. Abilene was a nice-size town in the middle of the state. It had many things going for it.

Dean asked me to go inside and look around the house again. He pointed out that there was even some furniture left inside. Obviously this home was in good condition except for some minor storm damage. "You could grow strawberries like they do in Pasadena," Dean was trying to convince me.

"Then if the oil didn't come in at least we would have something to eat."

"It's close to town, and a nice size for boarders." Sean said coming from the kitchen.

I stepped back on the porch. The weather was beautiful, balmy in fact. The three of us stood and looked out over the scenic vista. Beaumont was nice and it was on the mainland.

"Perhaps I will buy this house and land if you don't," Sean took everyone by surprise with his words. Without even looking at us he said, "Jane sold more of our Aunt's things."

I was reminded of the old adage that it takes money to make money. Even though Sean was not wealthy, I knew his background gave him some access to funds he could transform into much more. Each of us drew our lot in life when we were born. Sean faced much different obstacles than John, Dean and myself.

"Imagine your china here in this glass-fronted cabinet," Dean was a salesman at heart.

"But look, the front door glass is broken out on the bottom panes," I pointed out. "Wild animals could walk right through."

"We'll get a new door. A special door." Dean countered.

"Let's look around upstairs one more time," Sean said.

"Okay, I'll take it, if you two will agree to live here and help me repair the roof," I said this as I poked the roof with an old cane I found in the corner. It made a hole right through, revealing blue sky.

"We can live in the small house I bought yesterday until this one is repaired." Dean said. "It's a small one bedroom, but it's sturdy with lots of land around it. Not too far from the hill we're drilling."

"You bought a house," I found myself saying out loud. Immediately I was embarrassed because it was obvious I thought he had no money.

"Yes I did, with my lucky one hundred dollar bill." Dean beamed his most charming gambler's smile at us, showing both dimples. "It was soaked in sea water from my ride through the hurricane, but the bank found it to be in acceptable condition."

"Let's go tell the real estate person we'll take this house and all the property around it," Sean jumped over the porch railing.

"I can only afford the house and some of the property." I called to him.

"I know. I'm going to buy the rest of the property. We'll be neighbors." Sean danced around in the front yard area. "'Cept maybe I'll take your offer to live in your house because there is only a fallen down barn on my portion."

"Let's hurry to make the deal because land prices may go up as Hansen is buying everything out." Dean ushered us toward the horse and buggy. "John bought a tract yesterday with the same salt dome formations as where we're working."

Once we were inside the tiny downtown real estate office, I started to think I was moving too fast. I didn't want to move fast, but Sean assured me we were doing the right thing. In business, he said, an opportunity might be lost in an hour's time. Let's be bold. Hansen would not steer us wrong. And just like that I became a landowner, as did Sean.

Sean listed his age as eighteen on the forms and he fibbed about his identification papers being washed away in the great September cyclone. "Never mind," the man said. "Your cash is good."

Dean wanted to celebrate by eating at a local diner, but he only had a few dollars, so we bought some things at the grocer and ate on the porch of my new house. Afterwards, Sean and Dean made plans to work on my roof between their drilling shifts. It would be difficult, Sean said, but worth it once it was done. It was interesting to watch Sean's work ethic as he seemed to have boundless enthusiasm and energy. "We need to order the roof slates right away as we may have to wait for them to arrive." Sean added, "Just about every house for miles around has had to have roof repairs."

"It's not too bad except for the room where Sarah Michelle punched the hole. I think I'll go tomorrow and patch that area while we wait for supplies." Dean leaned back on the porch steps and flashed another of his winning grins. "Wait 'til you see my lovely new abode." I smiled back and said, "Hope John's rested up today." I thought of him trying to take care of Lucky without me. "You three have an early shift tomorrow."

JOHN

It's always strange to me to move around in twilight. My body wanted to sleep so badly, but the alarm clock clanged that it was time to go. Drilling was hard physical work and dangerous if you didn't keep your mind alert.

I had established a routine of sorts to get myself moving on these early morning shifts. I put the coffee on to boil before I even got dressed. Next, I splashed cold water on my face. Today, I poured it over my head outside of the tent and shook my hair like a dog. I had brought a fresh towel and I started to wake as the first few rays of sun touched the morning sky. I stood in awe as the sun poked over the horizon like a sunny-side up egg. It was absolutely majestic. Other than the beautiful sunrise it was your normal, average day. I was glad to be alive.

Dean and Sean met up with me outside the tent. Sean was already drinking coffee, black. He had brought a cup for me too. We drank without talking other than to tell ourselves we would get to sleep earlier tonight.

Once Sarah Michelle had gotten back yesterday evening, I had left Lucky with her and went into town. Dean had followed and together we drank like we used to—only now neither one of us was carefree. We drank a sight more than we should have last night with our early morning shift.

Dean didn't say anything when I began kissing one of the saloon girls. If he had, I'd have reminded him I was not the married one. I'd never said anything to him about it, but I knew he was womanizing right up until the night of the storm and he must have been married to January by that time. He was keeping it a secret to protect her honor when he knew my heart was aching for her. I didn't dislike Dean, but I didn't really like him either, and it bothered me to see him getting closer to Sarah Michelle.

They were dancing like lovers the night I came upon them at the hotel when I begged Sarah Michelle to come with me to Beaumont. Dean was staring into her eyes and their faces glowed. Why did it make me feel bad to think of it? Sarah Michelle wasn't my usual type although I found myself highly attracted to her. She was a very handsome woman now that her bruises had healed. Anyone could see that, especially a rake like Dean.

In Houston, Jane had suggested a professional hairdresser to Sarah Michelle. The two of them went off together, and Sarah Michelle came back with her short hair cut in a polished new style. It was a look I know she would have considered way to modern in her past life. But what choice did she have when I chopped off her long hair in chunks to get her out of the tree branches? I could tell Dean noticed how nice Sarah Michelle was beginning to look these days. He was always staring at her.

Sean walked between us and soon we were getting about our business. As the sun climbed higher in the sky, the mugginess of the tropical climate made us sweat so we had to constantly hydrate ourselves.

We traded off taking frequent breaks out of the direct sun by standing in the shade of the few trees on the hill where we were working.

Dean and Sean were standing back away from the drilling site when I noticed we hit some kind of mud. Captain Lucas himself was standing near me and had just noted we were drilling at a depth of 1,139 feet. While he was inspecting the equipment, mud started to bubble out. "What the hell?" I said. Dean and Sean and several other roughnecks working with us that day started to come toward the drill.

Lucas turned and waved them back. "Get out of here!" he shouted. He ran and I followed. I didn't see behind me or I might have had a heart attack as six tons of four-inch drilling pipe came shooting out of the ground. Up ahead I could see everyone running. I could hear the tremendous sound of the earth boiling and blowing something upward. Pipe started to fall like rain around us as we ran.

When we reached a relative degree of safety, Lucas and I turned to look back. My pulse pounded so terrifically I couldn't focus. My heart seemed to explode in my chest as I looked at the now-quiet hole in the ground. I was halfway bent over with my hands on my knees trying to catch my breath. Lucas was doing the same thing. In the distance, I could see Dean and the others gesturing to each other. I was not anywhere near ready for what happened next, even though I had had several minutes to recover.

The hole gurgled up a geyser of mud that turned into a spewing fountain of gas that turned into a blowing mountain of oil that reached more than 100 feet high. I looked at Captain Lucas standing beside me, and he had fear in his eyes and a smile on his face as he watched the ship of his dreams come in on that average, ordinary day.

He winked at me and said, "Fortune has smiled on us." And for some reason my mind remembered a newspaper headline about Galveston's rise to glory that read "Flirting with Greatness..." It was a mighty strange thing to think of as Lucas half-pushed and half-pulled me away from his spurting fortune. Even though he had to sell out most of his stake in the oilfield to investors, he was going to be a very rich man and perhaps more importantly a man who proved himself to himself. Thank God he did not give up on his oil theories when others did. All would have been for naught.

The day was January 10, 1901. It would be nine days before the geyser named Spindletop was capped. Newspapers everywhere reported the Lucas Gusher, with its 100,000 barrels of oil a day, to be the beginning of a new age. Another Industrial Revolution, they screamed, this time fueled by oil instead of wood and coal. Life would never be the same, only we didn't realize it then. It took some time for the big picture to soak in to our subconscious.

Aye, all I knew is I was happy at that moment.

Later we celebrated with champagne in Dean's tiny shotgun house. His $120 tract of land would fetch more than $50,000 in the next year as Beaumont boomed. But we were only wealthy in friendship that night as we drank bubbling champagne out of a variety of mismatched glasses.

"'Tis good," I toasted. "'Tis good," they echoed back.

***

The next day, I rose early to send a letter to my Galveston neighbors asking them to ship my old front door to Beaumont. Sarah Michelle agreed that the very door I had ridden to safety at the height of the storm would be perfect in Sean's and her new home.

Slowly, I wrote in careful script just as Sean had taught me in the last few months.

Dear Seamus and Virginia, I hope all is well. I have found a new place to hang my old door, a new place for the five of us to call home. Please ship to me at the Spindletop oil field in Beaumont. Bless you for its safekeeping. John McLaren

My words were simple, but they brought tears to my eyes as I thought of the indentions my fingers had made in the sturdy wooden door as I clung to it for dear life.

Sister Elizabeth is who I was, but no longer. Now I am a part of the light. Don't be frightened, I whispered on the wind, and more than a few people in the world heard and seem to settle down. You are not alone. You were never alone. Even before the day you were born.

350

MORE BOOKS BY GINA HOOTEN POPP

Lucky's Way (Winds of Change Series – Book 2)

The Emigrant's Song (Winds of Change Series – Novella)

Chico Boy: A Novel